D0168857

*For all who are brave
enough to be afraid.*

AUTUMN
PUBLISHING

Published in 2020
First published in the UK by Autumn Publishing
An imprint of Igloo Books Ltd
Cottage Farm, NN6 0BJ, UK
Owned by Bonnier Books
Sveavägen 56, Stockholm, Sweden
www.igloobooks.com

0920 001
2 4 6 8 10 9 7 5 3 1
ISBN 978-1-80022-037-9

Printed and manufactured in Italy

DISNEY
FROZEN II

FOREST OF SHADOWS

An Original Tale by

Kamilla Benko

FEAR
WILL BE YOUR
ENEMY

— Grand Pabbie

Prologue

THE SKY WAS AWAKE and so was the forest.

Anna of Arendelle hugged her cloak tight as the bare branches clacked like teeth above her and the wind tugged at her braids. She peered into a bush. As far as she knew, bushes weren't supposed to have eyes. But then again, five-year-old princesses weren't *supposed* to be alone outside the castle at night, either. And yet here she was... although Anna hadn't started off the night alone. Her sister, Elsa, was somewhere out here in the snowy woods, too. Possibly hiding in the very bush that Anna was tiptoeing closer to.

Three years older than Anna, with wide blue eyes and a shy smile, Elsa was the kind of girl who could sit for hours without swinging her legs and whose tidy white-blonde plait always hung straight down her back.

Grown-ups often remarked how well-behaved Anna's big sister was... but they didn't know Elsa the way Anna did. Underneath the polite and poised exterior was a mischievous sense of fun. All Elsa needed was an excuse, and Anna was happy to be just that: Elsa's excuse to slip into her cloak and sneak out of the castle to build a snowman and play hide-and-seek under the northern lights. Which was exactly what they were doing now. Elsa had already found Anna in a tree's hollow, but Anna had been looking for Elsa for what seemed like forever... or at least five minutes.

The leaves rustled again and Anna clapped her hands over her mouth to stop a giggle from escaping. Yes, there was *definitely* someone watching her from the snow-covered thicket. Holding her breath, she stepped closer. She was pretty sure it was Elsa, but there was always a chance it could be a Huldrefólk, one of the rumoured hidden people who dwelled in the streams, under the rocks and in the bedtime stories told by their mother, Queen Iduna. Anna's heart beat faster. If it *was* a Huldrefólk, she just *had* to see their tail. She'd always wondered if their tails were flowing like a horse's or bushy like a fox's or long and skinny like a mouse's.

But Anna had a feeling she knew who the figure

hiding behind the bush was. Anna parted the leaves and in the colourful glow of the dancing sky, she caught a glimpse of blonde hair. So, not a Huldrefólk. Just a sister.

Laughing, Anna shook the bush. "I found you! Your turn to be the Crusty Troll!"

Elsa didn't respond.

"I said, I *found* you." Anna peered through the foliage. "It's my turn to hide – that's the rule. Come on out!"

Anna's sister turned her head, and that's when Anna realised her mistake. It wasn't blonde hair she had spotted in the shifting light.

It was white *fur*.

Anna's scream stuck in her throat as a giant white wolf prowled out from the thicket with unusual grace, its long limbs uncurling like smoke. Its fierce yellow gaze fixed on her. Anna's eyes ran down its huge, horse-sized body... to see four fearsome paws, each the size of one of the large shields that belonged to her father, King Agnarr. But that wasn't the worst of it.

No, the *worst* was the red-stained fur around its claws and jaw.

Red. The colour of blood.

What had happened to her sister?

"Elsa!" Anna screamed. "Where are you?"

The wolf leapt.

Anna ran.

Her heart slammed in her chest, each breath a sharp knife as she tried to run faster and faster – but she knew she couldn't outrun a wolf. Spotting a fallen log, she dived behind it, her knees tucked to her chest as she tried to make herself as small as possible. Though her lungs ached for air, Anna held her breath, not wanting to give herself away with even the tiniest exhale. One second passed, then another, and another. Had she lost the wolf?

Snow fell thick and silent. Anna shivered, wishing she'd listened to Elsa when she'd told her not to wear her most beautiful green cloak, but to put on her everyday thick woolly brown one instead.

Elsa. Where was Elsa?

As quiet as a shadow, Anna peered around the log, half expecting to come nose-to-snout with the wolf. Instead, all she saw was an army of trees casting ghastly shadows onto the snow-covered ground. And as the wind picked up, so did Anna's ice-cold fear. If she walked through the fresh snow, the wolf would be able to see exactly which direction she'd gone. And if she didn't walk through the snow... she might never find her sister.

Red on white.

Blood on fur.

Anna couldn't stay behind the log forever. Peeling off her cloak, she arranged it on the ground, bunching it into the shape of a five-year-old girl taking a nap. Then she moved into a crouching position. So far, so good. She took a slow, steady step backwards. And then another, and another, carefully weaving her way in reverse between the trees, the same way the Huldrefólk in her mother's bedtime stories were said to travel so they could keep their tails hidden. But Anna didn't have a tail to hide. Instead, she was leaving a fresh trail of footprints in the snow – footprints that would always lead *away* from where she actually was.

"Elsa," she whispered, "you've won hide-and-seek. Please come out."

But still there was no reply. The snow fell faster, so Anna moved faster, darting between trees, diving behind boulders, all the while scanning the snowy woods for a sign of her sister – any sign. But there was not a footprint to be seen. It was as though her sister had been erased. As though... but the thought was too horrible for Anna to finish.

From somewhere nearby, the wolf howled.

Anna froze. She knew that sound. It was the same sound her father's hunting dogs made when they'd picked up the scent of a fox. The wolf howled again, but this time it was a little farther away. Anna's decoy had worked! She spun round and ran. The snow fell faster, the thick flakes clumping on her eyelashes and making it hard to see.

"Elsa!" The name ripped from her throat. "Elsaaaa! El–" She choked on the word.

There, standing in front of her, wasn't her sister, but the wolf.

Once more, its fierce yellow eyes were fixed right on her.

How had it got ahead of her? There was no time to think – only to run.

Anna pumped her legs, sending snow flying up around her. She couldn't stop. Her entire world was snow and fear and cold, and then suddenly – endless sky! Anna stumbled to a halt. She was at the edge of a cliff. An inky expanse of nothingness lay before her, but she knew whatever she found lurking behind her would be far worse.

Hot breath.

Sharp claws.

Sharper teeth.

"ELSA!" she yelled again.

But Elsa did not appear. If her sister wasn't here by now, something horrible *must* have happened. Pain seared itself across Anna's shoulder blades. She had hesitated for too long. The wolf's claws had connected with her back. Anna stumbled forward.

She plunged over the edge—

And woke up.

A cool, comforting hand was on her forehead, and as she blinked, Anna saw her mother's face sharpen into focus. The queen's blue-grey eyes shone with concern, and her chestnut brown hair cascaded down one shoulder, loose from its usual upsweep of braids. A large burgundy scarf, stitched with a multitude of snowflakes and complete with purple fringe, had been thrown over her shoulders and was covering up a lavender nightgown.

Anna shot up. "Where's Elsa? Did the wolf get her?"

"Anna, it's all right." Her mother sat and wrapped an arm around her. "All is well."

"There was snow," Anna said, her heart still pounding. "And trees! I was running, and then... I slipped!" She struggled to sit up against her pillows. "Elsa was there, and then she wasn't. I was so worried!"

Anna's father strode forward with a tray bearing mugs of hot chocolate. "You had a bad dream," he said. His ruddy blond hair, usually brushed back neatly, was tousled, as if he'd just come in from a midnight ride. For some reason, he was wearing his navy-blue uniform resplendent with badges and golden epaulettes instead of a nightshirt. Bending, he placed the tray on the bedside table. "Elsa is in her room, asleep, as we all should be at this hour."

But that didn't seem quite right. The last thing Anna remembered was being awake in this same bed, watching the dancing sky through her window, wanting to wake Elsa up to... do something. But what? Anna squinted her eyes, trying to remember through the pounding in her head. Odd. That's all she *could* remember. The only thing after that was the outline of her nightmare: a mountain, a wolf and bitter cold.

Her father settled next to her mother and handed

a warm mug to Anna. "Drink up," he said. The steam uncurled from the mug, moving with the same effortless grace as the wolf.

Anna shivered, still a bit shaken, but she had never said no to hot chocolate. She took a sip, and as the liquid slipped down to her belly, it warmed her stomach.

Her mother patted her knee. "You know, when I have a bad dream, I always imagine crumpling up the nightmare and tossing it out the window so that Frigg has something else to fish for besides the moon and the sun. You remember the old story I used to tell you about Frigg the Fisherman, right?"

Anna did, but she shook her head. She wanted her mother to keep talking. She leaned back as her mother began the tale of the boastful fisherman who kept casting his nets for bigger prizes and accidentally found himself stuck in a night-time ocean of stars. Anna soaked in the comforting presence of her mother, who always smelled like calming lavender.

The memory of the nightmare faded, replaced by what was real: her cosy bedroom decorated with pink wallpaper, thick ornate rugs, an oval painting of Arendelle Castle that she loved to admire, a tapestry of queens and flickering candles in the sconces on the walls. Though no flames burned in the fireplace, a few embers still glowed like dropped jewels. And her parents there beside her were the cosiest details of all. Anna's eyes grew heavy.

"Feeling better?" her father whispered when her mother finished her tale.

Anna nodded, and he smiled.

"Everything is always better with hot chocolate," he said.

"We should wake Elsa up." Anna's eyes fluttered as she held up her empty mug. "She'd like this."

She almost missed her mother and father exchange a fleeting glance at her words. There was a shift in the room, as if a cloud had drifted past the window.

"Elsa needs her sleep," her mother said. "And you should try to get some rest, too. Agnarr, can you please hand me that extra pillow?"

Anna's father stood and walked over to the white-painted chair that had been dragged from its place by the wall and now stood between Anna and the fireplace. Another pillow and a crumpled pile of blankets lay on the floor around it, as if it were a makeshift bed.

Anna looked from the floor to her parents. They only stayed in her room if she was really ill... "Were you sleeping in here?" Anna asked. "Am I sick?"

"You're just fine," her father said with a soft smile. Picking up the pillow, he placed it under Anna's head while her mother tucked the blankets tight. Anna wiggled her toes to loosen the covers just a bit as her parents extinguished the lights and headed for the door.

"Sweet dreams, Anna," her mother whispered from the doorway, the light from the hallway outlining her and Anna's father.

"Sweet dreams..." Anna murmured back, sinking deeper into her pillow.

The patch of light grew smaller and smaller, until, at last, it vanished as the door clicked shut. Anna listened to the sound of her parents' footsteps recede before she turned her cheek to stare out her window.

The sky was asleep now, the ribbons of colour from the northern lights tucked beneath a patchwork quilt of clouds. But the moon stayed bright. It glared down at her like one of the wolf's yellow eyes. Watching. And waiting. But for what?

Cold again, Anna pulled the covers over her head, but sleep never came.

Sixteen Years Later...

Chapter One

ANNA FLEW DOWN the carpeted castle stairs of the second great hall, taking them two at a time.

She nearly tripped on the landing, but she didn't bother to slow down. The clock tower had already tolled ten in the morning, and she'd *promised* Elsa she wouldn't be late. For a second, she thought about sliding down the banister. It really was the fastest way to get around, but at twenty-one she was too old for such things... right? Right. But...

Anna's feet slowed. The white wood of the banister gleamed with a recent polish and the promise of speed. And her new riding boots with heels – a gift from a dignitary from Zaria – hadn't been broken in yet and weren't exactly the best for running. She glanced over her shoulder. No one was around. Decision made, she hauled the skirt of her dress into her arms, slung a leg over the banister and slid the rest of the way down, landing with ease as she reached the first-floor landing. She flew through the castle doors and raced outside, towards the stables.

"Elsa! I'm here!" Anna whisper-called as she moved through the barn doors and entered the quiet world of sweet hay and softly munching horses. She smoothed down the back of her black dress and checked to make sure that her long chestnut brown hair was still pinned in place by a double braid. "I'm not late! Well," she amended, "not *that* late. But I was having the most fascinating dream where..." She trailed off and looked around.

Her only audience was the alert ears of the castle horses and the litter of barn kittens that came stumbling towards the stables' entrance whenever someone entered. But there was no sign of Elsa. Anna brushed her fringe off her forehead, confused. Somehow, even though she'd overslept, she had managed to beat Elsa. Which was odd. Very, very odd. Elsa was *always* on time; it was one of the many reasons she was such a great queen, beloved by all of Arendelle.

Picking up a purring grey kitten that had begun to bat at her bootlaces, Anna took a step towards the livery. Maybe Elsa had got here *so* early that she'd decided to inspect the recent delivery of apples. Careful to keep her voice low so as not to startle the horses, Anna called out again. "Elsa?"

"You're looking in the wrong place," a friendly voice called from the far end of the stables, and a second later, Kristoff Bjorgman's head popped over a stall door, a pitchfork in his hand and a bit of straw in his hair.

Anna grinned. She always did whenever she was around Kristoff – she couldn't help it. When Kristoff had first started to visit the castle frequently three years before, Gerda, one of the people who had known the girls since they were young, and who also helped them schedule their time, had remarked to the sisters that he resembled the mountains from which he harvested ice: broad and solid. Elsa had whispered back that he seemed 'nice'. When Anna had pushed her for a little bit more, Elsa had added 'blond'. All of which was true, but to Anna, Kristoff wasn't just a mountain man or 'nice' or 'blond', he was her best friend – and definitely something *more,* even if he did sometimes smell like a reindeer. Which was completely understandable, given his other best friend, Sven, *was* a reindeer.

Sven's head popped over the stall door to look at Anna, and he twitched his ears in a friendly hello. Though Anna had invited both Sven and Kristoff multiple times to take up residence in one of the many spare rooms of the castle, they both preferred to stay in the stables. Anna suspected they enjoyed the less confined living space of the barn after spending the summer months in the mountains harvesting ice for the kingdom.

"She's not here?" Anna asked, bending to set the kitten down gently. It scampered away to join the others.

Kristoff moved his hand under Sven's lower lip and began to wiggle it as he said in Sven's voice, "Someone's not *listening.*"

Anna smiled at Kristoff's "Sven Talk" – he was always dialoguing for his reindeer friend. It was silly, but she loved it, and so she took 'Sven's' advice and listened to her surroundings. At first, all she could make out was the occasional swish of a horse's tail flicking flies away and the mewling of the kittens tumbling around one of the water troughs, but eventually, beneath the usual sounds, she heard an odd buzz that sounded like...

"Oh!" Anna's eyes widened and she hurried to the far end of the stables, where there was a little window. Peering through it, she saw just what she had suspected: a small crowd of villagers gathered in the courtyard. And though Anna couldn't see exactly *what* they were surrounding, she knew exactly *who* it would be: Elsa.

Wherever Elsa went, people seemed to follow. They were there in the morning, asking her questions about what should be done in the afternoon, asking what they should be doing in the evening, asking what they should do tomorrow. Elsa's table in the council chambers was always heaped with papers, and more often than not, Anna only caught a glimpse of her sister as Gerda ushered her from one appointment to another, always tapping the comically large calendar like a metronome to keep Elsa on the day's beat.

And Elsa's frantic schedule had only got busier over the last month, because at the end of this week, she would at last follow the tradition started by their grandfather King Runeard: setting off on a grand tour of the world. In five days, Elsa would leave from the Arenfjord, the body of water on which Arendelle was built, sailing past Weselton and the Southern Isles before heading east to explore lands like Zaria, Royaume, Chatho, Tikaani, Eldora, Torres and Corona, to name a few. Elsa would meet *everyone*: dignitaries and dancers, scientists, painters and prized mountain goats. And she would be going without Anna.

When Kai, the castle's old steward, had first mentioned it was time for Elsa to start planning for her grand tour, Anna had assumed she would be going with her older sister. But as the months dwindled down to weeks and then to days, Elsa still hadn't invited her. And it wasn't as though Anna hadn't given Elsa plenty of chances to ask her. Only last week, Anna had oh-so-casually mentioned that it had always been a dream of hers to see the Chathoan ballet – and she'd said so in Chathoanese. She'd spent days perfecting her accent. Before that, she'd performed Tikaani's national anthem for everyone at the castle, with an accompaniment by Olaf, the snowman whom Elsa had created three years ago with her magical ice powers, on a carrot-nose flute.

So far, though, none of Anna's efforts had worked.

But that was going to change today.

Or so she had planned.

Still peering through the window, Anna frowned as even more villagers in brightly coloured shawls and jackets entered through the castle gates and hurried to join the crowd around Elsa.

Anna had been racking her mind all week and had finally decided that the perfect time would be *this* morning, during their last scheduled sisterly ride through the woods before Elsa's departure. Anna knew that Elsa found the quiet of the forest peaceful, and she hoped that it would lead to the perfect moment to ask Elsa if she could go on the grand tour with her. A ride was also a good opportunity to prove that Anna could be a useful travelling companion. That she was helpful and wouldn't get in the way. But that was part of the trouble. Elsa didn't seem to need any help.

Though Elsa had only been crowned queen three years before, Anna already knew her older sister would be remembered as one of the great rulers of Arendelle, like the ones who appeared on the tapestry that hung across from Anna's bed. Her sister appeared to always have everything under control

– even her magical powers – with a regal presence that all respected. Whenever Elsa listened to Anna, she made Anna feel special and important, and at twenty-four years old, Elsa carried herself the same way she seemed to do everything: effortlessly.

"It's been like that since she got here," Kristoff said, coming to stand next to Anna and looking out the stables' window. "Which," he said, giving her a teasing look, "was half an hour ago."

Anna made a face. "I know, I know— I overslept... again." She needed to find some way to pull Elsa out of the crowd for their horseback ride. Before Elsa left her.

Something tugged on Anna's foot, and she looked down to see that the tiny grey kitten had returned, determined, it seemed, to catch those devious laces.

"Hey, Kristoff?" Anna said slowly, still watching the persistent kitten, only the size her palm, take on her large boot. "I think I have an idea. Do you have a minute?"

"For you?" Kristoff winked. "Always."

Anna grinned as she wrenched the kitten off her laces and placed it into Kristoff's arms. "Perfect! So, here's the plan..."

A few minutes later, Anna left the stables and hurried out to the friendly crowd in the courtyard. As she got closer, she could hear their questions piling up all around Elsa.

"Your Majesty, the chimney in our forge has cracks, and I'm worried it won't be mended in time for the winter," called Ada Diaz, a woman with curly brown hair standing next to her wife, Tuva Diaz, who had even curlier brown hair. They were the best blacksmiths on the continent and were known for making the luckiest horseshoes, though it seemed even an abundance of lucky horseshoes weren't as helpful as their queen's collected wisdom.

"I was here first," another familiar-looking villager sniped at Ada before turning in Elsa's direction and bowing. "Your Majesty, you promised that the rocks in my garden would be removed by the beginning of autumn, and look—" He held up a red oak leaf. "It's autumn!"

"Ah-hem," yet another said. "The *Village Crown* is waiting for you to announce who the judges will be for the harvest festival this year, Your Majesty. Do you have the names?" Though Anna couldn't see this particular person in the crowd, she knew, just by hearing his voice and grating, know-it-all cough, that it was Wael, the self-proclaimed reporter for the village, whose slick black hair always matched his ink-stained hands.

Sidling towards Elsa, Anna counted down silently. *Three... two... one...* Then she signalled for Kristoff.

"Oh, my goodness, Sven!" Kristoff proclaimed loudly from the stables' entrance. "Look at these adorable kittens!"

"They're cuter than you!" he said in Sven's voice.

And during the brief second that everyone in the crowd turned to look at the kittens frolicking in the far corner of the courtyard, Anna darted into the throng, grabbed Elsa's hand and pulled her round the back of the stables and inside.

"Anna!" Elsa gasped as they ducked round a corner, where the fully saddled Havski and Fjøra, the swiftest horses in the stables, stood waiting for them. "What are you doing?"

Anna grinned. "Breaking you free!"

"But..." Elsa protested, sweeping a loose tendril of ice-blonde hair off her forehead, "the villagers, they need my help—"

"I know!" Anna nodded. "But Kai and Gerda can

handle their requests, and it's important for you to ride out one last time before you set sail – just to make sure everything is in order. Don't you agree? Besides," she added, beaming even wider, "don't you *want* to spend some time with me?"

Even though she'd been handling complaints all morning, Elsa still seemed regal and calm. The wind blew through an open door and buffeted her diaphanous blue split cape and coat, and tugged at the fishtail braid hanging over her left shoulder. For a moment, she looked like a timeless, valiant queen from one of Anna's history books. But the next second, she flashed a grin at Anna, and it was like it had been before – when they were just two children sneaking out of their bedrooms for a night-time adventure.

"I suppose I could let Kai and Gerda take care of things – just this once," Elsa said.

Anna let out a whoop of joy. She swung up onto Havski's back while Elsa took a moment to clamber on top of Fjøra, a beautiful horse with a black-and-white striped tail. Finally, after a few attempts, Elsa mounted. Together, they trotted out of the stables and left the courtyard, with Anna waving to Kristoff, who smiled from under a pile of kittens batting at his face.

The sisters crossed the Bridge of Arches and took in the wild, fresh autumn air. Behind them, nestled in the shadow of soaring mountains, the castle sparkled and shone with the decorative touches of Elsa's ice magic. Anna kicked her horse into a canter, and Elsa did the same.

Arendelle was a kingdom of wilderness, of rugged coasts, deep blue waters and towering ships. Lots and lots of ships. They came from everywhere, bringing people from all over the world who were happy to settle down in the picturesque kingdom – people who were happy to answer Anna's invitation to share memories of their own countries so she could learn about their customs. Memories that could help Anna prepare Elsa for the grand tour... if only Elsa would let her. Because while ships brought people to the kingdom, they also left with people. The royal ship currently sat in the harbour, loaded with goods and waiting for Elsa to board.

As they rode past the expanding village and people waving excitedly at them, a delighted fizziness filled Anna's body. This was the *best* part of opening the kingdom gates three years ago – all the new people and new ideas that had trickled in. Although the village was more populous than ever before, with more and more people having moved there, Arendelle would always be Anna's heart and home. That was one thing that would never change.

As they moved beyond the houses and shops, the forest of Arendelle flourished around them, showing off in bright yellows, deep reds and burnt oranges that reminded Anna of bonfires and melted caramels. A happy sigh slipped from Anna. The autumn leaves had just begun to turn and change, and the living things of the forest seemed to be settling into themselves, the same way Elsa had settled into being queen. Anna didn't particularly like change. She always wanted things to stay the same. These days, Anna barely got to see Elsa, who was constantly cooped up in the council chambers poring over paperwork, or else leading important meetings that Anna also attended. But she was happy watching Elsa come into her own, even if it meant their relationship was evolving as a side effect of it.

The horses slowed, picking up an easy trot side by side. Wondering if *now* was the moment, Anna glanced over at Elsa. Her sister wore a far-off and pensive look on her face.

"What are you thinking about?" Anna asked.

"Oh." Elsa looked up from her reins. "Nothing... just, you know, work."

"Want to tell me?" Anna said, trying to keep her eagerness down to about a level eight, instead of her usual level ten. "You remember what Father always said, right?"

Elsa tilted her head. "What, that 'burdens should be shared'?"

Something scraped in Anna, like a rough crumb caught in her throat. Because... well, her family's burdens and secrets *hadn't* been for everyone. Or at least, they hadn't been for Anna. Her father had let a mountain troll bundle away Anna's memories of Elsa's ice magic, and he, her mother and Elsa had all worked together to keep it a secret from Anna.

And it had stayed a very, *very* big secret, until Elsa's coronation day, when Anna had pushed the new queen a little too far and Elsa had lost control of her temper – and her ice powers. Which, at the time, had seemed as terrible as the vast and eternal winter that had taken root in the kingdom, but in hindsight had been the best thing to ever happen to Anna. Not only had it marked the beginning of a new era with her sister, but Anna had also narrowly managed to avoid a very... *hasty*... marriage with a prince who had deceived her.

"Nope! Not that one!" Anna shook her head, wishing she could shake away the uncomfortable feeling. "The *other* saying – the one about 'many hands make light work'."

"Oh." Elsa laughed. "He had a lot of sayings, didn't he?"

Anna waited for Elsa to keep talking, but she seemed to have forgotten Anna was there again even though she was trotting alongside her.

"Hey, Elsa?" she tried again.

"Hmm?"

"Bet I can beat you to the clearing!"

"What?"

But Anna had already kicked Havski back into a gallop. Havski surged forward, setting Anna's heart free. Riding the grey horse was like riding an avalanche: fast, thrilling and powerful. Adrenaline rushed through her, and without thinking, she let go of the reins.

"What are you doing?" Elsa shouted from behind her.

"Flying!" Anna shouted back. She flung out her arms. Cool wind flowed over her face, and it seemed to blow away that tight feeling that had settled on her chest since Elsa had announced she was leaving. Elsa yelled something, but the wind swept her words away.

"What?" Anna glanced over her shoulder.

"BRANCH!" Elsa yelled again.

Anna swung forward just in time to duck beneath a birch tree's low-hanging branch. Giggling, she hugged Havski's neck and the horse snorted in response, never missing a stride. And why should he? They'd grown up together, and for a long time, he'd been the closest thing Anna had had to a best friend. They'd dodged thicker branches and jumped across wider rivers together. Picking up the reins again, she kept them loose and let Havski settle into a breathless canter.

Gradually, his strides shortened and he transitioned into an easy trot before reaching a mossy clearing. There was a crunch and the sound of twigs snapping, and Anna twisted in her saddle just in time to see Elsa and Fjøra blunder into the clearing. A single scarlet leaf had snagged on Elsa's hair, and it looked almost as though the forest had crowned her its autumn queen.

Anna grinned. "Isn't this fun?"

Sweeping away loose strands of her blonde hair, Elsa plucked the leaf off her head, looked at it, and began to laugh. "It is," she agreed.

Anna felt like a miniature sun had ignited in her chest.

Eventually, they neared the tamed, bountiful farmlands, and Anna, sneaking glances at Elsa, saw that her sister had finally settled into her saddle and was looking around the landscape with curious eyes. She seemed at ease. She seemed relaxed. Maybe it was time for Anna to finally ask her burning question. As they turned left, they passed a beautiful orchard with bright red apples and autumn leaves so orange that the world looked like it had been set aflame. *Apples. Perfect.*

Anna pointed at them. "Did you know that there's an apple on the royal flag of Zaria?" she said oh-so-casually. "And that's because it's always customary for a guest to present an apple to the host." A worry pricked Anna's thoughts. "Your ship *does* have apples on board, right?"

Elsa shook her head. "Yes, Anna – you've made sure of it! If I have any more barrels of gifts you've suggested for everyone, my ship will be too heavy to leave the harbour!"

Anna swept her fringe out of her eyes and laughed. "What would you do without me?" She tugged on the reins, gently pulling Havski to a halt. "Elsa, I wanted to ask you something. I was wondering if I could join—" But before she could finish, Havski's ears flattened as a rustling came from nearby.

A villager burst from the underbrush, panting heavily as she lifted her green skirts high so she could run.

It took Anna a moment to place her – there were so many new villagers in Arendelle these days – but then she recognised SoYun Lim, a girl Anna's own age who'd recently started to herd cattle on a farm not far from there. Anna had talked to her over the summer, during one of the castle's hosted bonfire nights, and had asked her about her native country of Chatho. Research, of course, for the grand tour. In fact, SoYun had been the one to help Anna perfect her Chathoanese accent.

But that girl always seemed as calm as a lake on a windless morning, her quiet nature soothing the animals she tended. The girl standing in front of her now was dishevelled. Her jet-black braid, which usually hung as straight and tidy as a clothesline, was a series of escaping loops, and she had on two different boots – the left foot was clad in a tall black boot, while the right foot wore a soft brown leather one. But it wasn't the strange state of her clothes or hair that sent warning bells tolling through Anna. It was the girl's expression – wide-eyed, as though she'd seen a ghost – and the frantic way in which she flailed her arms to catch their attention.

"Your Majesty!" SoYun bobbed her head towards Elsa in a slight bow. "Thank goodness I caught up with you – something *terrible* has happened!"

Chapter Two

"SOYUN! WHAT'S WRONG?" Anna swung off Havski, landing in a pile of leaves before hurrying towards her.

"It's my cattle," SoYun said, looking from Elsa, who was cautiously dismounting from Fjøra, to Anna. "They're—oh!" SoYun shook her head. "I don't even know where to begin!" Tears formed in her eyes.

Anna opened her mouth to respond, but stopped herself to give Elsa a chance.

Elsa stepped a little closer. "How about if you take us to your cattle, and you can tell us all about it on the way? Say whatever comes first, and we'll piece it together, all right?"

SoYun blew her nose, then nodded. "I'm just up that way," she said, and broke into such a fast walk that it almost could have been a jog. Holding on to the horses' reins, the sisters followed, trying to catch SoYun's story as she told it.

"It started a few days ago," SoYun said, her voice ragged, "when I tried to call the cattle in – you know how it usually works like a charm."

Anna did. Calling cattle was an old Arendellian custom of singing high notes to summon the animals home. Much practice and control was required in order to do it properly, as it was so much more than a simple call. It was a fairy-like sound. A sound that raised the hair on the back of Anna's neck and let her know – really, truly, deeply *know* – for one single instant that any difference between her and the earth and wind and sky was only an illusion. SoYun was now one of the best cattle callers in the village. She never had any trouble. In fact, when the cows wouldn't come home, people always went to SoYun for help.

"And so, I went out into the fields," SoYun continued, "and tried to sing them home. But..." Her shoulders slumped. "They never came. Not even when I pulled out my bukkehorn. I went out looking, and when I finally found them..." SoYun's voice broke off.

"What happened?" Elsa pressed as they cleared a copse of maple trees and entered into a meadow nestled at the foothill of a blue mountain, where Anna could just make out a neat farmhouse among even neater rows of golden fields, and a herd of cattle circled around a large white boulder.

"*This* is what happened." SoYun led them forward. As they got closer to the herd, Anna realised the cows weren't ringing a white boulder after all, but a sleeping bull.

"That's Hebert," SoYun said. "The leader of my herd."

Hebert. The name struck a familiar chord in Anna, and she remembered that a year before, during the harvest festival best-in-show competition, a large energetic bull with that name had won first place. But that bull's hide had been as black as a raven's wing, while this one was entirely white.

SoYun took a shuddery breath. "A few days ago, I noticed he had a sprinkle of white hairs, which wasn't too strange. He's getting up there in age. But then, the next morning, the white increased pretty dramatically, until he was as you see him now."

Elsa raised her eyebrows, as if to say, *That's it? Some white hair?*

But Anna remembered when a lock of her own hair had turned white as a result of an accidental strike from Elsa's ice magic when they were children.

SoYun tugged on the end of her long braid and bit her bottom lip. "But I wouldn't have bothered you just because of that, Your Majesty. There's... there's more."

"Like...?" Anna didn't take her eyes off the figure of the sleeping bull, his great horns curved up to the sky in twin points.

"He'd been acting funny for a few days, too – at first it seemed like he was scared of something he couldn't see, like a draug," SoYun said, referencing a terrifying mythological zombie Anna had heard spoken of around castle bonfires. "And then," SoYun continued, "he ran round the field until he broke into a panicked sweat, which seemed to turn his fur white. And finally, his pupils grew wide, *huge*, until his eyes were completely swallowed by inky black." SoYun made her eyes wide as she looked at them. "And then he started groaning like he was in horrible pain, and fell down, until, at last, he slept."

Anna exchanged a confused look with Elsa. Anna didn't usually think of sleep as a *bad* thing. In fact, the more sleep she got, the better.

Elsa's eyebrow quirked again. "Slept?" she asked.

"Yes," SoYun nodded vigorously. "But not a *usual* sleep. A *deep* sleep. No matter what we do – yell, shake him, splash water on him – he won't wake up. It's been days. Which means he also hasn't been eating."

Now that SoYun had mentioned it, Anna could see the bull's ribs jutting from its sides, the white fur making it far too easy to imagine him as a pile of bones bleached by the sun. Anna wrapped her fingers in Havski's long silky mane – she didn't know what she would do if something like that happened to him. At the same time, any thoughts Anna had about a connection between her once-white streak of hair and the blanched bull fell away. After all, when Elsa had turned her hair white, Anna had been in danger of turning to ice, not falling asleep.

SoYun looked from the bull to the girls, and a tear rolled down her cheek. "He's fading away right in front of us – and the other cattle are showing similar symptoms, too!" SoYun gestured to a sweet-looking cow with long lashes and eyes that moved back and forth like the pendulum in a grandfather clock. It was as if the cow was tracking something that wasn't there. Or rather, tracking something invisible that only the cow could see.

"What if," SoYun continued, "they *all* fall into the deep sleep, and then..." The fear in the girl's voice was tangible and sharp.

Anna reached out and hugged her close. "They'll be okay," Anna said. "Don't worry. We'll find a way to help, won't we, Elsa?"

Elsa reached out and patted SoYun's shoulder a few times. "Yes. You did exactly right by coming to tell me."

Me. That small word echoed through Anna's whole body. There had been a time, she was sure, when Elsa would have said *us.*

Anna spun to Elsa. "I have an idea," she whispered. "We should visit the trolls." Though only as tall as Anna's waist and covered in moss, the tiny mountain trolls were the most powerful creatures Anna knew. Grand Pabbie, the oldest and arguably the wisest troll, would sometimes use the aurora's glow to show glimpses of what might be or, occasionally, to deal with all matters that could involve magic. If anyone could help SoYun and her cattle, Anna knew it was the trolls. Because as she had learned, when mysterious happenings occurred that raised questions, it was best to visit mystical creatures for answers.

Elsa smiled. "That's a great idea, but I think we may only have time to look in the castle library. Why don't we try that first? Remember what Father used to say."

Anna scrunched up her face, trying to remember which of Father's many sayings Elsa could be referring to. "'Anna and Elsa, always lean on each other for help'?" she guessed.

A slight smile appeared on Elsa's lips, though it was tinged with sadness. "He did say that. But he also said, 'The past has a way of returning'. We should find out if this has happened before, and at the very least, gather information that might be of use for the trolls."

Elsa made an excellent point, and Anna was suddenly excited to check the library together. Both sisters enjoyed curling up with a good storybook there, but the library also held books about the histories of the kingdom, the royal family and the townspeople. If any place in the castle had answers, it would be there.

"Does anything help with the symptoms?" Elsa asked SoYun.

SoYun, who'd knelt down to stroke Hebert's nose, glanced up. "Mint seems to help them stay alert. The smell is sharp for their noses, but it doesn't last for long."

"Mint," Elsa repeated. "I'll make sure to write that down in the report. Remind me, Anna, won't you?" After making sure they had taken in all there was to know regarding the symptoms, they bade their farewells to SoYun, Hebert and the rest of the cattle.

As Anna hauled herself onto Havski, she called back, "Don't worry, SoYun! We'll fix this. I promise."

Anna and Elsa spent the rest of the afternoon in the castle library. So far, absolutely nothing mentioned sick cattle ever falling into seemingly endless sleeps in all of Arendelle's history. Which meant that there were no suggestions for a cure for the Blight, as Elsa had decided to call the sleeping sickness.

Elsa sat in the window seat, flipping through a book, while Anna sprawled out on the couch in front of the fire, lifting a book overhead to read. A sharp knock resounded throughout the library, followed by

Kai's urgent voice. "Your Majesty, are you in there?"

"I'm here, Kai!" Elsa called.

The ornate door slammed open, and the usually calm man entered looking flustered, his scarf undone instead of knotted neatly at his neck and his ruddy eyebrows knitted together. Anna's heart sped up. As steward of the castle, Kai was a man of decorum and protocol. He *always* bowed when he greeted them, no matter how many times the sisters had begged him to stop. But not now.

"What's wrong, Kai?" Elsa stood up from the window alcove and hurried towards him as Anna set down her book and bolted up from the couch.

"Grave news," Kai gasped out, sounding as though he'd run to get there. "The Westens' entire herd of goats have seemingly dropped down in the middle of the field, and they simply won't wake up. The family is asking for you to come quickly, Your Majesty."

Dread crept over Anna and she turned to Elsa. "Do you think...?"

Elsa nodded. "It's certainly possible. But we still haven't found an answer." She looked from the tall piles of books to the high, full bookcases, then back at Kai, clearly torn about what she should do next.

"You should go," Anna urged her. "Just to make sure it's the same thing."

Elsa tugged at her fingers, a habit Anna knew was left over from the days when Elsa always wore silk gloves to repress her powers. Anna reached out to rest a hand on Elsa's forearm. Startled, Elsa looked down and, realising what she had been doing, gave Anna a small smile as if to thank her. She folded her hands neatly in front of her.

"If you're worried," Anna said, "we should divide and conquer. Send Kristoff and Sven to the trolls, since we haven't found anything useful, and I'll stay here to keep looking for answers. I can handle it."

Still, Elsa hesitated, and Anna wondered why. Did Elsa not like her recommendation? Or did Elsa not trust her to handle this job? But at last, Elsa nodded, and relief settled over Anna as her sister said, "That's a good idea. I'll let Kristoff know before I go, but I promise I'll come right back." And with that, Elsa hurried out after Kai, leaving Anna to search for solutions on her own.

Hours passed, and the wax from the candles cascaded onto the table in little pools, but Anna hardly noticed – she kept bouncing from book to book, trying to find answers... and failing. A gentle breeze twirled in from the open window, sending many of the open books' pages fluttering, as well as scattering a sprinkle of goosebumps across Anna's arm and stirring up the ash in the fireplace. Soon, that very same breeze would be filling Elsa's sails to take her far, far away.

Travel by ship made Anna nervous. Seven years had passed since their parents had set out on a voyage to the Southern Sea that had been meant to last only two weeks, but had turned into forever. The days following the news had been the darkest of Anna's life, and the nights had been worse. Sleep had been impossible. The insides of her eyelids were the colour of the fathomless waves that she imagined took her parents. Sometimes, even now, her parents' absence would startle her all over again, fresh and sudden as a bee sting. But as the years went by, the pain had become less immediate, old childhood nightmares faded and she could remember her parents – her mother's loving lullabies, her father's teasing humour and tall tales – with joy.

Her reunion with Elsa had helped. When Elsa had shut herself away as a little girl, Anna was left with only her own memories of their parents. But since Elsa's bedroom door had opened, Anna's collection of stories about their parents had multiplied. And while the stories didn't fill the hole in her heart, they did help smooth out the jagged edges.

She may not have her parents any more, but she had her sister, and that was enough. Enough to make her wish Elsa wasn't leaving her behind. She would be leaving her... *unless* Anna could prove her worth. Unless she could prove she was more than just the silly little girl who had talked to the portraits in the gallery and said yes to an offer of marriage to the evil (and thankfully now exiled) Prince Hans after less than twenty-four hours of knowing him. Anna knew Elsa valued her despite those things, but she still felt lingering insecurity.

Anna glanced at the stone statue of the horse that stood in the corner of the library as if it would have the answers they needed. But all it had were delicate stone seashells and starfish carved into its mane, and an angry expression on its face. It was an old statue, and Anna had been afraid of its bared teeth, its two front hooves furiously out in the air and its blank eyes. Once, when she was four, she'd used up all of her mother's cosmetics trying to make the horse look happier before her mother had discovered her

CHAPTER TWO

and carried her out of the room, warning her not to touch the statue again. Young Anna was always being told not to touch things, like guitar strings and oil paintings and her father's swords and...

"Wow, what happened in here?"

Anna startled at the sound of the voice. Dragging her eyes away from the statue, she looked up to see the round shape of Olaf standing in the doorway.

As children, Elsa and Anna had made up stories about a snowman named Olaf with branches for arms and a carrot for a nose. Years later, on the day of Elsa's coronation, Elsa had accidentally lost control of her ice powers and brought Olaf to life. Since then, he'd become the castle's resident snowman and a member of the sisters' family. He used to have a snow flurry hovering over his head that prevented him from melting, but since Elsa's powers had grown and changed, she was able to do away with it and instead enchant him with a permafrost that served the same purpose. Now, Olaf's eyes widened as he took in the library. Or rather, the *mess* in the library.

"It's easier for me if I sort things into piles," Anna explained, following his gaze to the towers of books scattered across the floor. She hadn't realised how...

enthusiastic she'd been when she'd pulled titles. There might actually have been more books on the floor than there were left on the shelves. It certainly wasn't Elsa's neat and methodical system, judging by the volumes Elsa had left standing in perfect stacks in the window alcove.

Olaf nodded. "That makes sense. When you build a snowman, you always have to start with piles. Unless you're Elsa, of course." He pointed. "Which ones are those?"

"Books about sicknesses," Anna said. "The pile next to that is about animal anatomy, and the one next to that is about sleep." Each title was bursting with possibilities.

Olaf moved to the last pile, his twiggy hair just visible over the stack. "And this massive one?"

"That's my 'to be read' pile."

"Oooh, it's so much bigger than all the rest," he observed.

Anna shrugged. She had set aside these books as not currently useful but interesting enough that she wanted to check them out later. Poems were great because of their beautiful imagery and brevity, but she also loved the thick tomes of artists through the ages. And, of course, there were novels where people found true love or undertook a dangerous quest or were reunited with loved ones lost.

Anna rubbed her eyes and adjusted the skirt of her dress, which had begun to bunch around her uncomfortably. "Where have you been?" she asked.

Olaf wandered from pile to pile. "The village library, listening to a lecture on *Dante's Inferno* – the hotter the tale, the better."

Anna smiled. After her first birthday party following Elsa's eternal winter, Anna had taught Olaf how to read, and ever since, the snowman had become obsessed. He liked books of all sizes, but his favourites were the thick tomes on philosophy – and beach reads, which he so often insisted were just as important as the classics. Anna didn't disagree.

"So, why are you rearranging the library, anyway?" Olaf asked.

Taking a deep breath, Anna quickly explained about SoYun and her cattle and how Elsa was out now, checking on the Westens' goats.

"It seems that you could use some help," Olaf said, straightening a coal button. "And in the wise words of many a philosopher, four eyeballs are better than three."

"Is that what they say?" Anna asked, resting her head on her palm.

Olaf whipped out his favourite pair of ice spectacles, specially made for him by Elsa. "Indeed," he said. "They also say to 'start at the beginning'. So, we'll start with the letter B, for *beginning*." He pointed, and Anna followed his scraggly finger to the middle shelf of the nearest bookshelf behind the horse statue.

"Sure," Anna said. "You look at that while I finish this one."

Olaf clambered onto a table beneath a portrait of King Agnarr's coronation, then jumped onto the stone horse's back. Carefully, he shimmied onto one of the rearing legs and pulled himself up, wobbling precariously from side to side. "Almost..." he said, reaching out.

Anna could see he was struggling, so she leapt up and hurried over to him.

"Just a little bit further—whoops!" There was a click followed by a great grinding, like the sound of gears turning on each other, as the horse's rearing leg that Olaf stood on sank down like a lever. Dust swirled into the air and Anna squeezed her eyes shut, turning her head away to avoid swallowing any more of the grime. And then... everything was still.

Everything was silent.

"Wow," Olaf breathed. "Now that's something you don't see every day."

Anna's eyes flew open and she gasped.

The bookcase behind the statue had swung inwards like a door. No, not *like* a door. It was an *actual* door, opening to reveal an arched entryway and, beyond it, darkness. And maybe – just maybe – something that would hold answers and help Elsa figure out how to cure the Blight.

Squealing, Anna plunged into the secret room – and immediately crashed her shins against something. She winced. Whatever she'd hit was definitely going to leave a bruise. Why hadn't she thought to grab a candle? Turning to head back, she saw Olaf waddling towards her, a candle in his hand. He stopped in front of her, the flame casting a creamy orange glow across his concerned face.

He raised a sceptical eyebrow. "I thought you couldn't see in the dark."

"I can't," Anna said. "Do you mind sharing the light?"

"Nope!" Olaf handed it to her. "You'll need it to see that person standing right behind you."

Chapter Three

ANNA WHIRLED ROUND, stifling a shout.

But as she held up the candle, she realised it wasn't a person at all, but a metal helmet expertly forged to create the illusion of a fearsome grimace and sharp teeth. It had thrown her off at first, out of sheer surprise and because it was different from the helmets that Arendellian soldiers wore. In fact, the more she looked at it, the more Anna was certain that this helmet came from the same era as Aren of Arendelle, from that long-ago age of heroes that was now more legend than history.

As she raised the candle higher, the sphere of light widened to reveal the rest of what they had found: a windowless room filled from flagstone floor to vaulted ceiling with sparkling shelves.

The shelves had been carved into the stone walls, and unlike the rest of the castle, these walls hadn't been papered or painted over or decorated with rosemaling. They were left bare, and the tiny crystals embedded in the rock seemed to wink a friendly greeting as the candle's light passed over them. It wasn't just the rock that glittered underneath a layer of dust, but also the many strange and wondrous objects that sat on the shelves: a gleaming pair of silver scales, schematics of what looked like a dam, glass beakers and bottles filled with fascinating specimens of flora and fauna suspended in brackish water.

And there were books. They spiralled upwards into the rafters of the ceiling, the only surface that had been painted and resembled a sky alive with the northern lights along with familiar constellations: Ulf the Wolf, Frigg the Fisherman and many others. There were wide books with thick leather spines, tall books with thin spines, books with yellow pages, books with ragged pages, squat books, medium-sized books and tiny books no bigger than a thumb. Anna's mouth dropped open. No matter how different they looked, each book had the possibility of containing the answers that she so desperately needed.

Olaf teetered forward into the room. "Oooh, more books! *Secret* books!"

"Secret books..." Anna mused, and her initial excitement dimmed. She knew she should have been more excited at the discovery of the secret room, but something about the *secretness* of it all pinched, leaving her feeling slightly bruised. She slowly made her way to the shelves. She wondered who had used this room. Arendelle's royal family had lived in the castle for decades – ever since her grandfather King Runeard had overseen its construction when her father was just a boy. Perhaps this room had been a place of solace for a long-ago aunt or uncle.

Anna skimmed the titles. Some were written in languages that she didn't know but recognised from her research for the grand tour. Others were in indecipherable symbols. But the ones that she could read made her heart backflip: *Hulda's Hideout*; *Scrolls of Trolls*; *Of Nightmares and Nixies*; *Quests of Yore*; *Sorcerer's Craft and Games*; *Legends of Magic*; *Deciphering Magic...*

Magic. Anna's thoughts pulsed with the thump of her heart. Magic. Magic. *Magic!*

Magic was not *unknown* in Arendelle. After all, Elsa had magical abilities that no one in the kingdom had ever seen before. Or at least, no one alive had ever seen. In some of the old stories that were favourites of Queen Iduna's, magic abounded. She'd told tales about tablecloths that could produce banquet-sized feasts in the blink of an eye, and boots that could travel seven leagues in a single step – of shape-shifters who lived in an enchanted forest, and stones that could turn lead into gold... but those were made up. Make believe. Pretend.

However, in the last three years, Anna had seen incredible things, *impossible* things, come to be. A sister who could be one with the earth and sky and build ice palaces with a few breaths and some nimble flicks of her wrist. A queen who could harness the cold. If Elsa could exist, as Anna very much knew she did, then why couldn't other impossibilities exist as well?

Why couldn't there be a spell of sorts, or an enchantment, that could fix whatever was happening with the Blight? Sure, Anna was hoping to find something in this room to help with the problem at hand, but *after* that, who knew? Maybe there was knowledge somewhere in there that could stop horseshoes from ever rusting, bread from ever going stale or candles from ever melting down to stubs and going out. She'd be a hero.

"Aha." Anna pulled a thick volume from a shelf and plopped it down onto a bare worktable in the centre of the room alongside the candle. "This one might have something helpful." She tapped at the title and read it out loud to Olaf. "*The Alchemist's Almanac: A Guide to the Care and Keeping of Fields, Accurate Accounting of the Weather and Wheat.*"

Olaf looked down his pair of ice spectacles at Anna. "Not exactly my genre."

Anna smiled.

"Ooh, this one seems cryptic and dense!" Olaf said, tugging out another thick book. "Here! You might like it, too!" He held it up for Anna to see. Its cover was a beautiful brown with black lettering. The title wasn't written in an alphabet Anna recognised, but as she squinted at the book, a forgotten memory – more of an impression of sound and colour, really – coalesced: the soft fabric of her mother's dress beneath her cheek as Anna snuggled into her lap. A warm pressure at her side – Elsa, who'd climbed up to join. Words, low and gentle and hazy as her mother read out loud from a book, its cover the colour of Anna's new riding boots.

Lullabies about secret white rivers and Earth Giants and lost legends of yore... Could it be?

Setting the almanac back on the shelf, Anna cracked open the new book and saw the title again written in runes. Someone had written next to them, in pencil, the words *Secrets of the Magic Makers*.

Anna's breath caught.

It was her mother's handwriting.

Anna would know it anywhere.

This book. This *room*: her mother had known about it; she had been here. These books and objects about magic were *hers*. Suddenly, Anna's chest felt too small for her heart. Or maybe her heart was too big for her chest. *Secrets*. This castle was full of secrets she had not known – was not *allowed* to know. Questions rattled through her: Why was Anna always shut out? Why had her mother collected all these books about magic? And... did Elsa already know about this room? Like when they were children, was Anna the last to know again?

"Anna?" She felt a gentle pat on her shoulder. "Don't judge a book by its cover."

At Olaf's words, Anna felt her ribcage loosen, just a tad, but it was enough that she could breathe again.

Olaf had been the friend of both sisters; he was a little bit of Elsa and a little bit of Anna, created by them together. And looking around, Anna didn't think Elsa knew about this secret room. After all, Elsa had been so good about filling Anna in on everything she had missed during the time when her head had been under the troll's persuasion, when she'd been made to forget Elsa's magic even existed. Elsa didn't keep things from Anna, not any more.

"I'm not, Olaf." Anna flung back a braid. "This book... it was my mother's."

"Oh." Olaf peered down through his spectacles. "Her reading selection appears to have been very *specific*. I'd rather check out this book." He waved a slender black volume in his hand. "It's about dangerous shape-shifters living in a cursed forest."

"Why don't you give it a read?" Anna asked. "Who knows – maybe it'll mention cursed animals, too."

"Shout if you need me!" Olaf plopped down at the worktable to page through it.

Meanwhile, Anna's eyes prickled. Her mother's book. She flipped through the rest of the thick pages. The runes looked like meaningless constellations, but the translations next to them had been made by her mother, and she would follow her mother's footprints, or fingerprints, as they were, anywhere.

Secrets of the Magic Makers seemed to be a book of old tales, brief histories and maps showing the way to the Valley of the Living Rock, but also a glossary of sorts, naming all kinds of creatures that only existed in lore. Spirits of wind, water and fire. Earth Giants. Nattmara. Huldrefólk. They all sounded so familiar, but it was like Anna was trying to stare through a bedsheet hung out to dry. At some point in her life, she'd known what these bedtime-story words had meant in crystal-clear detail, but now she could not make out any more than the slightest shape. Sadness crept over her.

Mother would have known. Anna hadn't just lost her mother when the ship sank beneath the Southern Sea's waves. The world had lost Queen Iduna's stories and lullabies, and there was no way to recover them. Or was there? Anna kept turning the pages. There were too many emotions at war within her to settle on any one page, on any one definition. Faster and faster she flipped through the book until fragile pages slipped out and flitted to the floor.

Anna froze. As carefully as she could, she picked

up the papers to realise with relief that they weren't pages from *Secrets of the Magic Makers* at all, but scraps of research that had not yet been bound in. One page displayed some familiar-looking blueprints: it was Arendelle Castle. Anna squinted at the page. She, like Gerda, already knew all the secret passages and places that were marked, except for one that drew her attention now and the one she was currently *in.*

Below the castle, something called the Earth Giant's Passage seemed to run from somewhere beneath the ice room next to the kitchen and then turn south, under the waters of Arenfjord, to... to somewhere. Anna couldn't tell. The black ink ran off the page, unfinished. But instructions had been printed in the margins. *Three flagstones in, two across.*

"*Fascinating,*" Anna whispered and set aside the blueprints. As soon as she found something to help the animals, she would *definitely* be taking a trip to the ice room. She shuffled to the next piece of paper. It was a map of Arendelle and the land that surrounded it. Markings circled a black sandy beach and a place called the Dark Sea, and scrawled across it in that same clean flourish that distinguished her mother's handwriting was one of her father's many sayings.

The past has a way of returning.

It was underlined twice, as if it meant something important. Anna squinted at the words, trying to make sense of them. But she was confused. The past *was* the past, so how could it ever come back? And why would her mother have written it on a map... a map that was stored in this particular book in this secret room? Was it supposed to mean something?

Anna yawned. Maybe the words didn't mean anything special at all. Most likely, she was only looking for meaning because she so badly wanted meaning to exist. And because she dearly missed her mother and, for a moment, had felt close to her again as she read her book. Or maybe it was because she was tired. So very, very tired.

Anna had no idea how much time had passed since she and Olaf had entered the secret room, and with no window, it was impossible to tell. Tucking the map back inside the tome, she looked up to find Olaf balancing on a dusty wooden chair as he pulled a snow globe from a shelf.

"Hey, look what I found!" Olaf called. "Snow that can exist in summer – just like me!" He plopped a kiss on the globe. "Hello, little pocket flurry." Giving it a shake, he sent the glittering snow swirling around a miniature of Arendelle Castle carved from a seashell. It was pretty, and Anna had definitely seen that snow globe before: not the actual snow globe, but a sketch of it in her father's sketchbook she still kept in a place of honour on her dressing table.

"I think my father also knew about this secret room," Anna said, "which means that there's only one family member who might not know about it yet." She snapped *Secrets of the Magic Makers* shut. "We have to go tell Elsa!"

"Tell me what?"

Chapter Four

ELSA HAD RETURNED.

And though Anna knew her sister had been up since way before her, had held a meeting for the villagers, visited a farm, scoured the library, then visited another farm, she was still crisp and clean, her blonde braid a streak of sunshine against the burgundy of their mother's cosy scarf, which was now wrapped around her shoulders. Elsa stood still, her mouth open, staring in what could only be called astonishment at Anna and Olaf inside the secret room.

"H-how? I mean, did you…" Elsa sputtered. "What *is* this place?"

Happiness and relief washed over Anna. From the expression on Elsa's face and the way her voice shook, Anna knew – the same way she knew that ice was cold and fire was hot – that Elsa had not known about this particular secret. For once, Anna had not been the last to know.

"We found a clandestine room," Olaf said. "*Clandestine* means secret. But I guess now it's not so clandestine. Unless you can keep a... what's the noun form of *clandestine*? Keep a *clandestiny*?" He still held the snow globe in his hands. "Do you mind if I show this to Sven?" And before the sisters could reply, he skipped out of the room.

"I don't know, exactly," Anna said in reply to Elsa's question. "But isn't it *wonderful*?" She gestured to the secret room's shelves and fought the urge to giggle as Elsa took a few steps into the room and looked around, her eyes wide, taking in the dried herbs, the gleaming copper spyglass and the creamy swirl of what appeared to be a narwhal tusk. Elsa moved closer to the shelves.

"How did you *find* this place?" Elsa asked.

"Olaf," Anna said. She filled Elsa in on the items, the map, the notes and the book she felt could hold the answers to their problems. At the mention of their parents having been in this room, Elsa gasped.

"And so," Anna concluded, "I bet we can find something in here about the Blight."

"I don't know about that," Elsa said. "But whatever is affecting SoYun's cows is also affecting the Westens' goats. I couldn't wake them up. I tried everything."

"I mean, look at this title!" Anna plucked the *Alchemist's Almanac* from the shelf and turned back to Elsa, but Elsa's attention seemed to have snagged elsewhere, onto an old golden frame that had been carefully leaning against a wall. The painting inside of it was muddied by grime, but Anna thought she could just make out a pair of eyes and a strong jaw: a portrait.

Picking it up, Elsa blew and a puff of dust ballooned into the air, settling on Anna's face. Anna sneezed while Elsa held out the painting at arm's length and squinted. "I *think* this is supposed to be Aren of Arendelle. The painting is so dirty, though, it's hard to tell."

Anna placed the almanac back on the shelf and peered over Elsa's shoulder. "What makes you think it's Aren?"

Aren was a legendary leader from times of old – the very, *very* old, before the last ice age, even. So old, in fact, that it was most likely the famous warrior had never even existed.

"See that?" Elsa pointed at a dark smudge. "I think that's supposed to be Revolute, his sword with a 'yellow diamond, bright as an eye.'"

Anna stared at her sister. "Are you... quoting something?"

"Yeah," Elsa admitted. "That's a line from the *Saga of Aren*, written by an unknown poet whom some claimed was actually Aren's true love."

It sounded kind of familiar to Anna. While she knew everything that there was to know about Arendelle, there were still *some* things, like these fine details, that she knew she'd *once* known but had forgotten. The things that she'd forgotten were usually stories her parents had shared. Embarrassment crept through her. She hated when she forgot things!

She tried to remember everything she could about Aren. There were endless stories and epic poems about his brave deeds – from helping the Huldrefólk hide their tails to journeying under the sea to sing with mermaids or questing to mountaintops to meet the sun. According to that particular story, Anna recalled, the sun had been so impressed with Aren that she'd given him a sword called the Revolute Blade. With the sun's sword in his hand, Aren had carved the fjord between the mountains. And not just any fjord, but *this* fjord: Arenfjord, the backbone of the kingdom of Arendelle.

"Is that the one that goes, 'Revolving moon and spinning sun, forged a crescent blade', and... something, something, something, 'May the flags of Arendelle ever wave'?" Anna asked.

Elsa nodded. "Exactly." Anna's embarrassment subsided as Elsa pointed a little above the smudge to a blur. "I think that might be the yellow diamond in the pommel, and then there" – she moved her hand – "see how the blade curves? According to myth, the curve is where the sword first struck the earth. That's how the sword got its name. 'Revolute' means 'curved'."

"Magic swords are nice and all," Anna said, tilting her head and fanning herself with her hand. It was getting hot in the windowless room. "But I don't really see why it would be helpful to be able to make cuts into the earth."

Elsa fiddled with her braid as she looked at the painting. "Apparently, the sun bestowed Revolute with great powers, and with the sword in his hand,

Aren became known as the protector of the people, unifying them against a dark fright. He was a great leader." A strange expression settled on Elsa's face. "History seems to be *full* of great leaders."

Anna glanced at her sister. For some reason she did not quite understand, Elsa seemed to have left the room, even though she hadn't physically gone anywhere. She no longer looked at Anna. Instead, her gaze was fixed on a shelf full of books, bottles and jars.

"Why were they studying magic? And why did they seal off the room and never tell us about it?" Elsa asked, her voice so soft that Anna wondered if she'd meant to say anything at all. Elsa stood there, with her back impossibly straight, standing the way a queen should. But at that exact moment, Anna didn't see Elsa, queen of Arendelle. She saw Elsa the lonely child, who'd spent her days alone in her room with only patterns of frost to keep her company.

Anna reached out to touch Elsa's arm. Her sister was stiff, as if she didn't just wield cold and snow, but were made of it. "I have the same question," Anna admitted, glad they were in this together. "But think about it: why do people study art?" she asked. "Why does Baker Blodget spend her entire life in pursuit of baking the best butter biscuits in the world? Why does Kristoff keep trying to sing?"

Elsa remained silent, so Anna answered for her, reaching down to pick up *Secrets of the Magic Makers*. "Because talents are worth exploring. Because butter biscuits are delicious, singing is fun and your magic is beautiful, Elsa. Maybe they wanted to know more about it."

She slipped a hand in Elsa's and waited. A few seconds later, Elsa squeezed her fingers, and Anna squeezed back. Without meeting Anna's eye, Elsa moved away from her and towards the exit.

"I need to go." Elsa's voice was quiet. "This place creeps me out."

"What do you mean?" Anna didn't think she had ever been in a more beautiful room with still so much to explore. The possibilities were endless!

"It's all these things in jars." Elsa waved her hands. "Contained and locked away."

"Well," Anna said, tucking *Secrets of the Magic Makers* under her arm, "maybe that just means it's time for them all to be brought to the light of day." Excitement again rose within her. "The answers to how to stop the Blight could be in here! Maybe there's even more magic out there, magic that can actually help us!"

Elsa flinched.

"I—I didn't mean it like that," Anna said. "Your magic is really helpful. Just not in *this* situation."

Elsa took a step back. "I need to help the livestock before we can start really delving into this room, okay?" Elsa said. "There's no time to waste. I... I have to go."

"Of course. But—but *we*... I can stay here and keep looking for clues," Anna suggested. "We may be able to find the answers to what's happening to—"

Elsa shook her head. "I really think we should leave this place alone for now."

"Hold on," Anna said, desperate to keep her plan in place, desperate to help. "There's so much we haven't uncovered! The books might have the answers!"

"I have to go now." Elsa's voice was sharp as an icicle.

"But we—"

"*We* should leave this room in the past. There has to be a reason Mother and Father wanted to keep it secret. Besides," she said as she gestured towards the door, "the answers to our problems are out there."

No, Anna thought, her fear big and full and pressing

against her chest. It was happening again. Her plan to prove herself to Elsa was falling apart! Who cared about being able to go on some silly grand tour? Anna wanted to do what was best for everyone, but she seemed to have a knack for doing the complete opposite these days.

"Stay away from this room, Anna," Elsa continued, turning away from her and stepping towards the library. "It was left hidden for a reason. Let's keep it that way."

"*Elsa—*"

"Leave it alone." And when Elsa spoke in *that* tone, more like a queen than a sister, Anna knew there was no point in arguing.

Silently, Anna nodded. As she placed *Secrets of the Magic Makers* back onto a shelf, Elsa returned to the library and strode to her next scheduled appointment. But Anna couldn't bring herself to leave – not just yet. She let herself look one last time at this secret room, imagining how her mother might have sat at that worktable, translating symbols into words, while her father studied the objects on the shelves and cracked a clever joke.

Without really thinking about it, Anna reached

her fingers back towards *Secrets of the Magic Makers*, but they stopped just short of touching the soft leather. Elsa might be really upset with her if she found out what Anna was thinking, but Elsa would be even *more* upset if the animals kept getting sick. It would be worth it, Anna told herself firmly, when everything had been fixed – when *Anna* had fixed things. Besides, Elsa had only said that Anna needed to stay out of this room, but she hadn't said – or at least, hadn't said *specifically* – that Anna couldn't take some of the room *with* her.

And with that, Anna tugged her mother's book free and hurried away.

Chapter Five

IT WAS VERY LATE NOW and Anna was hungry.

Stopping to grab a plate of cheese, crackers and apple slices from the kitchen, she chatted with the castle cooks, catching up on local gossip: who was most likely to grow the biggest pumpkin in the village patch this year, how many people would attend the annual harvest feast, and the very exciting rumour that an engagement ring had been purchased at the jeweller's shop, but by whom?

Usually, Anna would have loved to stay and muse, but she knew the more time she spent down there, the less time she'd have to research. And so, excusing herself with her cheese plate, Anna rushed into her warm bedroom, clambered into her most comfortable pyjamas and began to read.

Secrets of the Magic Makers was more than just a collection of stories. It almost seemed like a field guide, as if someone had traipsed through the wilderness collecting information on various mythological creatures while also gathering ingredients for turning flowers into frogs. There were histories of enchanted forests, and things that looked like recipes. And while several of the text passages had not been translated by her mother, many had.

Anna followed her mother's handwriting like a hungry bird trailing crumbs. Crunching on her crackers, she read of shape-shifters who lived with herds of reindeer; talking trees; draugs; and boys who were no larger than a thumb. There were pages and pages of the unknown language, and every so often an illustration accompanied the symbols. Anna wondered if Kristoff would know anything about the runes, or if he had ever come across anything in the Valley of the Living Rock that might help. Were they runes of the mountain trolls? Or something else?

Her mother seemed to have skipped translating the pages with the more creepy-looking sketches. Anna flipped past a sketch of a man seemingly screaming in agony, then one of another man lying on a stone table as blue smoke curled from his head and a troll stood over him with its arms held high. Finally, she landed on a page that, based on its illustrations, seemed to detail the *Saga of Aren*.

The physical features of the legendary hero were much easier to see in this book than they had been in the portrait Elsa had uncovered. Aren had a shaggy head of yellow hair and a bright blond beard with a few skinny braids tucked into it. His face was more square than it was round, and his hooked nose put Anna in mind of an eagle. Though there were only runes on the page – no translation – Anna recognised some of his more famous exploits. In the corner was a sketch of the waterfall whom Aren had tricked into helping him breathe underwater. And just to the right of that, a sketch of the sun, each ray a delicate sword with a yellow diamond in its pommel, just like Aren's famed Revolute Blade. And in the last corner, far right and down, lounged a scrawled dragon. Anna turned the page and cringed.

A sketch of a wolf, so realistic that Anna half thought she could feel its hot breath blasting from the pages, snarled up at her. Her mother seemed to have only got to the very beginning of the page, and had translated only a single word: *Nattmara.* Anna frowned. Yet another one of those once-known-now-forgotten words from her childhood. In frustration, she flipped the page. She'd had enough of not knowing – and enough, as a five-year-old, of that scary recurring nightmare, thank you very much.

The next installment that made her pause was a recipe. It was a loose page, simply tucked into the binding, but it had been neatly titled in her mother's handwriting: *MAKE DREAMS COME TRUE.* There was another word scrawled in the margins in the same handwriting: *SPELL?* Anna's fingers traced the word *spell.* Not a recipe – *magic.*

She had never known anyone other than Elsa to be able to use magic before, and Elsa certainly didn't incant words or spells when she created and manipulated snow and ice. The magic was part of Elsa. It ran within her. Shortly after their reunion, Anna had asked Elsa what it felt like when she twirled her hands. Elsa had described it as an overwhelming emotion, a *feeling* that would eventually grow so big it had to find release in some way.

"Like when you want to cry but you hold on to

it because you don't want others to see?" Anna had asked.

"Yes," Elsa had said, "but not just crying. Sometimes, it's the feeling of clamping in a giant laugh in a time you're supposed to be quiet, like in the chapel. It seems that if I listen to the feeling, to the magic, and release it, I can manage it."

A poem in a book didn't seem like the kind of magic Elsa possessed, but that didn't necessarily mean these words would *not* hold any power. These words. This *spell.* Excitement trilled through Anna.

The more she looked at the words, the more certain she felt that everything they needed was right here, in their parents' research. She just wished she knew what knowledge lay behind the untranslated sections. Anna squinted at the symbols, as though by simply staring at them she would come to understand. But no knowledge came, only heavy eyelids.

She wondered if Kristoff had found out anything helpful on his trek to the valley. She wondered if SoYun was still out in the field, trying to keep her cattle awake through the night. But most of all, she wondered what her parents would have done in this situation.

"Anna and Elsa, always lean on each other for help,"

Father had said. He'd have wanted her to tell Elsa about this spell, but first, she just needed to rest her eyes. Anna's thoughts slipped over and past each other like darting fish as her eyelids drooped lower and lower and lower... She needed to fix the Blight...

The court of Royaume was just as beautiful as Anna had always dreamed, and she knew she was dreaming – not only because she'd never been to Royaume, but also because everything felt too perfect and fragile to be real. Besides, Elsa would never be caught dancing in real life, and there she was, spinning on the dance floor, arms flung wide as if she were trying to embrace the chandeliered ceiling above them.

Anna grinned. "You look like a tree caught in a gale!" she shouted over the high song of violins and flutes.

"And you look like you're dizzy," Elsa said.

Anna shook her head. "Dizzy? Why—oh!"

Before she could finish her question, Elsa grabbed her hand and began to twirl her, her diaphanous white skirts fanning around her like a skein of sparkling snow.

Anna threw back her head and laughed, imagining what a sight they must make on the dance floor. Elsa, dressed all in white spangled with pearl seeds, was the very embodiment of winter, while Anna's headdress and gold skirts helped her masquerade as summer.

CHAPTER FIVE

*The grand ballroom blurred around her, seeming to turn
into streaks of paint. Her head began to pound, but it was so
rare to see Elsa silly and carefree that she didn't want to tell
her to stop. Instead, Anna closed her eyes, trying to hold on to
this moment, even if it was only pretend... but was it?*

*She was feeling really dizzy now. No matter how much fun
Elsa was having, it was time to stop.*

*"Hey, Elsa? That's enough!" Anna opened her eyes and
gasped.*

Her sister was no longer twirling her.

*Instead, a tall stranger in coat-tails and a silver wolf mask
stood where Elsa had been.*

*Anna stumbled to a halt. "Pardon me." She removed her
hand. "I need to find my sister."*

*The dancer bowed, the silver wolf mask nearly tipping off
his nose. "As you wish, Princess Anna."*

*The blood in her veins turned to ice. Anna knew that
voice. It was a voice she didn't want to hear again. She peered
uncertainly through the dark eyeholes of the mask. "Prince—
Prince Hans?"*

*"The very same." A diamond ring suddenly materialised
in his hand. "Your sister said I should give this to you when I
ask for your hand."*

"My—my hand?"

Hans grabbed her wrist and jammed the ring onto her finger. "Your hand in marriage, of course. Your sister has given her blessing. She has no use for you."

Anna yanked her hand away. "I don't believe that," she said, craning her neck to see if she could spot her sister in the glittering hall. But no one was there. The decorations, the musicians, the dancers... all had vanished, leaving her completely alone with the prince of the Southern Isles – her villainous almost-husband, who had tricked her and the rest of the kingdom before Anna uncovered his awful plans to kill Elsa and take over Arendelle.

Hans laughed, an awful sound, made worse by the way it turned up into a howl at the end. As Anna watched, the silver hair of his wolf mask rippled in the draught as if it were real fur, and his nose elongated, becoming more and more snout like.

More and more wolf like.

Until suddenly, there was no Hans, just a great white wolf with amber eyes and teeth the size of dinner knives. It was the same wolf that had stalked her childhood dreams. But while most things from childhood seem to become smaller as one grows, the wolf had, in fact, only grown with Anna. He was fiercer now. Hungrier.

The wolf licked his maw and advanced.

Wake up, Anna, *she thought frantically, tripping on her skirts as she tried to scramble backwards.* Wake up! Wake up! Wake up—

"Wake up!" Anna sat straight up. The sound of her own voice shattered her nightmare. Relief, warm and sweet as fresh honey, coursed through her. It had been so long since she'd had this particular dream, this particular nightmare, and the fear it spawned was unfortunately as familiar as the ache of missing her parents. And this time, there was no Mother to tell her a distracting story or Father to bring her hot chocolate.

Always rely on each other for help.

Leaning forward, Anna grabbed *Secrets of the Magic Makers,* which had slid to the foot of her bed. She tucked it close to her chest and raced into her parents' old bedroom. Not because she thought they would be there, but because Elsa had moved into it after her coronation, abandoning her childhood bedroom. But looking around the room and at the dying fire, Anna wondered why Elsa had not yet returned. She reassured herself that sometimes queenly duties could last all night.

She walked back to her room. Before clambering into bed, she stopped by her dressing table and took hold of her father's sketchbook. King Agnarr had been a talented artist, wielding both his pencil and sword with ease. On the bad days, when Anna felt most alone, she liked to open his sketchbook up and see the world as he once had. There were images of Arendelle Castle, as well as the far-off lands he'd seen on his grand tour.

Elsa would leave on her own grand tour in just four – no, now *three* days – and if Anna could heal the animals before then, there was still a chance she'd be able to sail away with Elsa.

Returning to her bed, Anna decided that she'd wake up extra early to show Elsa the spell first thing. And so, with her father's sketchbook on one side of her pillow and her mother's book on the other, she at last dared to close her eyes.

The wolf did not return.

Chapter Six

ANNA HEARD THE SOUND of chimes and footsteps from somewhere in the castle.

Dawn had broken, spilling warm autumn sunlight across her face. Keeping her eyes closed, Anna stretched, enjoying the cosiness of her quilt and the softness of her pillow. Just a few more minutes. She could afford to wait before she found Elsa, asked more about the Westens' goats and told her about what she'd found last night in their mother's book. After all, she was so comfortable that it would be a *crime* to untuck herself, and—

Her thoughts screeched to a halt.

Secrets of the Magic Makers. The book with spells in it. The book with a potential cure for the animals.

Anna lurched up, eyes flying open – only to be blinded not by the light of dawn, but by golden mid-morning sun. She'd overslept again!

Faster than Sven could chomp a carrot, Anna tumbled out of bed before she could even untwist herself from her quilt. She grabbed *Secrets of the Magic Makers*, and with her blanket flapping behind her, she sprinted through the dressing room and downstairs. Not bothering to knock, she flung open the door to her parents' old bedroom. The bed was neatly made, the ashes cold in their hearth.

Of course – her sister would have been up for hours at this point. Elsa, for some strange reason, enjoyed mornings. She said they made her feel fresh as new snow, while they made Anna feel as fresh as chicken droppings. A headache pounded at her temples. Even though she'd overslept by hours, it had been a restless sleep, as it had taken her long hours to relax after the return of the childhood nightmare.

Think. Where would Elsa be at this time of day? Whirling from the bedchamber, Anna ran down the hallway to peer through open doors. Elsa wasn't in the library or council chambers. Maybe the portrait gallery? Anna flew downstairs and made a sharp turn on the landing – and barrelled into something warm and solid.

Anna flew backwards, sprawling onto the ground. A dull pain rattled through her backside, but thankfully, the majority of her fall had been cushioned by the carpet. *Ow.*

"Hey!" the warm wall grumbled from above. "Watch where you're going!"

"You watch where *you're* going!" Anna replied, and instantly regretted it. That's not what someone hoping to be a royal ambassador on a grand tour should say. "I'm sorry," she added, looking up to see the old, wrinkled face of Madam Eniola staring down at her.

"Anna!" Madam Eniola bobbed a curtsy, her long brown skirt contrasting with the bundle of white ribbons she held in her arms. "My apologies, I didn't recognise you in your..." Her eyes swept up and down. "Quilt?"

Anna winced. Royal ambassadors should also probably remember to put on proper clothes before carrying out their important missions – and to comb their hair, too. Her hair didn't look so much like hair as it resembled a bird's nest. "That's all right." Anna clambered to her feet. "I should have been paying attention." *Like always.* She pulled her quilt tighter around her and hoped it looked more dignified than her ruffled pale green nightgown and bare feet.

Anna knew Eniola as one of the new villagers who'd moved to Arendelle from Tikaani, and specifically as the one who had taught Tikaani's national anthem to Anna. Eniola lived in a cosy cottage on the outskirts of the farmlands. Holding her chin up, Anna asked, "What brings you to the castle, Madam Eniola?"

Eniola sighed, and the creases on her face, which already held more lines than King Agnarr's old sailing charts, seemed to increase tenfold as she frowned. "I'm here to speak to the queen." She pursed her lips. "We *all* are."

Anna arched an eyebrow. *"We?"*

Eniola stepped back to reveal more villagers lined up outside the Great Hall, staring at Anna. She recognised many of her friends – the sweet-maker, the farmer, the gas lamp lighter, the miller, the two blacksmiths and many more. Many, *many* more.

Anna's eyes widened as she saw that the line of villagers extended from the double doors that led into the Great Hall all the way through the second great hall and into the portrait gallery. Anna's mouth went dry and she cleared her throat. "Why do you need to see Elsa? Erm, *Queen* Elsa?" she asked.

Eniola held out her bundle of ribbons, which Anna saw now were not actually ribbons at all. They were strands of wheat, but instead of the long golden straws Anna was used to seeing from the tower window, *these* strands were short and mottled white – mouldy and rotten all the way through and recognisable only by the heads of grains at the tops. Even as Anna stared, a few seeds crumbled off into white dust. First the animals, then the crops. What was going on?

"We woke this morning," Eniola said, "and it's all like this – everything!"

The villagers grumbled in agreement behind her.

Anna needed to tell Elsa about all these villagers – *now*.

"Excuse me." Anna tore her eyes away from the pitiful bundle in Madam Eniola's arms and hurried downstairs in the direction of the Great Hall. "Pardon me, coming through!" The line shifted to allow Anna to wiggle by, and as she did, she saw that each and every person held white bundles similar to the one that Madam Eniola held: the pumpkins, usually the colour of the sunset, had large unsightly splotches splashed across them, while the apples, usually red, round and crisp, seemed to have the same consistency as raw dough. Up and down the line, Anna saw dried corn husks, white-mottled potatoes and carrots as pale as cream. Every crop, every vegetable, every grain Anna could think of, was destroyed. Rotten.

The Blight.

Anna picked up the pace. Squeezing past a harried-looking woman, she at last made it through the doors and into the Great Hall.

The Great Hall, as its name suggested, was exactly that: *great.* It was the largest room in the castle, with tall windows and a gleaming chandelier, capable of fitting a hundred dashing lords and twirling ladies, Elsa's throne and a massive chocolate fountain all at the same time. Once, it had even hosted an entire ice skating rink when a late winter storm had threatened the annual ice dance competition.

But now, for the first time Anna could remember, the Great Hall felt small. The single file line cutting through the portrait gallery hadn't prepared her for the absolute crush of people that filled the Great Hall. Even on the busiest market day on record

– shortly after Elsa's coronation, when everyone had come to see their new magical sovereign – there had not been *this* many people. Or maybe there had been, but joy didn't take up nearly as much room as fear. Fear filled the hall, as large and present as one of the Earth Giants in her mother's tales. The voices all around Anna were pulled tight, sounding as if they would break at any moment.

"Everything is gone! It's been ruined!"

"My cattle! They won't wake up!"

"Never in all my days! It's as if the very earth has gone awry!"

"Do you think this has to do with the Northuldra?"

"No," someone grunted. "King Runeard, may he rest in greatest peace, made sure they would never trouble Arendelle again."

"And the animals…"

Anna heard a strange noise from outside. It sounded like a mix of children learning how to play the violin crossed with the sounds of a zoo. Peering through the window, Anna gasped. The courtyard was just as full as the Great Hall, filled to the brim with farmers and animals. Sheep had broken loose from their shepherds, and the herding dogs, usually so careful, seemed distracted, following something in the air that no one else could see. All the animals looked like walking ghosts, their fur and hides the same sickly yellow-white. And even as Anna watched, a cow and two horses knelt to the ground, their eyes as large and black as lumps of coal, their mouths open and tongues lolling out until, suddenly, they fell asleep.

Anna's stomach turned. "Excuse me," she said over and over again as she tried to wade her way to the front of the hall, towards the throne where Elsa must be. Grumbling people followed in her wake as she weaved in and out of the crowd, and more than once, she had to tug her quilt from beneath someone's boot.

But with one last push, she made it to the throne, relief washing over her as she found Elsa standing there, just as Wael, the local journalist, yelled out, "That's not going to help us!"

"Wael," Elsa said, "if you would please only just—"

"*Ah-hem!* Winter is fast approaching." Wael's ink-stained fingers gestured wildly. "We will have nothing to eat! We deserve answers – and it's *your* responsibility as queen to give us answers and take care of your people! We don't have enough food to last the week!"

A hush fell over the Great Hall at his words.

Elsa stood tall, not backing down, but Anna knew her sister. She could see the overbright sheen of her eyes. It wasn't just ice that could sparkle in chandelier light. Tears could, too.

Anger, bright and hot, swept through Anna. "Don't speak to my sister that way!" she burst out as she reached Elsa's side.

"Anna," Elsa said, her voice low, "I've got this, it's fine—"

Anna glared at Wael. "No, it's not!"

The man glared right back.

"Elsa is doing her best," Anna ploughed on, her words coming fast and furious. "She has a plan! She'll fix everything before she leaves on the grand tour!"

Next to her, she heard Elsa's breath catch. "Anna—"

"That's in just three days," a tired-looking villager said, her arms full of what Anna thought was supposed to be emerald courgette but now looked more like great white slugs. "Can the queen really—"

"Anna—" Elsa tried again.

But Anna didn't listen. She was going to stick up

for her sister. Elsa might be able to stand there and listen to people doubt her, but Anna wasn't going to have any of it.

"Of *course* Elsa can!" Anna said, holding on to their glowing secret, the promise of the mysterious book.

"ANNA." Elsa flung out her hand. There was a time when icy spears would have sprouted from the floor, but Elsa had control of her magical powers now. Instead of a dangerously pointed ice spear, it was now just a gesture – to remind her sister to watch what she said. "I apologise for my sister," Elsa said to the Great Hall at large. Her chin had lifted in the exact same way Anna remembered her father lifting his during special ceremonies, when he was trying to be his most regal.

Anna opened her mouth to protest, but one glance at Elsa's expression squashed any words she had left. Her cheeks flushed. Burning anger transformed into burning embarrassment. What had she done?

"I understand your concern," Elsa continued, her voice steady and cool. "And I share it. What I've been trying to say is, to show my commitment to solving the problem of the ruined crops and sick animals,

I'm postponing my grand tour until I can sort out this troubling matter at hand."

"What?" Anna gasped before she could stop herself, shocked her sister would cancel her grand tour. She didn't understand what Elsa was thinking – what if postponement convinced the dignitaries and people from other lands that Arendelle wasn't, in fact, opening its gates, but closing them once again? And from the shocked look on Wael's face and the murmur of the crowd, Anna knew she wasn't the only one surprised by this announcement.

If they hadn't been standing in front of a large crowd of stressed villagers, Anna imagined Elsa would be rubbing her temples and sighing right about now. But they *were* standing in front of stressed villagers, and her sister never failed to live up to what was expected of her: she was queen, regal and unflappable.

"Because," Elsa said, speaking loud enough for all to hear, "the royal ship is loaded with rations of food, apples, wheat, dried vegetables, cheeses, cans of pickled herring and sausages. We need to share our surplus or else the villagers with Blight-stricken farms will suffer further." Once again, Elsa had come up with the perfect solution – one so obvious Anna wondered why she hadn't thought of it herself. Elsa was *so good* at seeing the larger tapestry, while Anna let herself get distracted by whatever thread was dangling in front of her at that very moment.

"That amount of food will only last us all three days at the *most*," Wael protested. "And what makes you think the food on your ship hasn't soured, *Your Majesty*?" There was something about his all-knowing attitude that made Anna want to release Marshmallow, Elsa's dangerous giant snowman – and Olaf's little brother – on him. But seeing as that wasn't an option, since Marshmallow was currently the housekeeper for the ice palace on top of the North Mountain, she'd settle for glaring at Wael instead.

"I'll scour our kitchen here," Elsa offered.

Beside her, Kai scribbled a note onto a ream of parchment, while brown-haired and kind Olina, in charge of overseeing the kitchen staff, clasped her gloved hands together in deep thought. Nothing ever missed Olina's careful eye, and Anna knew that she was probably already running through a mental list of food the castle kitchen could provide.

"What if *that* food's gone bad, too?" cried a voice from the crowd.

Anna held her breath while everyone stared at Elsa.

Elsa, however, looked at only one person: Olina. The woman gave a slight shake of her head: the kitchen was still fine. Anna exhaled, thankful that at least this one piece of news wasn't terrible.

"As your queen," Elsa said loudly, her voice strong, "I will see to it that you have food."

The crowd murmured, but Anna could hear the shift in tone. The conversation around her no longer vibrated with the intensity of a string pulled too tight. Instead, the words loosened and the conversation relaxed as the villagers considered Elsa's proposal.

"I think it's a good idea," Tuva called out. "My wife and I accept." And the two blacksmiths nodded in agreement.

"I accept, too," Eniola called out, and soon other villagers voiced their agreement as well. All except for Wael, who only reluctantly nodded, but not before adding, "Fine, but the *Village Crown* will make sure that you keep Anna's promise that the solution will be found before three days are up."

Pride filled Anna as Kai led the disgruntled villagers back out of the castle and towards the harbour to collect the supplies from the royal ship. She felt like cheering, but instead she settled on a quiet squeal and whispered to Elsa, "That was *brilliant*."

But Elsa didn't smile back. Instead, she walked to one of the more secretive side entrances to the Great Hall, hidden from view by a tapestry. "Anna," she said without turning round, "can we talk for a minute, please?"

Anna's smile slipped away as she followed her older sister. She might not know why the farm animals were sleeping or why their fur was turning white, or why the kingdom's food seemed to be turning to dust and ash, but she did know one thing: she was absolutely, completely, 100 per cent in trouble.

"Three days?!" Elsa whirled on Anna as soon as the tapestry fell back in place, obscuring them from view. "Anna of Arendelle, how on earth can I fix this mess, and so soon?" Even though Elsa didn't raise her voice, Anna could hear her frustration boiling underneath. "Between this and Kristoff—"

"Kristoff?" Anna interrupted, furrowing her eyebrows. "What about Kristoff?"

Elsa closed her eyes and rubbed her temples, just as Anna had suspected Elsa had wanted to do earlier.

"He's not here. I thought he'd be back by now, but..."

Worry zipped through Anna, but she forced herself to shrug. "I'm sure he's fine," she said. "You know how happy Bulda is whenever he visits." She smiled, thinking of the mountain troll who'd raised Kristoff as her own. "I bet you he's delayed because he's so full of mushroom stew that he's too heavy for Sven to carry and they have to walk."

But it seemed Elsa couldn't be distracted from her worry, not even with the funny image. Elsa shook her head. "It's so much pressure. I don't know what I can do."

"You mean, what *we* can do... with a secret book full of magic!" Anna said.

Elsa groaned. *"Oh, Anna!"* She shook her head. "I know you want it to be, but I don't think magic is the answer to all of our problems."

"Okay, I hear you, but *look.*" Anna held out *Secrets of the Magic Makers.* "There is so much information in here." She flipped through the pages until she found the one she was looking for. "See? This one grants your *dreams.*"

Elsa sighed. "Anna, I told you not to go back in the secret room."

"I didn't go *back* into it. I grabbed this book before I left the first time. Look at it!"

Reluctantly, Elsa glanced down at the page that had been pushed under her nose, but before she had a chance to skim, Gerda pulled back the tapestry, wearing her signature green skirt, jacket and cap, and holding Elsa's great big calendar.

"Your Majesty, I'm sorry," the woman said, and Anna could hear the sympathy in her voice, "but even with the grand tour postponed, this fiasco with the sickness has put us behind schedule. And now you must write explanations to all the different dignitaries and heads of countries to explain why you can't make it."

Elsa took a deep breath. "Yes, of course, Gerda, you're right. The work of a queen is never complete." She glanced over at Anna, who held her breath. "Here. Let me have that book. Maybe you're right. I promise I'll look at it as soon as I have a spare minute."

"Of—of course," Anna said, happy to share. But she would have been even *happier* if Elsa had told Gerda that Anna had found something important. That they were working on discovering a solution *together*.

"I'd like to meet with an animal expert now to get their opinion," Elsa said, and Anna noticed again that she was tugging on her fingers. "And a botanist. I'm not sure what should be done first..."

"If you need someone to write letters, I can help with that," Anna offered. "I've read up on all the different etiquettes of each country."

"That should be just fine, dear," Gerda said, her pencil already flying over the calendar to adjust it. "Just make sure Elsa signs them before you mail them."

"I will!" Anna promised, happy to help Elsa and happy to have something to do while she waited for Kristoff to return to the castle. She had so many things she wanted to ask him, starting with, *How do the trolls say we can cure the Blight?* and leading to, *Do you know how to read the mysterious ancient runes in my mother's book?*

"Thanks, Anna," Elsa said as Gerda hurried away to arrange everything. "If that's all taken care of, then I need to get going. I'll make sure I visit you before I go to bed, okay?"

But she turned before Anna could even nod.

And though Anna stood in the middle of a

crowded castle still bursting to the brim with villagers, the sight of Elsa walking away from her had never made Anna feel more alone.

Chapter Seven

THROUGH HER BEDROOM WINDOW, Anna watched the exodus of the castle staff trailing over the Bridge of Arches and into the darkening village.

That afternoon, Elsa had given the staff the option of leaving work with pay so that they could go help their nearby relatives whose animals and crops were suffering from the Blight. After she had written the letters, Anna had changed into her travel cloak and spent the rest of the day helping unload food from the royal ship and handing it out to the villagers amidst the groaning of sick animals.

She'd wanted to cover her ears, but then she thought that would be the cowardly thing to do. She couldn't just ignore the ugly things in the world around her. If people did that, no one would ever help at all, and nothing would become well again. And so Anna had gone to help the farmers dab white fur with wet washcloths to try to keep their livestock alert. She'd stroked a sad little foal's fuzzy ears as it curled up next to the sleeping form of its mother, who did not so much as stir at the foal's pitiful nickers.

Anna turned away from the window and paced, still in her travel cloak from earlier. Just as she'd thought, Elsa hadn't come to see her. She knew her sister was busy, but... Anna glanced out the window again, and made up her mind. Lighting an oil lamp, she quickly made her way through the now empty halls of the castle to Elsa's council chambers.

As Anna approached the doors, she was surprised to see no yellow light trickling out from beneath. Her breath quickened. Maybe something else had gone wrong in the village, something so bad that it had pulled Elsa away from the signing of the dignitaries' letters.

Anna knocked and when there was no answer, she let herself in.

Elsa was nowhere to be found.

But—Anna felt her mouth tighten.

There, lying unopened on the desk, was *Secrets of*

the Magic Makers. It was clear Elsa hadn't touched it. But she *needed* to! Anna knew people said she was too optimistic, naive about the way the world worked, and maybe that was true, but she had faith in stories. And she had faith that there was a solution to any problem, just as long as one kept looking. She just needed to get Elsa to listen to her.

Anna hurried back through the castle, gripping *Secrets of the Magic Makers*. She looked everywhere for her sister, until her eyes grew heavy with sleep as the sky continued to darken outside the castle. Maybe Elsa wasn't in the castle at all. Reluctantly, Anna trudged back to her room.

And then...

Voices.

Voices coming from Elsa's bedroom. Anna pressed her ear to the bedroom door, and though she couldn't make out the words, she recognised the low timbre of Kai's voice as well as Gerda's northern cadence.

Anna staggered from the door. Elsa was having a meeting without her! There was a time when Anna knew Elsa would have invited her to each and every single meeting, would have sought out her advice, but now... now it seemed Elsa no longer had any need for her little sister at all. Elsa had chosen to shut her out once more.

With all the dignity she could muster, Anna walked slowly away from the door, but as soon as she was out of sight from Elsa's bedroom, she broke into a run, trying to escape the emotion that threatened to overwhelm her. Rushing into the sanctuary of her own bedroom, Anna slammed the door shut and sat cross-legged on her shaggy pink rug, *Secrets of the Magic Makers* spread open in front of her. She studied the book, which blurred slightly in her gaze from unshed tears. Anna flipped through it again, and a loose page fell out, one that looked like it was ripped from another book.

Reaching for it, Anna was reminded of the same loose page that had given her so much hope the previous night. The page with a spell to make your dreams come true. Her tears dried up and Anna felt her sadness replaced by another rising emotion, one growing so fast and so big that it seemed to take on a life of its own. For a moment, she thought she understood what Elsa experienced when she used her magic. Anna *had* to let this wild, untamed hope free – even if Elsa didn't think it would work, there could be no downside to trying. And if it worked, maybe the doors to council meetings would reopen to Anna. Maybe the strained tension between Anna and Elsa would disappear. Because that was her dearest dream: Anna hoped she could help the people of Arendelle, working together with Elsa to find a solution that would make everything right again. And in the process, Anna hoped Elsa would realise she needed her sister, just the same way that Anna needed Elsa.

Tugging out the loose page, Anna whispered the words out loud:

"Wild, awake!
Wind and snow!
Plant the seed
And watch it grow!
Say this spell,
And you shall see
All your dreams
Come to be!"

A beat of silence. Anna felt foolish. What had she thought would happen after she read the spell? That her sister would materialise in front of her? Come racing in with open arms and lead her back to the secret room? Without her wild hope tugging her forward, Anna deflated. She crumpled up the dream spell page and put it in her cloak pocket, not wanting to look at it any more.

From the dressing room, Anna suddenly heard footsteps followed by voices.

"Poor thing, there is so much on her mind," a voice floated through the door. Anna recognised it as Gerda's.

"She bears so much," Kai agreed, his voice loud and clear as they passed right by her door.

The council meeting must be over by now. Which meant that at any second, there would be a knock on her door and Elsa would ask to come in. Any second now, she'd tell Anna how sorry she was that it took her so long to listen to Anna's suggestion and that Anna was right, they needed to look at the books in the secret room. Then Anna would show her *Secrets of the Magic Makers* and the loose page with the spell and they would fix everything. They would do it together. After all, they were sisters.

Anna sat up straighter on her rug and waited... and waited. The knock never came.

———

Anna's dreams were nightmare-tossed yet again. She dreamed of dark shadows in treetops, Earth Giants destroying the village, and a shipwreck on a stormy sea. And then ice. Anna had told Elsa she did not remember the moments during which she'd turned to ice. But that was a lie. She would never forget the horror of warm flesh turning cold, then all sensation fleeing as her warm blood frosted into stone-cold crystal. She would never forget the last bit of heat escaping through her final breath, would never forget seeing her sister sob and the unique pain of not being able to do absolutely anything at all. Tonight, Anna's nightmares would not *let* her forget. And so Anna's dream morphed...

She was a girl of ice, standing outside the castle, only able to peer into the window and never enter through the doors. Inside, she could see Elsa reading aloud to a girl, whose glossy white hair was pulled back in two braids. Anna didn't recognise the girl – her back was to the window – but she did recognise the girl's dress, a soft green one with sunflowers embroidered on the hem. Anna's birthday dress. She could see Kristoff entering the room, strumming his guitar and smiling at the girl.

Who are you? *Anna wanted to yell at the ivory-haired*

girl. Turn round! *But her frozen lips could not speak and Anna had to wait, impatiently and horribly, until, at last, the girl turned round to reveal... Anna's eyes. Anna's nose. Anna's smile. The white-haired girl was Anna – but she wasn't. Anna had been replaced. By this other person. And no one in the room, not Kristoff, Olaf, Kai, Gerda – not even her own sister – realised it. Or maybe they did and they simply did not care. A high howl pierced the air and the ice shattered. It broke away from Anna like a suit of armour, revealing her true self beneath. Suddenly, she could run, but the castle had shifted into a wide white tundra and there was no place to hide before the wolf appeared. Because it was already there.*

Without turning round, Anna felt the yellow eyes of the wolf fixed on her back. She ran. Yet, no matter how hard she pumped her legs or how fast her heart beat, nothing seemed to change. There was just a flat expanse of grey snow below her and even greyer sky above. The world was colourless and bleak and without hope, and then—

An explosion of red pain burst through her vision as the wolf's claws raked and sank into her back.

Anna expected to wake up – she always woke up.

But this time, she didn't.

Instead, the wolf flipped her over onto her back, opened its huge jaws and swallowed her whole.

Anna's eyes flew open. Sweat sheened her skin and she felt hollow, as if her insides had been scooped out, like a gutted pumpkin. Something prodded her back.

"Troll's toes!" Anna exclaimed to nobody as she pulled the book out from beneath her. Sometime in the night, she must have dozed off on the floor and rolled onto the book, its thick spine digging into her own, explaining the sharp pain of the wolf's claws in her nightmare. Anna let her head sink back onto the floor and flung her hand over her eyes.

"This is getting ridiculous," she muttered, hoping the sound of her voice would chase away the lingering fear. "You're too old for this kind of stuff." Though, she didn't *feel* old. In fact, that was kind of the problem. These last two days, she had felt *oh so very young* indeed. And that ache that always lurked just beneath the sea of her thoughts surfaced, sending a ripple of sadness through her.

How she missed her parents. Her mother would have fixed everything with a story or two about silly and magical things, like shaggy goats outwitting trolls or an empress who forgot her clothes. And her father, he would have chased away any lingering fear with a candle that crackled and emitted a sweet, soothing scent or a warm mug of hot chocolate.

Mmmm... hot chocolate... with marshmallows.

"Come on, Anna." She spoke out loud again, trying to shake the loneliness. "They're not here, but you can definitely get your own mug of hot chocolate. It's not like the wolf is hiding beneath the bed or something." She let out a soft little "Ha!" for good measure. The sound wasn't very convincing, but there was no one she had to convince but herself. And so, she got off the floor, and the terrible, awful nightmare that had ended differently than it ever had before – with the wolf finally winning – slipped from her tired mind.

Anna realised she was still in her travel cloak, but she didn't care. She could change into her pyjamas once she got back. Taking a flickering candle from her bedside table, Anna was her own source of light in a castle of darkness. The flame was weak, yet just bright enough for her to make her way through the familiar halls and down to the kitchen. And—wait. What was that?

Lifting the candle up a little higher, Anna paused on the stairs. She thought she'd seen a bit of movement, a skim of white. But as she strained her eyes to peer beyond the candle's light, Anna didn't see anything unusual or out of place or snarling with fangs...

"You're being silly," she chided herself. "Keep going. Remember: marshmallows!" Still, the memory of the nightmare resurfaced and trailed her through the corridors, down the stairs and into the kitchen.

The kitchen was the beating heart of the castle, the cheery red-glow of its stoves producing delicious banquets and even more delicious heat that cut through the autumn's creeping damp.

Tonight, though, the kitchen felt oddly empty and quiet. The pots and pans, instead of being clanged around by busy cooks, were hanging quietly on their hooks in neat lines next to colourful garlands of garlic, dried peppers and herbs that draped from the ceiling, dropping down to tickle the lids of jams, beetroot and pickled herring. Usually, at least one cook remained to keep an eye on the fire stoves, but Elsa had dismissed the cook staff, too, including Olina – which meant only Anna, Elsa, Olaf, Gerda and Kai were sleeping in the castle that night. Which explained why it felt particularly quiet, dark and empty.

That – and the fact that Sven and Kristoff still weren't back yet. At least, Anna didn't think they were back yet – she didn't know for sure. Usually, outings to the Valley of the Living Rock didn't last this long, and since he knew things weren't going too well with the villagers, he'd know not to linger. He was a mountain man; he could take care of himself. But still, Anna began to worry and hoped they had made it back. Despite her optimism, she always worried for those she loved. It was what made Anna... Anna.

She sighed, heart heavy, and shuffled over to the stove. Making hot chocolate was simple, and while she wasn't great with cooking that required twenty different detailed steps and ingredients and lots of fine chopping, she was adept at mixing delicious chocolate powder with milk and setting it on the stovetop. But as Anna stirred the pot of warming milk to stop a skin from forming, she heard a soft clatter.

She stopped stirring. "Hello?" she called hopefully. "Kristoff, is that you?"

No response.

She thought she heard the sound of footsteps fading away, but from the other side of the kitchen leading towards the stairs. Maybe Kristoff was wearing his earmuffs and hadn't been able to hear her through the fluff. Typical Kristoff. Or maybe it was Olaf. Perhaps he was up for a night of reading a gripping passage about existentialism or a book on another '-ism'.

Quickly, Anna turned off the stove and removed the milk. The hot chocolate would have to wait. The footsteps were too intriguing. If it was Olaf, she'd leave it alone. But if it *was* Kristoff, she had to know what the trolls had said about the Blight. Still... it wasn't really cold enough yet for Kristoff to be wearing his earmuffs. Like Elsa, the cold didn't seem to bother him as much as it did the non-mountain folk. After all, he'd grown up in the cold. Taking the candle, Anna followed the footsteps up the stairs to the rest of the castle.

"Kristoff? Is that you?" she asked.

It sounded like the person was walking through the portrait gallery, then the second great hall, and finally, the Great Hall. She stood in the doorway, lifting her candle as high as she could. It only shed light on the polished wooden floor. She hadn't heard the footsteps *leave* the Great Hall, which meant Kristoff, if it *was* him, was still there in the dark room with Anna.

She stepped inside, peering behind each column that lined the wall of the cavernous room. She yanked at curtains and moved from one to the next.

"Kristoff?" Anna called. Her candle's flame danced this way and that. Nothing, nothing, nothing, two yellow eyes, nothing, nothing – Anna stopped breathing.

Two yellow eyes.

She brought the candle back around and saw the form of a wolf.

White and massive, exactly like the one in her nightmare.

Except this time, it was different.

Because Anna was awake.

Chapter Eight

ANNA HAD ONCE HEARD that when someone faced death, their life flashed before them.

But as she stood there in the gloom of the Great Hall, with the yellow eyes of the wolf fixed on her, it wasn't her life that flashed through her mind – it was the details of the Great Hall. The quivering red curtains that outlined each pillar. The gleam of the curtain's rod in the glow of the candle. The heat of the candle wax as it dripped onto her skin. She noticed all of this in the breath it took for the wolf to growl. Then it leapt at her.

Anna jumped out of the way, the knife-sharp claws missing her by mere inches. The wolf growled in frustration, and the sound seemed to reach into Anna and scrape against her insides, but she managed to drop her candle, grab the curtain and tug – hard, sending the curtain's rod clattering onto the floor. Snatching it up, Anna half ran, half stumbled towards the great double doors that seemed as far away as the moon.

One stride, then another, and then – she was through!

Slamming the doors shut, she pushed the curtain rod through the two handles, locking the doors in place just as the wolf threw its bulk against the other side with all its might.

THUMP!

The doors rattled, but stayed shut.

THUMP! THUMP! THUMP!

How long would the curtain rod hold? Anna had never seen a wolf so large. Or rather, she had, but only in... Something stirred inside of her, something she knew she needed to examine closer, but the little feeling about what could have brought the wolf from her dreams into the castle would have to wait for when she wasn't running for her life.

"HELP!" Anna yelled as she sprinted away. "WOLF! BIG, MASSIVE WOLF! IN THE CASTLE!" The only thing that beat faster than her heart was the single insistent question pounding through her brain: *What to do? What to do? What to do?* She'd faced a pack of wolves before, when she and Kristoff had journeyed to the North Mountain to try to find Elsa – but Kristoff and Sven weren't here right now. She needed to find Elsa, and quickly. She flew up the stairs in the second great hall. She needed to find help. But as she sprinted down the hall that led to Elsa's bedroom, she saw a flash of white up ahead. The wolf – it had somehow escaped the Great Hall!

She groaned. It was just like in her dreams; the large-as-a-bull wolf seemed to outwit and outrun her at every turn. But *how*? She knew wolves were fast, but they couldn't possibly be *this* fast. Gasping for breath, Anna pivoted and sprinted down another hallway. She turned left, right and then left again. She didn't know exactly where her feet were taking her, but she realised she would be near Kai's room if she made a final left. Maybe she could hide in there!

As the castle's steward, Kai had protocol for everything, from the right way to hold a teacup to the exacting ritual of snuffing out the candles and oil lamps one wick at a time. There was a chance that maybe he already *had* a plan for a wolf breaking into the castle. *A wolf! A wolf! A wolf!* Her breath came short and fast. From somewhere behind her, she thought she heard a howl. Only twenty more feet until she reached Kai's room... five feet... one foot...

"KAI!" Anna catapulted into the steward's room and bolted the lock behind her. She noticed his form lying in his bed. "Kai, wake up! There's a wolf in the castle! What do we do?"

But the man remained completely still.

Unease trickled through Anna. It wasn't as if she were being quiet. In fact, she was being very loud. Why wasn't Kai waking up? She lit a candle from his bedside to see.

Kai twisted and turned under his blanket, and as the light hit his eyelids, he muttered, "No, please... don't!"

He was in the middle of a nightmare.

Anna knew from personal experience that no one should be woken in the middle of a bad dream.

But there was a wolf now pawing outside the room.

Usual rules did not apply.

"Kai, wake *up*!" Anna shook the steward's arm. "Please, please, *please* wake up."

Kai's eyes snapped open, and Anna staggered back. The steward's eyes were usually the same brown-green colour as changing autumn leaves or muddied creeks. But instead of looking into warm hazel eyes, she was staring into two inky pits. His pupils had swallowed his irises, turning his eyes completely black. *Just like the cattle.*

Suddenly, Kai sat upright and screamed.

And screamed.

And screamed.

And screamed.

He screamed as though long claws were tearing out his heart. As though sharp teeth were sinking into his skin. As though he were being eaten alive from the inside out.

Anna placed a hand on his shoulder to try to comfort him, but he didn't react to her touch. It was as though she were invisible. Kai couldn't see her – couldn't sense her. He was lost.

The pawing outside the door grew faster. Hungrier. More desperate. And as the scratching grew in intensity, Kai's black eyes suddenly shifted again. One moment, they were black, and the next, they were yellow... and glowing.

Anna's heart seemed to fly up into her throat and she almost choked as she staggered backwards.

What was *happening*?

The scratching stopped. Or had it? Anna couldn't be sure, as Kai's scream continued to fill the room, making her clutch her ears. She needed to get out of there. She needed to find Elsa, Olaf, Kristoff and Sven, to warn the others. The people of Arendelle were in danger. All of this was Anna's worst fear, worse than her wolf-filled nightmare. Because it was real. It was happening. How and why, she would still have to think about later.

She took a step towards the door. Kai's yellow eyes stayed transfixed somewhere beyond her, as though witnessing unseen horrors. She crept by him and pressed her ear to the door. Nothing. Not so much as a yip. But what if the wolf was out there, waiting for her in silence? And worse: what if it *wasn't* out there, and was headed for others instead?

"ELSA!" Her sister's name ripped from her throat as she undid the lock and ran out of Kai's room, leaving him screaming and writhing. "ELSA! ELSA! ELSA!" she yelled.

Minutes before, Anna had felt the quiet of her home. But it wasn't quiet any more. Now she could hear more screams echoing throughout the castle. Screams she recognised as Gerda's. Anna had the sinking feeling that if she went to her, she would be too late, that Gerda would have the glowing yellow eyes like Kai. She practically sobbed. *"ELSA!"*

The door to their parents' bedroom slammed open and a moment later, Elsa appeared in the hallway, still in her work dress but wrapped in their mother's scarf, and with heavy bags under her eyes. Olaf waddled behind her, in a fuzzy yellow robe and with a matching sleep mask pushed up on his forehead. He also held the snow globe from earlier.

"What's wrong?" Elsa asked.

At the sound of her sister's voice, Anna almost collapsed with relief that Elsa wasn't asleep and screaming. And Elsa's eyes were blue – blue as the sky, and blue as a song.

"A-a wolf!" Anna sputtered, wrapping Elsa and Olaf in a fierce embrace. "Wolf! Kai! Gerda!" she gasped and then choked out, "Eyes! Glowing yellow eyes!"

"Elsa," Olaf whispered, "she's not making any sense."

The next second, Anna felt a cool hand on her forehead as her sister checked her temperature. At Elsa's touch, Anna felt her frenzy subside, just a little.

She wasn't sure if it was Elsa's magic or if it was just because the gesture was so familiar and comforting, but it made her want to cry. Their mother had done the same thing whenever Anna had woken up in a sweat from the fearsome nightmare that had plagued her childhood.

Anna managed to take a deep, shuddering breath. "That's because nothing makes sense!" After they bolted upstairs into the council chambers and locked the doors, Anna told them what had happened. The story came out jumbled, details piling up all out of order. Elsa didn't interrupt. She listened, and when Anna at last came to the end of it, she gave her a firm and understanding nod.

"Are you sure you didn't just have a bad dream?" Elsa said.

"It sounds like it," said Olaf, pushing his sleep mask up a little higher.

Anna stared at Elsa. "What? No! There is a *wolf* in the castle!"

Elsa rubbed her temples. "It's late. We should get back to bed."

"*What?*" Anna pulled away from her sister. "You don't believe me?"

"Question." Olaf had unbolted the lock and peeked through the doors. "Wolves usually have four paws, two eyes and long, sharp teeth, right?" When the sisters nodded, he pressed a hand to his mouth and tilted his head. "Then I'm preeeetty sure we should believe Anna."

The door flew open, blowing off Olaf's robe and mask, and sending the snow globe falling to the floor with a *crack*. The wolf had found them. Its sharp shoulder blades jutted up and down as it moved, like some sort of terrifying carousel creature. Its long legs brought it closer and closer, following Anna, Elsa and Olaf as they backed up and skirted around the long table.

Before Anna could scream, a wall of ice erupted from the wooden floor. Jagged crystals raced up to the ceiling in the centre of the room, knitting themselves together to form a thick protective barrier, with Anna, Elsa and Olaf by the doors and the wolf walled off on the fireplace end. Anna's gasp of surprise turned white in the cold of Elsa's magic.

"*Now* do you believe me?" Anna asked her sister.

Elsa ignored her. Her eyes swept the room. "We need to go find—"

But Elsa's words were cut off.

THUMP. THUMP. SCREEEECH!

Cobweb-thin lines scattered across the ice wall as the wolf pawed at it, its claws screeching. It was a terrible sound, even worse than the sound of teeth scraping against a fork, which until then Anna had thought to be the most awful sound imaginable. The ice wall wasn't holding. It was shattering.

"*Run!*" Elsa shouted, raising both her arms.

Anna didn't need to be told twice – and Olaf was already right by her side. Sprinting out the doors of the council chambers, they made their way for the stairs, down towards the great front doors that would take them to the castle bridge. But as Anna and Olaf neared the landing to the first floor, two pairs of yellow eyes shone at them from the shadows, blocking their path to the front entrance. Kai. Gerda.

Anna's stomach twisted. She'd been right, but oh! How she wished she'd been wrong. Gerda's friendly face was now an oval of agony – her eyes and mouth were all wide and round as she screamed and lurched towards them, something glistening in her hand: a pair of sewing scissors. And next to her, Kai clutched a red-hot poker.

"Put out the flames. The house is burning," Kai croaked, jabbing the iron at them as though *they* were the phantom flames attacking him. "It's burning!" he cried.

"Well, this can't be good," Olaf whispered as Gerda stepped forward with the blades of the scissors snapping open and shut, open and shut.

The look in their yellow eyes was not human, but something else.

Predatory.

Wolf like.

It's a wolf pack, Anna realised with horror.

Suddenly, a great shattering sound erupted above them, as if a thousand crystal goblets had been smashed... or one gigantic wolf had managed to break through a magical ice wall. A second later, Anna heard her sister's footsteps on the stairs behind her and Olaf.

"KEEP GOING!" Elsa shouted down to them.

"But Kai and Gerda want to prevent us from imminent escape and possibly cause us harm!" Olaf called back, darting behind Anna's travel cloak and away from the hot poker.

"Don't stop!" Elsa called.

Anna didn't know what to do – Kai and Gerda were blocking the only path to escape the castle and a massive wolf was barrelling down the stairs towards them. The only direction left was *down* – but there was no castle exit in the below-ground kitchen and they would end up trapped there, or worse, in the ice room.

Wait. The ice room. There was something important about the ice room. Something Anna had wanted to check out... the blueprints! The blueprints that had shown a secret passageway that led out from underneath the castle.

"Elsa!" Anna yelled at the top of her lungs. "Meet us in the ice room!"

Anna and Olaf practically flew down the rest of the stairs with Elsa bringing up the rear as she blasted the stair landing with mirror-smooth ice, making it difficult for the pack to follow them down the stairs. Anna didn't turn round, not even when she heard two *thuds* and a *whoosh* that she assumed were Kai and Gerda slipping on the ice, unable to chase any farther.

But that didn't mean the wolf, with its large hooked claws, couldn't navigate a bit of ice.

Anna, Olaf and Elsa continued racing downstairs. They burst into the kitchen, only to discover they weren't alone.

Kristoff sat in the middle of the room at the long table, scoffing down a sandwich, and by the number of crumbs scattered in front of him, it wasn't his first sandwich of the night.

Relief washed over Anna: Kristoff was back, and he was okay! Anna took stock of the details. Kristoff's blond hair was tangled, as if he'd spent the night in the woods or the mountains. His patched traveller's pack, lantern and pickaxe were slung across his shoulders, as if he'd been too hungry to wait even a second more. Sven made happy munching noises as he buried his nose in a bag of carrots. They must have only just returned from the Valley of the Living Rock. Horror collided with her relief. Horror, because she'd thought – she'd *hoped beyond hope* – that Kristoff and Sven were far, far away from the castle and somewhere safe in the woods. Relief, because she wouldn't have to face this terror without him. Kristoff looked up, a crumb dropping from his chin.

"Hi, Kristoff!" Olaf darted into the kitchen and sprinted past the table. "Bye, Kristoff!"

"RUN!" Anna yelled, barrelling towards him. With one hand, she grabbed Kristoff's elbow and pulled him after her.

"*Mwaf?*" he asked, his mouth full of sandwich.

But Anna didn't have time to explain, because the wolf was there, there in the kitchen. And though it was impossible – all of this was *impossible!* – the wolf seemed to have grown three feet since they had left it in the second great hall. Its shoulders brushed the sides of the door as it swaggered into the room, eyes glowing, jowls drooling a thick slime.

Kristoff dropped his sandwich onto the floor. "*MWAFFFF!*" he yelled.

Now all five of them – Sven, Elsa, Olaf and Kristoff, with Anna in the lead – sprinted towards the back of the kitchen, to the door that led into the ice room. Anna pushed open the heavy door and held it as Kristoff, Olaf and Elsa ran through. But where was Sven? Peering back, Anna's heart stopped.

Fear seemed to have frozen Sven in his tracks. He

remained still, a carrot in his mouth, as the wolf loped closer to him. It knocked aside the long wooden table with an ear-bleeding screech of its legs against stone.

"Sven!" Anna shouted. *"Run!"*

But it was as if Sven couldn't hear her. Instead, his eyes remained fixed on the wolf's glowing ones. He lifted a hoof and took a step... *towards* the wolf.

"SVEN!" Kristoff yelled from over Anna's shoulder.

At the sound of his best friend's voice, the wolf's strange hypnosis over Sven seemed to shatter. Sven staggered backwards, tripping over his hooves as he twisted on his haunches and stumbled through the door, leaving Anna just enough time to slam it shut on the wolf's slick snout. Sven wobbled beside her, shaky but safe, and Kristoff threw his arms around him. Elsa blasted the door with ice to hold it, and with a wave of her hand, thirty or so blocks of ice scraped across the rough stone floor to settle in front of the door, for good measure. But would it be enough?

Elsa panted and tucked a loose strand of hair behind her ear. "It might be a strange wolf with glowing yellow eyes, but it has to have a hard time clawing through stone and ice!"

The sounds of the wolf clawing and pawing against

the door made it sound like perhaps, just maybe, it was making impossible progress.

"Now what?" Elsa called, taking in the room. "Why did you want us in here?"

"One second!" Anna said, squeezing her eyes shut, not just to try to keep out the mental image of the wolf hunting them, but to try to remember what the blueprints had said about the entrance to the Earth Giant's Passage. Something about *three flagstones...*

She counted three flagstones in and two across, and hurried to one in the centre of the room. As she knelt down and placed her fingers around the edge of the stone, she hoped with all her might that the blueprints had been complete, that they weren't just a fanciful wish of her heroic grandfather King Runeard, who had built the castle.

Holding her breath, Anna pulled and the flagstone lifted away, revealing carved stone steps leading down into darkness. "Yes!" Grinning, she gestured to the entrance. "Olaf, you first!"

"Oh, I can't wait to go somewhere new!" he said with an excited wave of his arms.

Aroooooooooooooooooo! The sound of the wolf's howl seemed to burrow its way towards them, twisting and tumbling around Anna, surrounding her, becoming both up and down and around.

"Me first!" Olaf hopped down the steps.

Covering her ears to drown out the howling, Anna followed him, along with Elsa and Sven. Kristoff was last, and as he clambered down, he pulled the flagstone securely back over them, plunging them into utter darkness. For a moment, Anna was aware of everyone's breathing, and she wondered if they could all hear the pounding of her heart.

"What *was* that thing?" Kristoff finally whispered.

No one responded, but Anna knew.

It was not just a wolf.

It was a nightmare.

Her nightmare.

And it was coming for them.

Chapter Nine

ANNA'S HEAD POUNDED, her stomach twisted and her heart hurt.

She wasn't sick, and yet, in a weird way, she wished she were, because colds came and went of their own accord, but this – this aching feeling – *she'd* brought that upon herself. Just as she *must* have brought the wolf upon the castle. She wanted to believe it was a coincidence that the wolf had appeared after she'd read aloud the 'Make Dreams Come True' spell, but she couldn't.

Anna had dreamed of the wolf her entire childhood. Now, Kai and Gerda – people who had loved and raised her – had yellow eyes and were trapped in their own nightmarish realities. Why hadn't she listened? Elsa had *told* her to leave the secret room alone, that their parents had probably left it a secret for a reason. And now, Anna had unleashed her nightmare on Arendelle.

"It's a good thing it's so dark," Olaf said from somewhere to Anna's left. "If there are flesh-eating monsters down here, at least we can't see them!"

"Always looking on the bright side," Kristoff's voice called back. "Anna, what is happening? What is a wolf doing in the castle? And where are we now?"

"Elsa," Anna said, fumbling in her cloak pocket for the scrap of spell with one hand, and reaching blindly out into the darkness for her sister's shoulder. "I need to tell you something—"

"One second, Anna," Elsa's voice said from a little further away. "Kristoff, can we get some light?"

There was a rustling, followed by a *scritch* as Kristoff struck a match and lit the lantern clipped to the outside of his traveller's pack. Usually, Anna felt better when there was light, but the wavering lantern flame cast huge shadows across the rough rock walls and across her friends' faces, distorting their familiar features and turning them into strangers. And

– Anna's breath lodged beneath her ribcage – was that a glint of yellow she'd spotted in Kristoff's eyes?

"Seriously," Kristoff said, his face twisting with frustration as he ran expert hands up and down Sven's withers and then peered into Sven's ear. The poor reindeer was trembling from his close encounter with the wolf, and was standing so close to Kristoff he was almost on the mountain man's toes. "Would someone *please* tell me what is going on?"

As he patted down Sven's quivering legs, he turned his head and the yellow speck Anna had thought she'd seen disappeared. It had only been the lantern reflected in eyes. Her panic dissolved, just a little, and she took in where she had led them. They were at the start of a tall, wide tunnel, hewn directly from the rough rock of the castle's tiny island. The path led away from them, disappearing into more darkness.

"Where are we?" Elsa tilted her head back and looked up, wide-eyed.

"It's called the Earth Giant's Passage," Anna said. "It was on the blueprints in the... the secret room."

Elsa looked at her for a long moment. "You and that secret room."

"What?" Anna said. "It *was*! And *that secret room's blueprints* got us away from the wolf!"

"So," Elsa said, clasping her hands together, "do you know where this passage goes?"

"Not... *exactly*," Anna admitted. "I think it goes under the fjord, but it wasn't clear on the blueprints."

"So, you're telling me it could lead to anywhere, including a dead end?"

Anna's stomach twisted. "I... I didn't think of that."

Elsa sighed and shook her head. "It's fine. I'll think of a solution."

The words stung Anna, as though Elsa had physically thrown them at her. Anna had let her down. If Elsa was *this* upset about just the blueprints, what would she say if Anna told her she had recited the spell? When exactly was a good time to admit to your sister you'd messed up big-time?

Suddenly, Sven bellowed. His eyes rolled back and Anna could see white ringing them. In that same instant, from high above, Anna could hear knives being sharpened. No, not knives. *Claws*, scraping against a flagstone floor. The wolf was digging for them.

"We have to go. Now!" Elsa whirled away

from Anna, transforming from annoyed sister to commanding queen. "I'll go first, in case... in case there's anything up ahead. Olaf, do you think you could...?"

"Put my eyes on the back of my head?" Olaf swivelled his entire head 180 degrees. "Already done."

Elsa nodded. "Thanks. And if things happen, I want you all to run without stopping. Got that?" Without waiting for a reply, Elsa took the lantern from Kristoff and strode forward through the tunnel, the lantern scattering pale shadows across the rough stone walls.

Kristoff offered his shoulder to Sven, who rested his head on it. "What kind of *things* do you think Elsa meant?" he whispered to Anna.

"I think she means if anything goes wrong, we're supposed to leave her to handle it," Anna explained.

"Like, if there's a cave-in," Olaf added helpfully. "Or an avalanche, or if there's a monster, or if you lose a nose, or if the wolf or Gerda or Kai attack us again, or if Kristoff's eyes turn yellow—?"

Anna threw a hand over Olaf's mouth, stopping the plethora of awful possibilities. "We'll be fine if we just stick together." She wished and hoped that was true. She withdrew her hand from Olaf and smiled. "Besides, we have something the wolf doesn't have."

Kristoff raised an eyebrow. "What's that?"

Sven's ear perked also, waiting for an answer.

Anna nodded towards the light and felt her own frustration fade. Even though her sister's outfit was simple enough – a sensible heather-blue split dress perfect for long days at a desk or afternoons visiting a farm – it still glimmered where the lantern's light kissed it, just the way that everything Elsa touched seemed to sparkle afterwards.

Anna smiled. "We have Elsa." And with that, she hurried to catch up.

They ran as fast as they could through the passage, which is to say not very fast at all. In part because the passage was so roughly hewn that it proved tedious to navigate, and in part because Sven still seemed shaken and terrified of the wolf, which was presumably still scrabbling at the flagstone somewhere far above them. Sympathy flitted through Anna. As terrified as she had been, it must have been a thousand times worse for a reindeer, whose greatest natural threat was the wolf. Anna noticed that Kristoff kept a hand on his best friend's neck, and now and then, she caught an occasional note as Kristoff sang to him.

Meanwhile, Olaf, his eyes facing backwards, kept treading on the hem of Anna's travel cloak. The third time it happened, Anna stopped, recalling how Elsa used to carry her long ago, and crouched in front of him. "Olaf, how about a piggyback ride?"

"Don't mind if I do!" Olaf said. But without his eyes facing forward, it took him more than a couple of attempts, one of which knocked Anna flat onto her belly. "Ta-da!" Olaf climbed onto her back. "I did it!"

"You did," Anna grunted. "Just stay put while I try to get up."

"Anna?" Olaf asked, sitting on her back. "Are you okay?"

Anna replied, somewhat breathlessly as she pushed down with her palms, "I'm fine."

And that's when Elsa screamed.

"ELSA!" Anna cried as a new strength flooded through her. She launched to her feet. Pulse in her throat, she flew down the passage, Olaf clinging to her neck. The tunnel was dark but for the slightest halo of light.

"Elsa! Kristoff! Sven!" Anna cried. "What's wrong?!"

Horrible thoughts stampeded through her mind,

but Anna was able to slam them all out except for one: an image of the wolf, silent as the moon, stalking Elsa, while Elsa's blue eyes drained of their colour and shifted to a glowing yellow.

The tunnel bent slightly and then there they were: Elsa, Kristoff and Sven. Anna scanned them for any signs of injury, but nothing seemed amiss. No one was bleeding. In fact, there was no sign of anything wrong. And, the more she thought about it, there was no way the wolf could have possibly passed her in the passage to have reached them up ahead.

"What's happening?" Anna panted. "Why did you scream?"

"Sorry," Elsa said, her cheeks flushed pink. "I guess I'm a little on edge, and then when I saw it, I, well..." She gestured behind her.

The tunnel had widened into a chamber, though Anna could see that it narrowed again on the far side of the hall. It looked like a python that had swallowed a whole egg, the egg visible in its gullet. And in the farthest shadows of the chamber, Anna saw—

"A dragon!" Anna exclaimed, stepping backwards only to tread on the hem of her cloak.

Olaf spun his head round to face forward again,

prodding Anna's ear with his carrot nose. "Silly Anna. It's not a dragon, it's a boat *shaped* like a dragon."

Kristoff rested a hand on Anna's shoulder. "Don't worry. Elsa thought it was a dragon, too," he said with a kind smile.

Anna squinted in the dimness. It was a boat. Or a longboat, actually. Unlike the tall, multi-decked and multi-masted ships with butterfly-wing sails in the harbour above them, *this* boat was sleek, and laid long and low to the ground like a canoe. It had one simple mast, and its only height came at the front and back, where its wooden planks were swept up into the graceful point of a dragon's tail at one end, and the dragon's fearsome teeth at the other. It took her breath away – though part of that was due to jogging with a snowman on her back.

"This isn't just a tunnel," said Elsa. "I think it's... a tumulus."

"Oooh. A tummy *what?*" Olaf asked.

Elsa smiled, but it seemed tinged with sadness. "It's a burial mound," she explained. "In the long-ago days, people used to build large dirt mounds called tumuli and lay their fallen leaders in their boats, along with everything they would need to take with them into the afterlife, favourite things like bronze shields, drinking goblets and gold coins."

"It's beautiful," Anna said, wanting to explore this unexpected treasure. She loved nothing more than answers, and a broken bit of pottery or a single glass bead from a long-ago age could tell a lot about the cultures and tales that had been lost to time.

Later, she told herself. *One more reason you have to fix what you've done.*

"I wish it were a real dragon," Olaf said, interrupting Anna's thoughts and pulling her back to the present.

"I think a wolf is more than enough to deal with right now," Elsa said, already holding up the lantern again and taking a few steps away.

Kristoff nodded. "If we don't move, this place may become a *new* grave site."

Olaf shook his head. "Poor Fredrick. I don't think he'd like this place very much."

"Who's Fredrick?" Anna asked.

"The wolf," Olaf said, as though it were obvious. "He looked like a Fredrick, don't you think?"

"I wasn't talking about the wolf," Kristoff said, and shrugged his traveller's pack higher onto his shoulder. "I was talking about *us.*"

They continued to move, faster now and silent. They needed to save their breath to navigate the dark and twisting shadows of the passageway. After a few minutes, Anna thought she felt the ground begin to slope upwards, but she couldn't be sure, and she didn't want to get her hopes up.

"Do you hear that?" Elsa asked suddenly.

Anna listened. She did hear something – a low rumbling. A sound that was almost like thunder, or what she imagined a sleeping Earth Giant's snore would sound like, or—

"A waterfall," Kristoff said. "I think we've gone under the waters of the Arenfjord and ended up on the other side."

New energy quickened their steps. A few minutes later, they turned a corner to see a frothy curtain of water cascading down rock and a weak, grey light trickling through into the tunnel. It was that time of night that wasn't night at all, but the earliest moments of morning, the few minutes before the sun would break the line of the horizon.

Night would soon be officially over, but... what other nightmares had Anna dreamed that could come true? Would her teeth start to fall out? Would she look down to see she was standing in only her underwear? Or maybe it would be a brand-new nightmare, one where Elsa exiled her from the kingdom once she learned about Anna's wayward spell.

The spell. Her stomach twisted. Anna didn't like when secrets were kept from her, but holding her own secret made her feel like she'd eaten some of the Blight-stricken food. Now that they were leaving the tunnel, away from the wolf for at least a moment, she needed to tell Elsa. Maybe together, they could figure out a counter spell. Anna took a deep breath.

"Elsa? I have something to tell you—"

Elsa held up her hand. "You don't have to say it."

Tilting her head, Anna squinted at her sister. "Say *what?*"

"'*I told you so,*'" Elsa said with a small, tired grin. "I get it. You found the passage, and it was helpful. I'm not going to say otherwise. Can we please make a truce?"

Anna gaped at her sister, not knowing what to do. On the one hand, she was pleased that her sister seemed happy with her. But on the other... Elsa didn't know that all of this was Anna's fault. And while Anna wasn't exactly *lying*, the more seconds that ticked by, the more uncomfortable the omission made her feel, as though she were more of a scribble of Anna than an Anna who fully filled in all her lines. She hated to keep a secret – but she was more afraid of losing her sister. Oh, *now* what should she do?

But she was spared making a decision when Olaf emitted a squeal of glee directly into Anna's ear. He jumped down from Anna's back and she stumbled slightly from the sudden lack of weight.

"Hooray!" Olaf cheered. "We're not going to die in a tummy lice!" And then he sprinted down the path. Anna's breath caught. He wasn't really going to run straight through a waterfall, was he? Turns out he was, because in the next second, the water pounded on Olaf's shoulders as he waded into it.

"Oooh! A somewhat *unpleasant* massage!" he said, and then the snowman was through to the other side.

Anna heaved a sigh of relief. Sometimes when Olaf tried something new, he'd fall apart and they'd have to take time to go looking for his arms or nose or other body parts. And there was no time to spare, not when the wolf could show up at any moment.

Even though she didn't *think* it could dig through solid rock, she couldn't be sure of anything any more.

She glanced over her shoulder for the billionth time, just to check again.

Kristoff reached out a finger to test the temperature of the waterfall. "Yikes!" He yanked his hand away, and the tip of his finger was bright pink. "That's ice-cold, even by my standards!"

"Hardly," Elsa said, examining it. "Or else it would be frozen." She smirked.

Kristoff made a face. "Touché."

"I've got this." With a flourish of Elsa's lantern-free hand, an arch of ice appeared in the middle of the falls, sending water flying into the breaking dawn and scattering rainbows everywhere.

And as Anna walked under the arch, leaving behind the shadows of the passageway, she felt her headache lift slightly. Her stomach untwisted just a bit, too.

Wolves did exist, yes, but so did rainbows and sisters. There *had* to be a way for Anna to fix her mistake. And there had to be a way she could fix it herself, without adding to Elsa's pile of work. She just needed time – *space* – to think it through.

The Earth Giant's Passage had deposited them on a small ledge that overlooked the village, and the group paused to take count. They were all there, though Anna noted in the dim light of dawn that Olaf's twiggy hair seemed a bit bent out of shape, and new purple crescents had appeared under Elsa's eyes. Kristoff, too, looked bedraggled, even by his usual standards. The cold, crisp air tugged at the fabric of Anna's attire, giving her goosebumps. She pulled her travel cloak closer around her and was thankful she hadn't changed into pyjamas.

"I think we should warn the village," Kristoff said, shifting his weight as Sven moved his head onto his shoulder.

Anna's headache returned with renewed vigour, but she tried to focus. Because Kristoff was right. "Yes! We warn the village! Tell them to stay inside!"

Elsa shook her head. "You saw that wolf. I don't think hiding is going to help."

"Then we need to tell them to get far away!" Anna said as she tried to push her loose hair out of her eyes. She wished she'd thought to grab a spare hair ribbon so that she could wrangle her hair into manageable braids, instead of letting it hang loose and tangled around her shoulders.

"But then again, what if the wolf is there now,

prowling the village?" Kristoff asked, and then switched to Sven Talk. "What if he's already full?"

It was almost *too* horrible of a thought, and Sven's ears, which usually pricked forward, seemed to droop like a pair of discarded socks as he swayed on his hooves, looking as though a sneeze from Kristoff would be enough to knock him over.

Anna glanced at her sister, waiting for her to decide what to do. But Elsa didn't say anything. Instead, she stared out across the Arenfjord towards the castle. And even though the castle looked the same, it didn't feel the same. Anna knew all too well that things didn't have to *look* different in order to *be* different. One morning, she'd gone to bed having two parents. The next morning, she'd woken up an orphan.

As she squinted at the castle, Anna caught a speck of white in the window of the guard tower. Beside her, Olaf had put his ice spectacles back on and was staring at the castle windows as well.

"Fredrick's looking for us," he said, adjusting the lenses so they sat better on his nose. "It doesn't seem like he knows we're gone..." Olaf lifted a hand to shield his eyes. "Oh, no, never mind. He does."

"How do you know?" Anna asked.

Olaf pulled his gaze away. "Well, I think he misinterpreted why I raised my hand."

"What does *that* mean?" Elsa asked.

"He definitely took it as a friendly wave to come and join us. Which I think is what he's going to do."

"Elsa?" Anna's voice squeaked.

Elsa's brow furrowed the way it always did when she was looking for something she'd misplaced, or, more likely, that Anna had removed and forgotten to put back. She seemed to be sinking deep within herself. Then, taking a deep breath, Elsa gave the lantern back to Kristoff and raised her hands, like a conductor about to direct a symphony.

At first, Anna didn't see any change, but then she noticed the waterfall's roar had grown quiet. Looking behind her, Anna gasped.

The water was no longer in the waterfall.

Instead of trickling down the sides of the fjord and into the sea, the water was rushing upwards, climbing the air as if it had been shot up from a geyser. It arced over the coloured rooftops of the village below, its glittering tail reminding Anna of a comet. Her gaze followed its path to the castle, where it dipped and played around it, circling once, twice, three times, again and again until a dome of ice – seamless as an eggshell – covered the entire castle. Elsa had isolated their home inside of its own gigantic snow globe, preventing anyone from getting into the castle – but more importantly, keeping what was already there inside.

She lowered her hands. Her pink cheeks flushed, but her eyes sparkled. Anna had always thought creating ice with magic seemed like it should be exhausting, like trying to run up a mountain in ten seconds, but Elsa always seemed the most *Elsa* after she'd wielded her magic. And she was only getting better at it with each passing day.

"That was beautiful," Kristoff said, awe making his voice sound more solemn than usual, and Anna understood exactly how he felt.

"Thanks." Elsa bit her lip. "I just hope it holds the wolf. Now, we need to go warn the villagers, and get them to safety – just in case."

Anna nodded her head in agreement, tearing her eyes away from the ice-domed castle. Elsa was right. They would go to the village, and then maybe she could—

But Anna's thoughts jumbled up like crooked

teeth as she looked away from the dome and back at her friends. The first true ray of morning sun had not just illuminated the beauty of Elsa's creation; it had also brought to light something else: an unmistakable smattering of white in Sven's dun coat.

The Blight had struck again.

Chapter Ten

"SVEN!" KRISTOFF CRIED, holding up his friend, whose head lolled so low to the ground that his antlers skimmed the frost-covered grass.

Sven let out a rumbling groan, and the sound squeezed the breath out of Anna's lungs. No – not Sven. He'd been fine only an hour ago!

"Mint," Elsa said faintly, and when Anna turned to look at her sister, she saw that Elsa looked as shaken as she herself felt. "SoYun said that mint helped Hebert, and it was effective with the goats I saw the other day, too."

"The botanist's shop!" Anna said, tearing her eyes away from Kristoff's devastated expression and looking out at the village below them. "Gabriella always has mint in her shop! And if *that* doesn't work, Baker Blodget—"

"It'll work," Elsa said, cutting in firmly. "I was there earlier to ask about herbal remedies, but no one was home," she added. "She must be back by now."

With that, they ran down the path to the village, Kristoff keeping a hand on Sven the entire time while Anna's eyes remained fixed on the homes and shops ahead. The sooner they could evacuate the villagers, the sooner they could come up with a plan for how to defeat both the Blight *and* the wolf.

How much bad luck could a single kingdom have at once?

But it could be far worse. Anna knew that. Sven was still in the early stages of the Blight, after all. He could be doubling over in pain, he could be falling over, plunging into that unshakable sleep that would leave him unable to run from the wolf's teeth.

The wolf. Did *it* have anything to do with the Blight? Anna remembered the way Sven had stood still in the kitchen as the wolf stalked towards him, as if those yellow eyes had pinned him in place. But that didn't make sense. The Blight came *before* the wolf, but maybe the wolf had so terrified Sven – had so rattled him to his reindeer core – that his body's defences had been jostled enough for the Blight to settle in and begin to creep through Sven like a thorny, resilient weed.

But at least Sven was moving. He was still strong enough to trot, and he carried Olaf on his back, the snowman holding his own carrot nose in front of the reindeer's muzzle on a string to keep Sven awake and motivated. Anna wished that she had something as simple as a carrot to cheer up Kristoff.

When she'd first met Kristoff, she'd thought he was just a perpetual grump, but as she spent more time with him, she realised that he was someone who loved to laugh and wore a smile easily. Now, though, she could see the solitary mountain man slowly returning. Worry carved lines into his face and his mouth tugged down.

Anna slowed to a walk and slipped her hand into his. "Hey. It'll be okay. I promised we'd fix this mess in three days, and we will. Wolf and all."

Kristoff shook his head, brown eyes troubled. "I just don't understand what's happening. First the Blight, and then I couldn't find the trolls, and then—"

"Wait, what?" Anna gasped. "What do you mean, you couldn't find the trolls?"

"They weren't in the Valley of the Living Rock, and they didn't leave behind any message," Kristoff explained. He shrugged carelessly, but Anna could see the tension in his broad shoulders. "They're mysterious creatures, I get it, but they usually at least leave me snail mail." Snail mail, as Anna knew from experience, was notes written on the bottom of leaves with the help of friendly forest snails. They tended to be a bit difficult to read, and very, very sticky.

"Have they ever done that before?" Anna asked, but before Kristoff could answer, Sven's head jerked up, his ears swivelling forward.

Kristoff dropped Anna's hand. "What is it, boy?"

But Anna thought she knew, as a soft, far-off wailing met their ears. It almost sounded like the wind, mournful and ghostly, but the pitch of it sent a rush of goosebumps cascading across Anna's arms. Because it was *not* the wind. *This* was an utterly human sound – and it was coming from the village.

"*No,*" Elsa breathed, and Anna felt sick again. They sprinted the rest of the way.

The village of Arendelle curved around the harbour, balancing along the bay like a flock of birds ringing the edge of a birdbath. Anna had always taken pride in the village's vibrant homes, painted with bright splashes of colour and trimmed with exquisite detail. Many villagers liked to add personal touches that matched the personality of those living inside – and Anna knew and loved each and every one of them. There hadn't been one week in the last three years that she hadn't made a trip into the village, even on the days when Elsa wasn't able to join her.

On a usual morning, the villagers woke early, gathering fresh loaves of bread for breakfast and exchanging news from the previous day. Anna much preferred the village to the castle, and she loved having friends. Friends like Baker Blodget, who always had a spare basket of fresh butter biscuits to share with the children – and, occasionally, Anna. Or Akim, the seamster who was deft with the knitting needles and had made Anna her very own hat with cat ears. And then there were the three sisters, Supriya, Deepa and Jaya, who couldn't wait to see Anna every week to discuss the latest books they'd read and turned into a play.

That was how a usual morning looked. But this was not a usual morning. Not at all. The cobblestoned streets were empty of people, but full of their screams.

Before the wolf had entered the castle, it must have attacked the village.

"NO—" Anna began to yell, but Elsa put a hand over her mouth, stifling her cry.

"Shhh." Elsa pointed to a window. Peering inside, Anna saw Madam Eniola fast asleep, her nightcap askew on her grey hair. Her eyes were closed, but her mouth was open in a blood-curdling scream. And Anna knew deep in her bones that if Madam Eniola's eyes were to flutter open, they would be as bright yellow as the wolf's. Like what happened to Kai and Gerda.

"If we provoke them," Elsa whispered, "I think they'll attack us."

Anna nodded, sensing that her sister was right. "We just need to get some mint leaves for Sven," she whispered. "Then we can go."

"We don't split up," Elsa said, looking each of them in the eye and taking Olaf's hand. "We stay together, we stay silent and we keep moving." Spoken like a true leader.

They moved through the cobblestoned paths towards the market. Anna shuddered as they rounded every corner. Though there was no one in the streets, she had the constant feeling that someone was watching – as if all the windows were eyes staring at them.

Or as though a wolf were in the shadows, just waiting to pounce.

But, Anna assured herself, Elsa had sealed off the castle. The wolf, *her* nightmare wolf, was trapped inside, contained until Anna could figure out a better plan. Once they got help for the exhausted Sven – who now lifted each hoof as though it were heavy as a boulder – Anna would figure out a way to sneak back into the castle and read through each and every book in the hidden room, page by page, searching for a counter spell. There had to be one, even if she couldn't remember having seen one. And if the counter spell's runes hadn't yet been translated... well, then she would just have to figure out how to decode the language, even if it took her twenty years.

Worry gnawed at her stomach. She knew she did not have twenty years. She might not even have a day. Who else would the wolf enchant with its nightmare bewitchment? What would happen to all of them in the end?

They reached the forest-green doors of the botanist's shop and Elsa turned towards her companions. "Stay with Anna," she instructed Kristoff, and before Anna could stop her sister, or join her, Elsa was inside Gabriella's shop. Anna went to follow her.

Kristoff stepped in front of her with a gentle smile. "Elsa said to stay," he said.

"I can't let her go in there alone!"

"I think she's got it covered," Kristoff said, even as he unhooked his pickaxe from across his shoulder. "She *is* queen."

"She's my sister first." Anna looked at Olaf. "Please stay with Sven and make sure he doesn't fall asleep." Olaf saluted her as she went through the doorway, Kristoff just behind her. Inside the shop, a wailing scream reverberated, a sound so loud and clear and *sad* that Anna wished she could stick one of the many bunches of dried herbs in her ears to drown it out. Then the screaming stopped. A moment later, Elsa came flying down the staircase.

"Go!" Elsa said, her voice wild with fear. "We need to leave now!"

They hurried out and slammed the door, and then Elsa sealed its seams with ice, for good measure. "I accidentally woke the botanist," Elsa said, panting. And indeed, Anna could hear footsteps as Gabriella moved inside.

"Did you get the mint?" Kristoff asked.

Elsa held out her hand, flashing a bit of green leaf under Sven's nose.

Sven's head jerked up, and Anna noticed with relief that his pupils contracted, ever so slightly as he inhaled the sharp scent.

"Then what are we waiting for?" Anna said. "Let's *go*." But before she could turn round, there was a flash of movement out of the corner of her eye.

Kristoff had raised his pickaxe over his head. "Quiet," he whispered, not taking his eyes from the road. "Something's coming."

A shadow moved towards them across the cobblestones. Anna held her breath. A figure came into view. Tall and quick. Elsa raised her hands, and then...

"Hoo-hoo," a voice whispered. "Girls, is that you?"

"*Oaken,*" Anna whispered.

Sure enough, there stood Oaken, a large, powerfully built man with shoulders as wide as a rowboat and legs as thick as tree trunks. But despite his rather formidable height, Oaken's round cheeks were as rosy as a porcelain doll's, and his auburn beard and the frizz poking out from under his cap clashed gloriously with the green wool knit sweater that Anna knew his nan had made for him.

Oaken lifted a finger to his lips. Then he clasped his fingers together. He looked as though he'd aged ten years since Anna had seen him just the other week during a visit to his trading post. Exhaustion sullied his face, and the cap on his head was askew. His ruddy muttonchops twitched as he blinked wide blue eyes. He beckoned.

Together, they walked quietly but quickly through the empty streets, following the dirt path that Anna knew would take them down into a grassy valley surrounded by silver birch trees. But even though Anna knew the path well, everything seemed different. Trees that should have felt as familiar as old friends became just another potential place for a wolf to hide. Had it escaped the hold of the castle? As soon as they stepped out of the village, Elsa turned round and again waved her hands, directing a rush of cold and a flurry of ice over the village.

A minute later, the village, too, was encased in an ice dome, the screaming sobs muffled. Elsa didn't say anything as she hurried to catch up with the group, but Anna could read the expression on her sister's face clear enough: *I had to. For their own good. And for ours.* And Anna knew her sister was right. What if the wolf got out of the castle, and was feeling hungry? What if the sleepwalkers accidentally wandered out of the village towards the castle and freed the wolf? What Elsa had done was the right thing to do.

Finally, it was safe for them to speak.

"Thank the glaciers you're all right," Oaken said. "We hoped you were okay when we saw the ice encase the castle."

Anna's hope, which had been slipping away from her since Gabriella's shop, caught on his word.

"*We?*" Elsa repeated excitedly, clearly thinking along similar lines. "So, not everyone is asleep?"

Oaken nodded. "A handful of us managed to flee to my Wandering Oaken's Trading Post—"

"And Sauna!" Olaf inserted. "Oh, I'd like to go into your sauna!"

"And Sauna, yes." Oaken nodded. "That's where we're going now." Oaken was a shopkeeper who sold a little bit of this and a little bit of that, from carrots to snow shovels to healing draughts and more. But most famous of all was his sauna, a room of cedarwood and steam that could make even the coldest winter nights feel like a balmy evening in the jungle.

His shop sat in a small pocket in the forest, a little way off from a small creek that fed into a larger river and on the path that led to the North Mountain and the sparkling ice palace Elsa had crafted when she'd first experimented with her powers three years before. The little wooden cabin had been built with loving attention to detail, with geometric patterns carved into its logs, and tall windows fitted with diamond-paned glass.

Oaken took great pride in his shop. He'd once admitted to Anna that he used to think about becoming a designer before figuring out his real joy in life came from taking care of people and making sure they could get whatever they needed from him – for a fair price. Kristoff would disagree with that last part.

Oaken's trading post was open around the clock, and weary travellers could always find the sauna and a pile of fluffy towels ready and waiting to warm them. But as they neared the shop, Anna saw that for the first time in three years, the curtains were drawn and a little painted sign hung in the window: CLOSED.

"This way," Oaken whispered, leading them round to a back entrance that Anna had only seen but never entered. He knocked on the door: one long tap, followed by three quick ones. Nothing happened, and then Anna spotted a tiny quiver behind the curtains.

"Password, please?" came a man's voice.

"*Surplus*," Oaken whispered.

There was the sound of footsteps, then several clicks and a jangle of metal before the door creaked open.

"Hurry, hurry," Oaken whispered. He swept Anna, Elsa, Kristoff, Sven and Olaf inside, then stepped into the cabin himself, twisting the doorknob to make sure it was locked. Satisfied with his work, he turned to face them, looking concerned. "Four-footed animals aren't usually allowed inside Wandering Oaken's Trading Post and Sauna. This is an exception, *ja*?"

"He's very well-behaved," Anna said of Sven. "I promise he won't be a problem."

Oaken's expression shifted and he nodded. At last, they were all safe.

Metal screeched again as Oaken slid several bolts shut and clicked no less than seven padlocks. The shopkeeper wasn't taking any chances of letting a wolf enter his cabin and mess up his tidy shop. Anna looked around. Well, what *used* to be his tidy shop.

"Oh, dear," Elsa murmured.

Oaken's shelves, stuffed with an odd assortment of goods – flowerpots sitting on top of books, next to a corner of rakes and barrels of candied nuts – usually marched in straight lines throughout the shop. But now, the shelves and all their wares had been pushed to the edges. Reinforcements for the windows, Anna guessed. In case someone – or some*wolf* – tried to break in. It looked as though the cabin itself were preparing for a great war, and it wasn't just the cabin that was ready for a fight. Looking around, she spotted two villagers in the storeroom. Tuva the blacksmith, her hammer dangling from a tool belt, stood guard at the front door, and at the counter, scribbling across old receipts, was Wael.

At the sight of him, Anna felt a twinge of embarrassment and an even stronger pinch of annoyance. If the journalist hadn't goaded her yesterday, maybe she wouldn't have promised everyone that Elsa could fix everything in three days, and then maybe Elsa wouldn't have had a council meeting without her. And then maybe Anna wouldn't have accidentally spelled the wolf out of her nightmare.

"Where is everyone else?" Olaf asked as he hopped off Sven, made his way into the centre of the room, and peered behind overturned bookshelves. "Are they all in the sauna?"

Tuva shook her head. "This is all of us. We're the only ones left."

Anna froze. Earlier, she had assumed she'd find at least thirty or forty other villagers crammed inside. Not just *two*. She looked over at Elsa, but if her older sister had been expecting to find more villagers in there, her expression didn't show it.

Elsa nodded. "Okay. If this is what we have, this is what we have." And though her voice was calm, Anna saw that she played with the tassels of their mother's scarf. "Can someone please tell me exactly what happened?"

"I can." Wael held up a piece of paper. "I'm writing everything down."

Elsa, Oaken and Tuva moved towards the countertop, but Anna made her way to the corner, where Oaken had dropped off a pile of thick wool blankets that Kristoff was now crunching into a soft nest around Sven.

"I don't understand." Kristoff shook his head. "He was fine when we were looking for the trolls, and even when we got back to the castle, he seemed good. I mean, hungry, but good." He shook his head. "I *know* it sounds ridiculous, but it's like he got the Blight by just *looking* at the wolf. He's been out of sorts ever since!"

"True." Anna leaned close to Sven and waved the mint leaves under his nose. "Come on, don't fall asleep!" she said.

But the reindeer's eyes drooped. It was exactly as SoYun had described. The Blight was coming on quickly and horribly. Kristoff gently shook his muzzle again and again. There was nothing they could do.

"At this point, we need a mystic," Anna said, thinking of the magically inclined wise-folk who existed in legends.

"Anna? Kristoff? Can you come here?" Elsa called.

Anna and Kristoff hurried over. As they neared,

Wael held out mugs to them. "No one wants to fall asleep, just in case."

"Just in case *what*?" Anna took a sip. She almost choked. It was the strongest cup of coffee she'd ever tasted, and she could practically feel the tips of her hair twist up as the coffee coursed through her. Based on Kristoff's now red cheeks and the tremor of Elsa's hand, Anna suspected that they, too, had not been ready for the jolt.

"Everyone who was asleep when the wolf ran through town has stayed asleep," Tuva said, her usually cheerful face sombre. "Only the people who were up late at night avoided falling under its sleeping curse," she continued. "That's why we made the coffee so strong. Who knows what will happen if we fall asleep?" It was a terrible thought, made all the more terrible by the sudden exhaustion that washed over Anna. All she wanted to do was curl up and sleep.

"I was awake, but Gerda and Kai, well, they must have been asleep, because, I mean, they would never..." Elsa trailed off, at a loss.

"Didn't they attack us?" Olaf asked.

"Well, they didn't know it was us!" Anna rushed

to clear her friends' names. "And they weren't exactly themselves... I think they thought we were part of their nightmares." Speaking about them, Anna hoped Kai and Gerda were okay, and that the wolf hadn't hurt them any more than it already had.

Tuva nodded. "Exactly the same with my wife. Ada attacked me, all the while screaming for me to come help her. And there was absolutely nothing I could do." The expression on Tuva's face broke Anna's heart. She knew only too well what it was like to feel helpless. Tuva collected herself and continued. "I left her at home. She just kept screaming and screaming..."

"Anna, you said we need a mystic, *ja*?" asked Oaken, tapping the tips of his fingers together. "Maybe Sorenson can help!"

"Sore-what?" Olaf asked.

"Sorenson," said Oaken. "He's what you'd call an expert in myths and lore. He's the mystic of Miner's Mountain."

"No one lives on that mountain but bears and lynx," Kristoff said.

The coffee was way too strong. Anna could have sworn she'd just heard Oaken say that an expert in myths and lore – a *mystic* – lived on Miner's Mountain.

Elsa tilted her head. "What?"

Oaken started to say something else, but Anna was too distracted to pay attention. Mystics didn't exist. They were just characters in stories Anna and Elsa's mother would tell them before bed as young girls. Mystics were rumoured to dabble in potions, enchantments and powerful spells – but such people simply didn't exist, or so Anna had thought.

But if anyone would know how to reverse an accidental spell, it would be a mystic. Suddenly, finding Sorenson seemed more promising than returning to the secret room. Anna shook her head. If anyone had told her a week ago that she would be seriously considering seeking out a mystic, she would have laughed. But then again, she never would have believed that a nightmare wolf would be stalking the kingdom.

"Why haven't we heard about Sorenson before?" Elsa demanded.

"He keeps to himself in a tall tower," Oaken explained. "But if this is a curse, he could help!"

"Is he..." Elsa waved her fingers, sending a dance of snowflakes twirling through the room. "Like me?"

"Why, no." Oaken shook his head. "No one is like you."

"We need to get to him!" Anna said, turning to her sister, who looked less than convinced. Anna whirled to Kristoff and, seeking backup, asked him, "Don't you agree?"

But Kristoff didn't seem to have heard her. He was looking in Sven's direction and mumbled, "Why is this happening?" His coffee splashed out of his mug as his hands shook – from worry or from the coffee, Anna could not tell. "Where did it come from?"

"Magic," Oaken said. "It has to be." His words seemed to suck the air out of the room as Anna cast a glance at Elsa, only to see that her sister seemed to have, at the same time, both curled into herself and become rigid, like a nautilus's shell.

"Did *you* do this?" Wael asked Elsa.

Anna's headache returned with furious force. "Elsa would *never*—"

"Of course she wouldn't!" Tuva said. "And no one is saying she would. But between the rotten crops, the sleeping animals and people, and now the wolf

– what else could it be but a curse or a spell of some sort?"

At the blacksmith's words, guilt surged through Anna. Now was the time for her to come clean. "Elsa?" she said tentatively. The entire room looked at her, and she winced. Her voice had gone *very* squeaky. "Er... could I... *talk* to you for a moment? In private?"

"It's not like this is a very big place," Elsa said.

"Excuse me?" Oaken interrupted. "What did you say?"

Elsa gaped. "I mean, I didn't—it's lovely, but it's not, you know, the biggest—"

Taking advantage of Elsa's fluster, Anna pulled her sister away from the others and ducked behind the shop counter. "We have to go see Sorenson," Anna whispered, fumbling in her travel cloak pocket for the loose page from *Secrets of the Magic Makers*.

Elsa looked up at the ceiling and sighed. "Anna, I've told you, magic isn't—"

"I know, I know." Anna nodded. "It's not the solution. But it might be the reason."

"What?" Elsa asked. "Anna, what are you trying to say?"

"Now, don't get mad," Anna said. "It's just—you

see, I heard you having a council meeting without me, which is fine, but for some reason it upset me. I took back *Secrets of the Magic Makers* for some light reading, you know, because Mother always used to tell us stories at night. So, I found this song, more of a poem really, well, maybe it was a spell, only it turns out that maybe, possibly, it just might have—"

"Anna." Elsa sighed, burying her face in her hands.

"The point is..." Anna took a deep breath and held out the loose page from the book. "Arendelle is cursed... and... I may be the one who cursed it."

Chapter Eleven

ANNA HELD HER BREATH as Elsa took the page, her eyes wide, scanning it line by line.

"Anna, did you see the small note at the bottom?"

"No," Anna said, turning red. "Why? What's it say?"

Elsa moved the paper in front of her, along with a magnifying glass made of ice that she'd crafted.

Peering through the ice, Anna read:

*SPELL NOT GUARANTEED TO BE EXACTLY WHAT YOU WISHED FOR.

**IF NOT REVERSED, SPELL SHALL TAKE ROOT PERMANENTLY ON ITS THIRD SUNRISE.

"Oh," Anna said. "Yeah, I... definitely didn't see that."

Elsa bit her lip and her eyes shimmered.

"I'm sorry." Anna shook her head, all the while hoping she could shake away the words. "I was only trying to help."

Elsa sighed. "I know. I can't be upset at you for that."

There was something about Elsa's words that made Anna want to curl up and cry. She almost would rather have had Elsa yell at her than sigh like she had. If Elsa *had* yelled at her, it would have meant that she thought of Anna as someone who had the ability to shape the kingdom's future, but that sigh... it was the same sound her parents had made when a five-year-old Anna accidentally broke a clay figurine of a salamander over the mantel. "I thought it was a dragon," a sorry Anna had told them. "I thought that it could fly!"

It's okay, they had said. *You didn't know any better.*

"Anna!"

Kristoff's yell cut through Anna's thought spiral. She shot to her feet. Kristoff never yelled like that. Not even the time Anna had set fire to his sleigh to save them from a pack of *normal* wolves, of the animal – not magical – variety.

"What's wrong?" she called. Because something *had* to be wrong for him to sound like that.

"Sven." Kristoff's eyes and hair were wild. "He fell asleep. He won't wake up."

Anna ran out from behind the counter, aware of Elsa following close behind. Sure enough, Sven's eyes were shut and his sides heaved with ragged, laboured breath.

Kristoff rubbed Sven's cheek with the back of his hand.

What to do, what to do, what to do!

But there was nothing Anna *could* do, except... "Elsa!" She whirled round to see her sister. "We *have* to meet this Sorenson person – he may be Sven's only chance!"

"But—"

"We can ask him about, you know." Anna bumped a little against the word *spell*, not wanting to admit to everyone just yet who exactly was responsible for the wolf. "And we can see if he knows how to cure the Blight!"

At least the Blight wasn't *her* fault. It had happened before Anna had said her spell, but still... it was rather curious that both the Blight and wolf shared similar symptoms: a strange kind of sleep and colour-changing eyes. Anna felt like she was looking at a puzzle with a shifting picture. They could be related, but Anna wasn't sure *how*.

"Oaken, where exactly in the mountain does Sorenson live?" Elsa asked as Anna hurried back over to the counter.

Oaken pulled out a map and spread it smooth in front of the register, then traced a path east, to Miner's Mountain. He tapped his finger at the base of the mountain. "Follow the Roaring River past the Black Mountains until you see the signs for the abandoned mines. Beware. They're dangerous."

Kristoff leaned forward to get a closer look. "Dangerous *how*?"

"They're known for awful cave-ins and terrible landslides," Oaken said.

"And the Huldrefólk who live in the heart of the mountain," Tuva added. "They're tricky. Sometimes, they help. Other times, they lure humans off the safest paths."

Wael rolled his eyes. "The Huldrefólk aren't *real*, you know. They're just bedtime stories, an excuse for people who can't follow directions and a scapegoat for when things go missing."

"The Huldrefólk are dangerous," Tuva continued, ignoring Wael. "*You* know the stories. They like to hide in the shadows. They're thieves – they steal things." The blacksmith dragged her eyes back to Elsa. "I think it would be wiser if you fled, Your Majesty. Maybe another country will have the answer and they can bring help."

Anna was too stunned to speak. She couldn't believe Tuva was suggesting they leave their home when it needed them most. And from the look on Elsa's face, she knew her sister felt the same way.

"Thank you for your advice." Elsa stood up to pick up her cloak. "I appreciate it. But it's my job to remain in Arendelle with everybody, and to find a solution, Huldrefólk or no. I'll leave now."

Anna shot up. "Don't you mean *we'll* leave now?"

With a flourish, Elsa swirled her cloak onto her shoulders. "No, Anna. You heard them. It's too dangerous. I think it would be best if you all left on the royal ship, at least until things are back to normal. I can protect myself."

Anna could hardly believe her ears. She couldn't

leave Arendelle in such a state of danger. "It's not about protection," she said, her thoughts flying fast, trying to come up with a winning argument that could convince Elsa. "It's about... about..." She looked down at the mug in her hand. "It's about keeping you awake!" she finished. "You need at least one person with you who can keep you awake—"

"And another who knows the way of the mountains," Kristoff added. Anna noted with gratitude that he'd already shouldered his traveller's pack and added a coil of rope to his belt, even though he did cast a worried look at his sleeping reindeer friend. Anna knew how it must feel to volunteer to be separated from a sick and sleeping Sven, but she also knew that it would be even harder for Kristoff to not at least try to help. It was the way she felt, too, and part of the reason why she loved him so much.

Olaf popped up from Sven's blanket nest. "And a snowman who likes warm hugs!"

For a moment, Elsa stood still, as though she'd been carved from ice. Anna had already started planning how she would sneak away from the royal ship if her sister ordered her aboard, but finally,

Elsa raised her hands in surrender. "All right. Anna and Kristoff will come with me. Oaken," she said, turning to him, "would you please lead the others to the royal ship? Set sail south as fast as you can, and stay there until you hear word from me."

"And if we don't hear back?" Wael asked.

Anna stuck her chin up. "I promise you – you will."

Oaken lifted a thick finger and pointed out the window. "Then I suggest you leave now. The morning is almost over, and you'll want to reach Sorenson's before nightfall. And remember: beware the Huldrefólk!"

As Elsa and Kristoff did a final check of their supplies, Anna fidgeted with the crumpled spell in her cloak pocket. It might have caused trouble, but it was something her mother had touched, and the thought comforted her. Fastening her cloak, Anna went over to Olaf, who was shovelling a few more carrots into his own traveller's pack.

"I'm coming, too. I'm a snowman adventurer! A snoventurer!"

Anna smiled and placed a hand on Olaf's back. At least bravery existed in her snow friend, even if it was lacking in others. "I know you are, but Olaf... I need to ask you to stay here."

Olaf's grin slid off his face. "You—you don't want me to come?"

"I do," Anna said, and it was the truth. Olaf might be silly, and he could occasionally lose his head, but he was wise in ways of the heart and he knew how to bring warmth to cold places. And Anna had a feeling that, soon, they would be in need of hugs more than ever. In fact, she could use one herself now. But the people standing before her could use him even more. She picked up his carrot nose and set it back in place. "Kristoff needs you here to keep an eye on Sven, and Elsa and I need you here to help the villagers stay awake as they carry Sven and head to the ship." Anna ruffled his twiggy hair.

"Oh, I already have tons of ideas to keep them awake!" Olaf assured her, brightening. "The question is: how will I choose *which* idea?" He began to tick off his repertoire on his fingers. "I could sing soothing lullabies, do an interpretive dance of falling autumn leaves, recite the names of all the best beaches in the world in alphabetical order—"

"Remember," Kristoff interrupted as he came over,

his traveller's pack heaped with the added supplies from Oaken, "you're trying to *stop* them from sleeping. Not *put* them to sleep."

Anna nudged Kristoff's boot with her toe. "Hush," she whispered.

"I'll start a rousing game of charades. Or, no. What about jokes?" Olaf said. "Everybody loves jokes. They'll be laughing too hard to sleep. Ahem." He straightened his top coal button. "What do snowmen eat for lunch?"

"What?" Oaken asked.

"I'm not really sure. Snowmen really don't eat anything, which is a bit perplexing. There was the time I tried eating fruitcake, but it kind of went right through me."

Kristoff cocked an eyebrow while Anna giggled.

"Perfect. See, Olaf? You'll be great!" Anna said. But as she followed Elsa and Kristoff to the door, the laughter within her faded. Dangerous things lurked outside these doors and in the mountains. Dangerous things lurked within books, too. Dangerous power, it seemed, also lurked somewhere within Anna.

But here was her chance to fix things. Here was

her chance to prove herself to Arendelle. To prove herself to Elsa. And if she didn't, if she *couldn't*, the nightmare would be complete.

The wolf would swallow the world, starting with everyone she loved.

Chapter Twelve

THE SUN SHONE with intensity in the sky, a bright flat disc that sparked the colourful splendour of autumn leaves.

Usually, Anna loved nothing more than sunny autumn days, those afternoons when the sky was as blue as could be and everything around her was golden. Usually. Today, though, the sun was *too* bright. It showed too many things: their footprints on the path, their shadows creeping across the ground, the bright gleam of Elsa's hair. All were as visible as could possibly be. Beacons for the wolf that might as well have screamed *DELICIOUS MEALS WENT THAT WAY.*

Even though they had all guessed that the wolf would not move during the day, and that it was still trapped in the castle, there was no real way to be sure. So they stayed away from the cleared wagon path that followed the Roaring River, and instead stuck to the interior of the forest, picking their way over fallen logs and stumbling against rocks hidden by piles of leaves. Anna tripped more than a few times over wayward roots. Sneaking through the woods while imagining a wolf chasing her was all too familiar to Anna.

After a little while, an embarrassed Anna admitted to Kristoff what she had done. And instead of being upset at her, he hugged her. He understood that all she had wanted to do was help, and he was optimistic about their plan to save Sven.

"I don't get it," Anna said, trying to keep her voice quiet enough not to attract attention, but loud enough for Kristoff and Elsa to hear her over the crunching of leaves. "I have good dreams all the time. I've dreamed about flying and living in a castle made of chocolate and unicorn quests and—"

"And me, obviously," Kristoff suggested with a cheeky grin.

Anna nudged his arm. "Focus," she said, trying

to sound stern, though she knew her cheeks were turning pink.

"I'm just glad you didn't dream of something *really* scary – like a land-walking shark," he said.

Anna smiled. "Is that *your* most terrifying nightmare?"

"No." Kristoff shook his head. "When I was little, I used to have nightmares about Bulda trying to spoon-feed me mushroom soup."

Anna paused to unhook her cloak from a thorny bush. "That's not scary at all."

Kristoff adjusted his traveller's pack. "Have *you* ever had a troll try to spoon-feed you?"

Anna giggled and turned to Elsa, trying to invite her to the conversation, but Elsa didn't so much as crack a smile. She'd been practically silent since they'd left Oaken's trading post, and Anna had the sinking suspicion her sister was upset with her.

"H-how about you, Elsa?" Anna tried to keep her tone light and airy. "What's your worst nightmare?"

Elsa pushed back a branch. "I don't have nightmares."

From out of the corner of her eye, Anna saw Kristoff pick up the pace. He always liked to avoid spats whenever he could. And he, like Anna, could detect one brewing.

"Come on, Elsa." Anna took a quick side step to avoid the branch whipping back towards her as Elsa released it. "*Everyone* has nightmares. I'm your sister. You can tell me. You all know my nightmare now – a massive, girl-stalking wolf."

Elsa flung their mother's scarf over her shoulder. "I don't know what to tell you, Anna, except that *I* don't have nightmares."

Anna's sinking suspicion was no longer sinking. It had hit rock bottom, and anchored in the pit of her stomach. Elsa was definitely upset with her, and the worst part – the absolute *worst* part – was that Anna didn't blame her. Anna was a little furious at herself.

Snowflakes drifted in the shafts of sunlight that trickled down through the trees. Anna looked up. The sky remained as blue as ever, which meant there could only be one other source of snow.

"Elsa, why are you making flurries?" Anna held out a finger to capture a minuscule ice crystal. "We can't have snow. We'll leave footprints. More than the ones we're already leaving in the mud."

Elsa stopped and looked at her. "It's not me."

"Then what do you call this?" Anna held out her finger.

Elsa inspected the flake, and her pale cheeks grew even paler. "That's not snow."

"Anna! Elsa!" Kristoff yelled from ahead. He stood on top of a wooded knoll, looking down at something on the other side. "Come quick!"

They stopped caring who – or what – might hear them, and ran, coming to a halt beside Kristoff. Anna gasped. The forest ended on top of the knoll, and a red farmhouse sat before them, cradled by fields of wheat; wheat that was all white, translucent even, in the sun's sharp light. As Anna looked, a breeze rippled through the field, dislodging the grains and sending up billows of what looked like ash.

The Blight was spreading.

"We can't keep tiptoeing around," Kristoff said, and Anna could tell he was thinking of Sven's white coat that matched the terrible white powder. "All this darting and dodging is taking way too long. We have to move way faster!" He was right. But Anna didn't know what to do.

Even from this distance, she could spot little white huddles among the fields. Cows that had fallen asleep. Horses that had dropped in their tracks. Any animal that could take them farther or faster had fallen sick. The only thing that looked normal in the bleached autumn landscape was the navy thread of the Roaring River that wound its way to the base of Miner's Mountain in the distance.

"Can you freeze the river?" Anna asked Elsa. "Then maybe we could cross it."

"Huh." Elsa tilted her head. "*That's* an idea! Maybe these will help, too."

Elsa waved her hands, and Anna felt like she'd grown three inches. Looking down at her feet, she realised why: Elsa had transformed Anna's walking boots into a pair of ice skates. Anna wobbled, but Kristoff grabbed her elbow, keeping her upright.

Elsa nodded at the rushing river. "We can ice-skate."

That was *not* what Anna had had in mind. She gulped. It was a good idea, but Elsa was the skater, not Anna. And when Anna did skate, she preferred to skate on smooth, solid ground. On a river, there was always the chance the ice could break, pitching her into icy water. "We'll be exposed on the open river," Anna said slowly. "We won't be able to hide."

"Luckily," Elsa said as she made her way down the

knoll and to the river's edge, "you're travelling with an expert in ice. I can make the ice just thin enough that it'll support our weight, but anything heavier – like a giant wolf – will crash right through it." And with that, she stepped out onto the water.

As the toe of Elsa's skate touched the surface, a bloom of ice crystals appeared on the river. The crystal blossoms doubled, then quadrupled, then further multiplied, until the entire surface of the river had transformed into a sheet of wild ice blossoms refracting over and over and over again in the blinding midday sun.

It was, Anna admitted to herself, another one of Elsa's great ideas and magical creations. But just not one she really cared for all that much. She trusted her sister, though, and so she moved to the river's edge. The ice was so thin she could see straight through it, as though it were the delicate pane of her bedroom window.

"Come on, Anna," Kristoff said, "we're losing time!" He jumped out onto the river with his own ice skates. The sheet of ice jounced like a trampoline beneath him, but it held, just as Elsa promised it would.

"I won't let anything happen to you, Anna," Elsa

said, reading her sister's worried expression. "This is our best chance, and we don't have much time to fix this nightmare."

Elsa was right. Anna had got them into this mess. And now she needed to fix it. Taking a breath, she stepped out onto the ice. Elsa led in front, each stroke of her feet scattering ice crystals across the surface.

Lined on either side by trees in their autumn splendour, the river looked like a diamond necklace set against a cushion of red. And as Anna got her feet under her, she felt her heart lighten, just a bit. The rattling, windswept leaves sounded like applause. She took courage in the sound. It was as though Arendelle were cheering for her, wanting her to succeed. And she would. She wouldn't stop until Arendelle was safe.

Hours passed. Wind snarled Anna's hair, and the constant rush of cold wind meant her nose had started to drip. Her feet were beginning to ache. Elsa's magical skates usually fit just right, but today they squeezed a bit too tight, as though Elsa had forgotten Anna had grown up. Disheartened by the thought, she tried to shake away her melancholy. Anna hit a divot – and tripped. Before she could smash her nose into the ice, a hand caught her arm.

"You okay there, Twinkle Toes?" Kristoff asked.

"Totally," Anna said. "I meant to do that." Even though her ice-skating had much improved since her first lesson with Elsa, she wasn't winning a competition anytime soon.

"Sorry," Kristoff said. "I didn't mean to ruin the Anna Axel."

Putting her nose in the air, Anna sniffed. "I guess I can forgive you."

Kristoff grinned, his hand slipping into hers. "Are you sure?" And then he was off, skating backwards as fast as he could, pulling Anna after him. The world around them blurred as he whirled her around, as confident on the ice as he was on solid ground. Faster and faster they skated, balancing on a thin edge between control and out-of-control. Ahead of them, Elsa cruised with ease, not noticing them tilting, slipping, flying, until—

"Look out!" Anna shouted as the river took an unexpected bend. But the warning came too late. Kristoff didn't have time to pull them to a new course, and they skidded off the river and into a tall pile of maple leaves. Lying back, Anna watched as a swirl of golden leaves fell around them.

"I meant to do that," Kristoff said.

"Mm-hmm. The same way I meant to do the Anna Axel?" she asked.

He nodded. "Exactly."

"ANNA!" Elsa's voice tore through the air.

"I'm here!" Anna stood up and shook out her travel cloak to send leaves skittering to the ground. "We had a bit of a misstep. Er, mis-*skate*."

Elsa's blade sent a spray of powder over them as she came to an abrupt stop in front of them. "This isn't a time for game-playing!"

The world as Anna knew it slowed, then froze. And though Elsa hadn't done any magic – there had been no twirl of her hand, no blast of her ice, no ice shard burrowing its way into Anna's heart – Elsa's words froze something deep within Anna. Her *hope*. And things that are frozen... shatter. Anna could feel the splinters of her broken hope tumbling through her like smashed glass, making every breath, every blink, painful as she looked at her sister, queen of Arendelle, who no longer had any place for her sister's silly antics.

"I *know* it's not a game," Anna retorted.

"I don't think you do," Elsa said, her voice carefully controlled. Anna wanted to shake her perfect sister, to see some sort of crack, to show her that she saw her as an equal. But that tone – that disappointed tone – revealed all too well exactly what Elsa thought of Anna. And then Anna was no longer hurt, no longer numb, no longer frozen. She *boiled*.

"I'm *not* a child," Anna said. She was grateful that the ice skates' blades made her taller than she usually was. "Do you think I don't know?" With each word, her voice got louder and louder until she practically shouted. "Do you think I haven't been *trying*?"

And before she could hear Elsa's reply, Anna flung herself out onto the ice.

Digging the blades in deep, she pushed and pushed, going faster and faster. Anna felt too much. She *was* too much. That was the trouble. She was too distracted. Too carefree. Too ridiculous for anyone – even for her sister – to see how she could be helpful to the kingdom.

The wind whipped her cloak behind her, but she leaned into it, wanting to feel the fresh iciness against her hot, angry skin. For a moment, she thought she heard Elsa calling out to her, but she didn't stop. She wanted to skate away from it all. Away from that disappointed note in Elsa's voice, away from Kristoff's undeserved gentle kindness and away from her own messy, tangled emotions.

Away from her giant, cursed mistake.

The ice groaned beneath her weight, her blades scratching out a mournful note that Anna couldn't escape. *Faster, faster, faster!* If only she could skate as quick as the wind, maybe she'd melt into it and be swept away from all that she'd done.

And that's when the ice cracked.

Chapter Thirteen

ONE SECOND, everything was cold and dry.

The next second, everything was cold and wet.

The water dragged at Anna like it had fingers.

She gasped once – a single great breath of air – before it pulled her under.

The world below the ice was dark and quiet, peaceful even, except for the wild scream that worked through Anna.

She was *cold* again! She would *freeze* again! And if she died... would the wolf win? Anna kicked. She couldn't let everyone down! But no matter how much she willed her feet to propel her back up to the surface, the heavy blades of her skates dragged her down...

... down...

... down into the dark.

Or was it *up*? *Sideways*? The dark, ice-cold quiet was disorienting, and her thoughts began to slow. And then, a beam of light shot past her as someone chopped through the ice from somewhere above. Anna felt the water underneath her move like a giant horse, a black wave of water that surged beneath her, and she was flying up through the water and towards the surface with all the strength of a geyser. The water didn't have the temperature of a hot spring, though, but of an icy slush. *Elsa*. Moments later, after much spluttering and coughing, Anna was in the arms of Kristoff and Elsa.

"Thank you for saving me," Anna whispered, shivering.

But Elsa didn't acknowledge her words. Instead, her sister said, "Kristoff, you need take her back to Oaken's."

"What?! No," Anna croaked. "I'm fine. I'll be fine."

"But Anna," Elsa said, throwing her hands up in protest, "you almost drowned."

"Almost," Anna protested. "I've *almost* done a lot of things. I have to help with this!"

Elsa shook her head. "I'm just not sure."

"Why are you always trying to push me away?" Anna asked.

Elsa looked stung. "What? Anna, what are you talking about? *When* do I push you away?"

Anna grew quiet. "I'm sorry. I... Please, I *need* to accompany you." For a second, Anna thought Elsa would say no, but then something seemed to melt in Elsa.

She wrapped Anna in a hug. "I'm sorry, too. I didn't mean to yell—I just... I'm upset, I guess."

"I didn't mean to cast a spell," Anna said, needing to get the words out now. "I had no way of knowing it would bring my nightmare about the wolf to life."

Elsa shook her head. "It just... When did you start having the nightmares?"

"When I was a little girl, and then, this week the nightmare came back." *Ever since I realised that you were going to leave me behind for the grand tour.* But Anna didn't say that last bit out loud.

There was the *scritch* of a match as Kristoff lit a small pile of branches he'd gathered. He gestured the sisters over to the fire.

"When did you *first* have the nightmare?" Elsa prodded as they huddled close to the flames. Steam rose from Anna's clothes as they slowly dried.

Anna thought back. "I think it was the night you...

you know." She touched the spot in her hair where the white streak had once been, recalling once more when Elsa had accidentally struck her there with magic as a young girl. "I can't believe you've never had bad dreams."

Elsa shrugged. "The last time I had a bad dream, I must have been eight years old. I woke up and my entire room had turned into a winter landscape." She shook her head. "I felt so bad! Everything got wet and they had to bring in new furniture and carpets for me."

"And you never had the nightmare again?"

"No." Elsa leaned her head back and looked up. "Father taught me a bunch of tricks to try to control my emotions, my magic. I remember he came into my room once with a mug of hot chocolate—"

"He used to do that for me, too!" Anna said.

Elsa smiled and Anna smiled back, enjoying the surprise bridge that linked them.

"And Mother joined him and told me to imagine bunching up all the nightmares and throwing them out the window," Elsa said. "I used to think that when I balled them up, I would throw them and pretend to feed them to the constellations in the sky."

"I used to do that, too!" Anna said, feeling closer to her sister than ever. "I'd pretend to give them to Frigg the Fisherman so he could fish for them. But the trick didn't stop me from having nightmares."

Elsa shrugged. "Mother's trick worked for me. I haven't had a nightmare since."

"I'm sorry to interrupt," Kristoff said, "but speaking of stars... it's getting late."

The sisters smiled, and Anna felt a little bit better, if not completely. Her clothes were still damp, but no longer dripping.

After putting out the fire, Kristoff stepped back on the ice and Anna followed after him. But the bright hope that had been so certain before now seemed to have been left behind in the maple leaf pile at the riverbank.

Soon enough, the sun began to set, casting long shadows on the ice as they continued to skate up the rest of the Roaring River. Anna couldn't help thinking that their shadows looked like drowning figures trapped beneath the ice.

They were quiet as they skated. Anna didn't want to accidentally step on the tenuous peace between her and Elsa, while Kristoff seemed to be lost again in his own worries. Kristoff's birth parents had died long ago, and for the early part of his life, Sven had been his only family – until they'd both been adopted by the mountain trolls. The farther they glided away from Sven, the quieter Kristoff became, until, at last, it became unbearable for Anna. She needed a distraction – for all of them.

"Kristoff, have you ever met the Huldrefólk?" she asked, blurting out the first thing she could think of. "Did they ever visit the trolls?"

He shook his head. "Not that I know of," he said. "The trolls like to hide, but the Huldrefólk – well, they *really* like to hide, right? I don't think anyone's ever seen one."

"They're known for finding lost things, too," Elsa said, slowing down so the other two could catch up with her. No one in Arendelle, or probably in the whole world, for that matter, was as comfortable on the ice as Elsa. While Elsa always moved with grace, when she skated, she was *more* than grace. She became someone with wind in her veins and wings on her feet. "It's said that Aren of Arendelle once went to visit them."

"But his adventures led him to many make-believe

creatures," Anna said as his tales gradually came back to her. "Like mermaids and dragons."

"Right," Elsa said with a nod. "So maybe the Huldrefólk are like dragons and don't exist at all. Maybe Aren never even existed."

Kristoff made a face. "So why do you two know so much about this guy if he may or may not have existed? He's just a legend, right? A myth?"

"Possibly. It's said he did a lot of great things for the land," Anna said. "He carved Arenfjord himself, you know. Or so the old myths go."

Kristoff snorted. "Yeah, right. That's the most ridiculous thing I've ever heard."

"You've never heard the story?" Anna asked in surprise. "I thought everyone knew it."

Kristoff jabbed a thumb at his chest. "Raised by trolls, remember? Some of us didn't have fancy lessons growing up." There was something strange lurking in his voice, as though Anna had hit a nerve. It must have had to do with his worry for Sven. She turned to Elsa and asked, "You know the saga verbatim, right?"

Elsa nodded. "It helped pass the time when I was growing up." She paused a moment, seeming to collect herself, and then spoke the familiar lines that signified the beginning of a story: "'A long time ago, in the time before time, a great darkness swept over the land...'"

Anna held her breath as Elsa recited the ancient tale and described how an everlasting night had set over the mountains, and how humankind had fled to their boats for safety. Humans then lived on the waters for hundreds of years, until the day a strange sickness smote them. Scared, the people had asked the most ancient of water spirits for help, and the Water Spirit had told them that they were withering away without a place to plant their roots – they needed to return home. But all were too scared, except for a young boy.

"'Young as the morning, as fierce as a twig, Aren stepped out onto the land...'" Elsa recited.

They skated in rhythm to Elsa's voice, a stroke of one leg, then the other, a beat that flowed through Anna and calmed her. Impossible things had happened in the past. So why couldn't they happen in the future?

She took heart as Elsa described how Aren had climbed up the highest mountain to bargain with night and bring back the sun, and how when he'd finally freed the sun, the sun had gifted him the Revolute Blade and told him how to bring his people home: by carving a new path for them, right between the protective mountains.

Elsa's voice picked up speed as she reached the crescendo of Aren's very first quest, and Anna couldn't help mouthing along with the words as she suddenly remembered.

"'Revolving moon and spinning sun, forged a crescent blade. From light and dark within the heart, the burnished sword was made. The curving arc of Revolute shimmered in his hand. He raised it high above his head and smote the edge of land.'"

Without missing a beat, Elsa reached out a hand for Anna, gesturing for her to join her on the final stanza of Aren's first adventure, which Anna found herself happily able to recall. Together, the sisters finished telling the tale: "'The sea rushed in as hidden power flowed from the gleaming sword and shaped the rock and forest crown of the first majestic fjord!'"

Their voices rang out as one, the words triumphantly echoing across the ice.

"Not too shabby," Kristoff said. "It kind of reminds

me of the troll ballad about Dagfinn the Dusty, a troll who was allergic to mountains and would accidentally cause avalanches wherever he went by sneezing boulders out of his nose."

"Wait, what?" Anna giggled. "That's what trolls say boulders are? Troll bogies?"

Kristoff shrugged. "Well, yeah. I can sing it for you, if you'd like."

"Maybe later," Elsa cut in, stopping with a spray of ice. "We're here." She pointed up at a sign:

MINER'S MOUNTAIN

WARNING: KEEP OUT

NO TRESPASSERS OR GOATS

HULDREFÓLK ARE WATCHING!

Anna looked up at the sparkling summit of Miner's Mountain. If she squinted her eyes just so, she thought she could make out the mystic's tower. But it was so high up and so far away that from where she stood it looked more like a chimney that had been stuck on top of a roof rather than a tower on a mountain. It would take *days* to climb all that distance.

For people who didn't have a magical sister, that is.

Elsa waited for Kristoff and Anna to step off the frozen river before she did so herself. As soon as Elsa was on the bank, the ice cracked and blue water began to flow once more. With a twirl of Elsa's hand, Anna's ice skates melted away to reveal her boots beneath, but Anna hardly realised it because of the great whirlwind that kicked up around her, snow climbing into the air higher and higher, until solidifying into a grand icy staircase.

Elsa had done it again. While the staircase of ice was long and ever so high, with nothing but a curving, slender handrail, it would be much easier to navigate than a treacherous and tedious rocky trail. There must have been at least a thousand steps in the ice staircase – Anna couldn't be bothered to count. Either way, they were going to climb it, because, at the very top, answers were waiting for them.

"Classic," Kristoff said to Elsa.

"Thanks," she replied.

One step, then another, they ascended.

At first, Anna didn't bother holding on to the

fragile railing, but about two-thirds of the way to the top, she looked down and gripped it tight. The staircase was clear as glass, and Anna – though brave – wasn't entirely comfortable with the sight of her feet seemingly dangling above thin air. From this height, the pines seemed to shrink, smaller and smaller and smaller. As they moved up, the sun moved down.

At long last, in the blazing sunset, they reached the top. From there, the tower was much taller than Anna had realised – and much more jumbled. The rocks that made up the tower seemed to be haphazardly arranged, and certain stones seemed to be on the verge of slipping out of place. In fact, the tower did not look unlike the staggered piles of books Anna had left in the library. Elsa reached the door to the tower first and paused. Her hand remained still, raised out in front of her, as if she couldn't decide whether she should knock.

Anna pulled her cloak to her chest as the wind sang around them. "What's wrong?"

"What do I say?" Elsa asked.

"You knock and say hi, and we'll go from there," Kristoff called. *"Hurry."*

"What Kristoff said," Anna said, watching the sun sink over the horizon.

Elsa threw back her shoulders and knocked.

Then the three of them stared at the door and waited, but nothing happened. Was no one home? The thought filled Anna with a heavy dread. They had come all this way and Sorenson was not there.

Elsa knocked again. Nothing.

"Stand back," Kristoff said. He moved in front of Elsa and put his shoulder to the door. But it was sturdier than it looked. He lifted his pickaxe high.

"Why don't you try the handle?" Elsa asked.

Kristoff raised an eyebrow and did just that. The door swung easily open.

"Huh," he said as he put his pickaxe away. Without saying another word, he went inside.

Anna exchanged an amused glance with her sister and they followed him through the doorway and into the tower. From the outside, the tower had looked about to topple, but the inside seemed solid enough, made up of rock and wood and books.

Anna had always imagined a mystic to be exacting, the kind of person who might label the spices in their kitchen cabinet, but everything seemed to be randomly placed. Plants sprawled on top of books, and books on top of statues. On the far side of the circular room was a spiral staircase. There was practically everything under the sun in the tower room.

Except for a mystic.

Chapter Fourteen

KRISTOFF GROANED, letting his traveller's pack thump to the floor. "He's not here. Now what?"

"I'm sure he'll come back," Anna said, unclasping her cloak. The tower felt especially stuffy after being in the wind all day long. "In the meantime, we wait."

Aroooooooooooooooo!

A long, low howl wrapped around the tower, carving a pit in Anna's stomach – was it the wolf? Had it escaped Elsa's ice dome?

Kristoff, however, remained calm. "It's just the wind. Trust me." He picked up a small guitar that leaned next to a potted plant. "Growing up with trolls, you know what's the wind, and what's a wolf." He strummed the guitar. The tinkling sound filtered through the air, pretty, if a bit off-key.

Anna's fear receded a little, and she hoped he was right. "I'd rather the wolf be stalking us here and leaving the villagers alone," she admitted.

"Very noble of you," Elsa said. "We'll stay, but just until we figure out a plan in case Sorenson doesn't come back soon."

"Maybe there's a book or something here that can undo the curse," Anna said. "One that's already been translated."

"That's a good idea," Kristoff said. "I'll take the upstairs. You two search down here." And with a nod at the girls, he lit his lantern and disappeared into the swirl of dark steps above them. Anna thought she knew why he wanted to search a floor by himself. When Anna was upset, she always sought company, but when Kristoff was upset, he liked to be by himself or with Sven. And with Sven in trouble, she knew Kristoff was having a hard time, too.

Elsa sighed. "Ugh. I knew coming here was a bad idea."

Anna felt herself bristle like the grey barn cat, but she didn't want to fight, not again, not so soon. They had come a long way, and they had more of a way to go. So she kept her voice light. "We don't know that yet. Let's just give this room a chance. Please?"

Elsa crossed her arms, but after a second, Anna knew she'd won. This round, anyway. They divided up the circular room. In the light of a dying fire, she could see the walls were plastered with detailed star charts and strange silver instruments that hummed, and a delicate gold miniature of the solar system that was so beautifully done, Anna thought it was a shame that she couldn't study it for hours and tell the children of the village all about it. She also found a calendar with all the phases of the moon laid out, three miniature telescopes, powder-filled glass vials, and an old sundial, its copper face green from the years it must have spent out in the harsh elements. And last but not least, a hunk of blue-black rock that was labelled: METEORITE.

"This mystic seems to really like the night sky," Anna called to Elsa.

"I noticed," Elsa said as she straightened a frame. "Did you see the ceiling?"

Anna tilted her head back and gasped. A star map had been painted above them in deep blues and indigos. Delicate lines of silver paint connected some of the stars, tracing the outlines of fantastical beasts, crowns and heroes. They were familiar images, and Anna recognised them as constellations. But there was something else about the illustrations that seemed familiar to her, though she couldn't quite place her finger on it...

"It's so pretty," Anna said. "It's the prettiest ceiling I've ever seen."

Elsa nodded. "I like it, too. It even has my favourite constellation – Ulf." She looked over at Anna and smiled. "Ulf the Wolf was always my favourite. I made Mother tell me all his stories."

The sisters kept searching.

Sorenson's thinking seemed random, and his shelves didn't appear to be organised in any particular order that Anna could tell. Though, when she peeled back the first book's cover, she wondered if maybe he had ranked them by stench. Many of the books had dark stains on their pages, and a couple of them even had their own furry patch of mould. But for someone who was known to be an expert in myths and lore, Sorenson didn't appear to have many books on those topics. The closest thing was a small slate covered with strange symbols in chalk, but upon examining it, Anna saw it wasn't magic, but physics.

Wandering over to the last bookshelf, Anna skimmed the titles: *Book of Later Han* by Zhang Heng, *Almanack* by Richard Saunders and *Book of Optics* by Hasan Ibn al-Haytham. Picking up the first title, Anna flipped through the pages to see sketches of instruments that looked quite similar to those sitting on the mystic's shelves, along with annotations of water clocks and wind flows. No mention of curses or of dream spells gone awry.

"It's funny," Anna called out to Elsa as she tapped the book back onto the shelf. "I wouldn't think that a mystic would have so many books on science. I thought he would have more spell books and stuff. You know?" She paused, waiting for her sister's response. But when Elsa didn't say anything, Anna called again. "Hey, Elsa?"

"Anna, can you come here?" Elsa asked.

Anna followed her sister's voice to where she stood in a back room, more of an alcove really, that contained a tiny kitchen. Anna hurried over to her sister to find her gaping open-mouthed at a table. It looked ordinary enough, but then Anna saw it: on the centre of the table was a pot of soup.

A *steaming* pot of soup.

Anna's stomach flipped. For that twist of steam to exist, someone had to have been there recently.

"Where's Kristoff?" Anna whispered. She'd planned on checking on him, but had become distracted by the many books and treasures. The mystic's mind seemed just as distracted as her own. And now Kristoff had been gone upstairs for at least ten minutes, and he'd not come back down.

"Anna," Elsa whispered, "I don't think we're alone here."

"Exactly so," said a low, raspy voice.

Anna spun round as a man stepped off the staircase landing and into the tower room. He was short, barely up to Anna's shoulders, and he wore his long silver beard down to the floor. Anna had the fleeting thought that he looked a bit like the nisse from her mother's tales, those tiny gnome-like creatures that would adopt a family to both hinder and help. The only thing he was missing was a nisse's traditional pointy red hat, but he did have a sharp, glinting spear – and it was aimed directly at her heart.

Anna stopped breathing. In the corner, she saw Elsa raise her hands. They were trembling. But there was Elsa, once again ready to step in. Anna knew better than anyone how much Elsa never again wanted to use her powers to harm another – not after the disastrous consequences that had occurred the last time, when she had turned Anna to ice by accident. But Anna also knew that Elsa *would* use her powers to protect Anna – and Anna could not allow that. Not when Anna could do something about it herself.

"Hi! I'm Anna! This is Elsa!" Anna smiled, trying to inject as much cheer and goodwill into her voice as possible. "We're sorry to intrude. We promise we weren't going to eat your soup – it smells a bit funny – er, that's so rude of me. I'm sorry. I mean, it doesn't smell bad, but I'm not really sure I recognise that spice? But we're not here for spices. Please don't hurt us!"

"Hurt you?" The man looked dizzy from trying to follow Anna's words. "Why would you think I would want to hurt you?" His voice was deep and grating like gravel.

"Umm." Anna's eyes flew to his hand. "Because of the spear you're holding?"

"What sp—? Oh!" The man lowered the point of his spear. "This isn't a spear, it's part of a weather vane. That *mountain man* upstairs broke it when he barged onto my peaceful observation deck unannounced! He's *exceedingly* lucky I finished my Highly Flammable and Very Dangerous Combustion Powder last night or he might not have ten fingers. Hmph."

Anna blinked as the man shoved the pointed weather vane under her nose and she took in the large golden *N* that twinkled in front of her. *N* for north. "Ha ha," she said, and pushed the golden point away from her. "What a silly mistake. Is the, er, mountain man... all right?"

"He *will* be, once he cleans up the mess he made," the short man said, shooting her a glare. "He's *also* lucky he didn't come next month and disturb my view of the meteor shower. But that's what *I'm* doing here. I live here. Always have. My question is: what are *you* doing here?"

"We're looking for the *great* mystic Sorenson," Anna said, trying to sweep a curtsy, but her knees were still shaky from misinterpreting the weather vane, and she almost knocked over a nearby bust of a man in round reading glasses. "We're assuming that's you?"

The old man snorted. "I'm Sorenson, but I'm no mystic."

Elsa stepped forward, her hands no longer raised, but now clenched in the folds of her cloak. "But the villagers say you *are* a mystic."

"I'm a *scientist*," the man said, using the weather vane to reach through his thick beard and scratch the underside of his chin. "Though I suppose the villagers might not see that much of a difference between me and the old mystics of legendary tales."

A scientist. Anna tried not to let her disappointment show. It was great to be a scientist, but not when one needed a mystic to save a kingdom from a vicious magical wolf. How would a scientist be able to help with a terrible curse? "We're sorry to have bothered you." Anna stepped aside as Sorenson shuffled past her to check on his soup. "Oaken had told us that you're an expert in myths and lore."

"Oh, but I am." Sorenson gave his pot a stir. "Mythology and science are familiar friends – both seek for the *why* behind things. Both look to provide an explanation for the natural phenomena of the world around us. And all myths contain a kernel of hard truth." He took a sip of his soup and winced before tossing in a pinch of salt. Only after he took another sip and nodded his head in satisfaction did he look back at the sisters. "Though I *am* curious as to why the queen and princess of Arendelle are here seeking an expert in myths and lore. Something must be truly wrong."

"Because," Elsa said, her voice low but steady, "Arendelle has been cursed."

"And we need your help to figure out how to undo it," Anna added, attempting to gloss over the fact that *she'd* been the one who'd cursed it. She tried not to look at anyone, but Elsa caught her eye and nodded. For a moment, it felt like an ember from the fireplace had broken away from the logs and settled somewhere in Anna's heart. Even though snow and ice flowed through Elsa, she always made Anna feel the warmest. Maybe everything wasn't lost, after all.

Except, Sorenson's reaction wasn't exactly encouraging. His bushy eyebrows shot up so fast that they almost skidded off his face, and Anna wondered for a minute if he would laugh. Instead, he opened an old trunk and began pulling out empty bowls.

"In that case," Sorenson said, "someone please fetch the mountain man from the observation deck and have him rebuild my fire. It seems as though you have a story to tell, and I'd rather be warm while I listen."

A few minutes and a roaring fire later, Anna, Elsa

and Kristoff gathered around Sorenson's table, each taking turns sharing all they knew. Anna heard Elsa describe the unnatural quiet that had befallen SoYun's farm and the way the trees in the kingdom's orchards were not only producing mushy grey apples, but had also become gnarled, as though they were twisting away from something – the wolf, Anna guessed – as it had passed by. But did that mean the wolf had been present before she read the spell? And if so, how?

Then it was Kristoff's turn, and he described how the forest, too, had been quiet, though he did not mention the trolls or their surprising absence. Arendelle's mountain trolls were private creatures, and for the most part, they liked to keep themselves hidden from humans, with a few special exceptions. Kristoff wouldn't mention them to just any person, and though Sorenson was now feeding them warm soup that tasted of mushrooms and roots, Kristoff was still protective of the concealed trolls who had raised him as part of their family, and, after all, Sorenson *had* forced Kristoff to clean up his mess out on a chilly observation deck.

Finally, it was Anna's turn. She began with the crumpled piece of paper with the 'Make Dreams Come True' spell on it, and how she'd had a nightmare, and gone to the kitchen to make some hot chocolate. She told him how she'd seen something out of the corner of her eye and followed it to the Great Hall, where she'd seen a wolf – the same wolf from her nightmare. And how her friends' eyes had turned inky black and then glowing yellow while they seemed to have lost themselves in the strong hold of a nightmare sleep. As she completed her tale, Sorenson stood and went to his shelves. Pulling out two books, he returned to the table, the wooden floorboards beneath his boots creaking slightly as he walked.

"I think," Sorenson said, placing the books on the table and slipping back into his stool, "that the answer can be found in one of these."

Anna looked at the books. One was a tome called *Psychologia*. The other was a slim leather volume with block letters stamped across its cover:

NATTMARA

"'*Nattmara*,'" Elsa read out loud. "I know that word."

Anna knew the word, too. She'd heard the word before, long, long ago, but she had *seen* that word recently as well, as a non-translated entry in *Secrets of the Magic Makers.* A vision sprang to her mind: a sketch of a man screaming in agony and the drawing of the wolf...

"Yes." Sorenson nodded. "You probably do. Nattmara often show up in the sagas of old, and those stories are often told to children as warning tales." Flipping open the ancient book, he pointed to an illustration of a child sleeping in bed. "Another name for a Nattmara is 'Nightmare', because that's what it is – the embodiment of our deepest fear."

"Embody-*what*?" Kristoff asked.

"It means that nightmares can take on a physical shape and exist outside of your mind," Elsa said.

"Precisely." Sorenson held up his index finger. "The act of burying fear is what manifests the Nattmara. And eventually, the fear is too big to keep inside. They can take the shape of anything, and this particular one seems to have taken the form of a wolf. Nattmara tend to roam the world, leaching energy from all living things. Their very presence can cause trees to twist away from them. They feed on fear and so they seek to *create* fear."

Anna's eyes widened as she listened, trying to grasp onto the strange ideas.

Sorenson flipped the page to another illustration, this one of a swirling storm of black sand. "A Nattmara is also able to turn itself into black sand in order to slip through cracks – cracks in doors and cracks within the heart. There is no escaping them, unless you're brave enough that there is no weakness for the Nattmara to enter through."

He looked up, his brown eyes locking on Anna. "And if a Nattmara is allowed to run loose for too long, then a kingdom and everyone in it can fall into an eternal nightmare sleep. And as it grows more powerful, more people can become afraid and it can gorge itself on fear, becoming bigger and bigger." He tapped the page. "Or so the age-old myth goes."

Anna blinked, breaking away from Sorenson's deep gaze. "You don't sound like you believe in this myth," she said, puzzled. "But doesn't what's happening in Arendelle now *prove* that the myth is real?"

"Not at all," Sorenson said, shaking his head and sending his long beard swaying. "What do they teach in schools these days? The Nattmara is a creature of myth, and like all myths, it's an explanation to a greater mystery. In this instance: where do nightmares come from?"

"Pardon me," Elsa said, while Anna and Kristoff exchanged puzzled glances, "but I don't understand your question."

Sighing, Sorenson shook his head. "Let's look at it a different way. Did you see the signs for the mines that warn to be wary of Huldrefólk?" He paused, and when they nodded, he continued. "The mines were abandoned nearly twenty years ago, because of strange and mysterious things that kept going wrong. Cave-ins started to occur with increased frequency, and miners that had worked their entire lives in these tunnels began to get lost. Now, what was the explanation?" Sorenson looked from Anna to Elsa to Kristoff.

"Huldrefólk," Anna said, thinking back to the sign they had passed and Oaken's warning. "The mysterious, elf-like people known as the Huldrefólk are rumoured to live throughout Arendelle in mounds and under rock. They are a mischievous bunch, not necessarily bad, but they enjoy pranks above all else. They have a bit of a reputation for being thieves, but some stories insist they are simply collectors, borrowers of lost things. But unlike the mountain trolls, they are just a story that parents tell their young ones to go to sleep."

"Exactly," Sorenson nodded. "The miners believed

the Huldrefólk were angry that they were impeding on their territory. They thought the Huldrefólk were creating the cave-ins to scare the humans away."

"It seemed to have worked," Kristoff remarked. "I noticed some boards over the mines' entrance."

"It did work," Sorenson agreed. "And a good thing, too, because the mines had been overworked. The miners weren't in danger from territorial Huldrefólk. The human miners were in the middle of a danger of their own making. It was *their* pickaxes that had made the rock walls too thin to hold the weight of a mountain. Nothing mythical about it; just old-fashioned greed."

"So," Elsa said slowly, "you're saying the Nattmara probably has a simple explanation, too?"

"A *scientific* one," Sorenson clarified. "Most likely, our answer is in this." He tapped the book labelled *Psychologia* with a grimy fingernail.

Anna turned this information over. What Sorenson had said seemed simple enough, but she had seen the wolf. She had seen Kai's and Gerda's eyes. The 'myth' had seemed very real as it had chased her and her friends through the rooms and halls of the castle.

"But say it *is* a Nattmara that is doing all of this,"

Anna argued, not wanting to leave empty-handed, not wanting to leave without at least *one* answer. "How can we defeat it?"

"That's easy enough," Sorenson said, pulling out another book, this one titled *Mythica Explainia*. "You can only defeat a myth *with* a thing of myth. But it's not like Revolute exists. None of it really truly does."

"Revolute?" Kristoff asked. "That was Aren's sword, right?"

"The very one." Sorenson nodded. "Aren was said to have defeated many a mythical beast with his sword. The very sword, some say, that the sun herself gifted to him for ripping holes in the night sky so that she could watch her children during the day. Those rips, of course, are what we call stars." He smiled up in the direction of his painted ceiling. "See? Another myth seeking to answer how things came to be."

"Great!" Anna felt hope lift within her for the first time since they'd arrived at the tower. "So we need Revolute! Where is it?"

Sorenson burst into laughter, but as he did, he took in the serious expression on her face and shook his head. "I'm sorry, but it's unlikely that Aren *himself* ever existed – *or* his mighty sword of myth. It's likely that there was a strong warrior from way back when, but he probably never met the sun or faced a great dragon, or carved out the Arenfjord. That's just legend – like the Huldrefólk or the mountain trolls."

"But the trolls exist," Kristoff said with a shrug. "They raised me."

Sorenson stared hard at Kristoff. Then he cupped his hand around his mouth and whispered in Elsa's ear, *"Is the mountain man okay?"*

"Kristoff," Anna corrected, "is amazing. And the trolls *do* exist. And the Nattmara exists. And the Huldrefólk, well, they probably exist, too!"

Sorenson sat back, snapping his book shut. "Magic and myth don't exist," he said.

Elsa smirked and flicked her wrist. A second later, Anna felt a cold kiss on her cheek. She looked up to see a delicate snow flurry hovering above their heads.

There was a loud clatter as Sorenson tumbled from his stool. "In all my days! The rumours are true!"

Elsa smiled. "You haven't come down your mountain in a very long time, have you, Sorenson?" And so, Elsa began to tell Sorenson all that had happened in the last three years. And with each new thing he learned, Sorenson had another question.

Kristoff drummed his fingers on the table impatiently, and only when Anna laid her hand over his did he stop. "Sorry," he whispered, "but while we're talking, Sven is still sick!"

Anna knew that Kristoff was right. "Let's keep looking," she said quietly.

Kristoff crept over to the bookshelves while Anna cracked open the volume on the table. She skipped past passages about talking trees and a playful wind spirit until, finally, she found what she had been looking for: NATTMARA.

Sure enough, all that Sorenson had said was written there, including a few additional pieces of information:

> *The Nattmara is created when a child's fear*
> *grows too big to be contained and the child's*
> *fearful heart calls out to them.*

And then, a little below that:

> *Trolls tremble at the Nattmara's howl*
> *while the Nattmara flees from the sun like a shadow.*

Nothing in the section said anything about a spell that was able to manifest a Nattmara or banish it. But it was useful to know that the Nattmara didn't like sunlight. And it explained why the trolls had most likely gone missing. Frowning, Anna thumbed through the pages and reread an entry about the Huldrefólk. She stopped upon a line:

Huldrefólk always find that which is lost.

That which is lost... Anna's heart quickened. Maybe, she thought with rising excitement, that also meant the Huldrefólk could find a mythical sword that was lost to history. It was a slim hope, but a hope she clung to nevertheless. Maybe they needed to go to the mines to find the Huldrefólk – *despite* the warnings.

But they didn't have much time.

They only had two more sunrises left before the spell became permanent – and the night was no longer young.

"You know," Sorenson said to Elsa, "your mother came here once, seeking answers. In fact, she was the one who painted my ceiling."

Anna froze. Their *mother* had been here? It couldn't be. Why on earth would their mother come to visit Sorenson? Answers to *what*? And suddenly, she realised why the painted ceiling looked familiar. It reminded her of the painting of the northern lights and constellations that decorated the ceiling of the secret room.

Slipping the book into Kristoff's traveller's pack, Anna opened her mouth to ask Sorenson more, and to tell the others her idea about going to the mines. But as Anna looked up, she noticed something strange across the tower room: an army of black ants pouring in from under the door. She shut her mouth.

No. Not ants.

Black sand.

The Nattmara had found them at last.

Chapter Fifteen

AS THE BLACK SAND trickled into the tower room from beneath the door, thoughts, dark and sticky, clung to Anna like oil.

Thoughts like bugs crawling into ears, teeth rotting and falling out, waves black and drowning, and a door. A large white door with purple flowers repeating over and over again, each one telling her that she was not good enough, that she was not wanted, that she was shut out. And as the thoughts hit her, pounding as relentlessly as a stormy sea, Anna felt it hard to breathe. Her heart tightened as if something was pressing on her chest. The weight made it hard to speak, but she must – she had to warn her friends.

"Y-you guys," Anna whispered, trying to get her mouth to work. But in those few precious seconds, the sand had spilled into the room, forming a dark puddle. The grains lifted and swirled into the air, as if each grain had its own pair of miniature wings, its own brain and then they swarmed, creating the outline of a shadow. A wolf's shadow.

Fear gave her strength. "Nattmara!" Anna yelled.

The sand solidified into the great white wolf. Now the creature was as big as the length of wall. Its head practically scraped the painted ceiling.

As if in slow motion, Anna saw the others turn. Kristoff's mouth dropped open, while Elsa's eyes widened in horror. But it was Sorenson – the old scientist who believed in the entanglement of science and myth, myth and science – who reacted first.

"Close your eyes!" He bolted up and grabbed for one of the many glass vials near him.

Anna shut her eyes. A second later, there was a bright flash even through her closed eyelids, followed by the yelp of the wolf. *No. Not a wolf,* Anna corrected herself. *Nattmara.*

"Upstairs!" Sorenson yelled. "Run!"

And even though she had closed her eyes to the flash, black dots still spotted her vision as she stood and ran with Kristoff towards the steps. Taking them two at a time, she was aware of screaming and a noise that sounded like sharpening knives. Glancing backwards, she saw Sorenson at the bottom of the stairs, and beside him, Elsa, shooting ice javelins at the wolf again and again and again.

But the ice javelins, sharp and lethal, seemed to do as much harm as a toothpick plunged into water. Each time Elsa let loose an ice javelin, it soared through the air towards its target – but it never *hit* its target.

The Nattmara didn't seem to be made of fur or bone or muscle. Or anything solid, really. Because as ice javelins were about to pin its paws down in place, the wolf's paws dissolved at their touch, shifting and morphing its shape like – *like sand*, Anna realised.

It was as Sorenson had said. The Nattmara could take any form. Seep through the cracks in any door. Slip into the fragile spots of a person's heart. It fed on fear, but how could they not be afraid of it? It *was* fear. A bit of black sand floated towards Anna and her breath caught again. The sticky thoughts rushed back into her mind: *she'd* done this. She couldn't do anything right. She never could. She'd failed Elsa.

"ANNA!" Kristoff, his traveller's pack dangling from his shoulder, pulled her arm. "KEEP GOING!"

The sound of his voice – full of worry and care – snapped Anna back into herself. She ran with him, and didn't stop racing up the dizzying, tight spiral of steps until she exploded out into the cold, open air of Sorenson's observation deck.

Any other time, she knew she would have loved to stay up there. The mountain air was so clear that the stars above pulsed bright. The moon overhead was round and ripe, just begging to be plucked from the sky and put into her pocket as a sweet treat for later. And in the centre of the circular deck, standing like a newborn colt on spindly legs, gleamed a copper telescope. It pointed to the heavens, an instrument that helped seek answers in the celestial dance. It was all strange, fascinating and beautiful. And a dead end.

Just like in Anna's nightmare, there was no place to run.

The wolf, still behind them on the tower stairs, had cornered her, this time on a wooden deck, hundreds of feet in the air, and the only means of escape – jumping – definitely didn't bode well for any of them. They were trapped!

Sorenson's shoulder collided with hers as he shot past her to the edge of the deck. Leaning over the simple wooden railing, he grasped at the night air and then pulled back. In the light of the full moon, Anna could make out the silver glint of something in his palm: a wire cable – one so thin it seemed to vanish only a foot away from the tower.

"Grab the tablecloth!" He gestured to the long wooden workbench that stood next to the telescope. It was covered in beakers, thermometers and barometers, pencils and quills, abacuses, rulers, flasks and pages of calculations. And seemingly all of Sorenson's life's work sat on a little lavender tablecloth neatly embroidered with a crocus. If the tablecloth were pulled, all of that work – years and years of it – would smash onto the deck, lost forever. Anna hesitated.

"Do it!" Sorenson roared at her.

But Anna couldn't, she just couldn't. It was a table of answers, the work of a lifetime of gathering information. So Kristoff reached behind her and tugged the tablecloth free. With a tremendous clash, the beautiful and strange devices fell to the floor, the sound something similar to the breaking of a heart.

"Now tear the cloth!" Sorenson commanded.

The sound of the wolf's vicious barks and the

scrape of ice filled the air. Elsa had made it to the observation deck and stood at the entrance, flinging her hand out again and again and again. With each flick of her wrist, the doorway filled to the brim with ice – fresh ice, new ice, ice without cracks.

For a moment, anyway.

Because then the Nattmara would slam itself against it, sending cracks scattering across the surface, and a little more black sand wisped through the cracks each time.

Smooth ice.

Shattered ice.

Smooth. Shattered. Elsa was holding the Nattmara and its sandy paws at bay, but even Elsa – brave, strong, wise, magical Elsa – couldn't keep at it forever. Already, Anna could see the weariness in the slope of her shoulders. The snap of her wrist grew looser with each deft gesture.

Riiiiiip! Anna turned to see Kristoff obeying Sorenson's orders and tearing the tablecloth into thick strips, but Anna didn't offer to help. Instead, her mind had become preoccupied by something else. Each time Elsa flung out her wrist and filled the doorway with ice, Anna thought the Nattmara grew a little bigger. Smooth ice. Shattered ice. Smooth ice. Yes, Anna was sure of it now. Whenever Elsa shot a magical blast of ice at the creature of myth, its paws expanded, its teeth sharpened and its strength doubled.

"Elsa!" Anna cried. "Elsa, stop! Your magic! It's making it stronger!" But between the snarling of the Nattmara, the tearing of the cloth and the sound of ice cracking again and again and again, Elsa couldn't hear her. Their only way of surviving in this moment would be if they escaped.

"Hurry!" Sorenson cried. "Take some!"

Anna took a bit of tablecloth from Kristoff and stumbled towards the scientist. Grabbing the strip, Sorenson looped the cloth over the thin wire, making a *U* with the fabric.

"Hands," he grunted.

Anna obliged, holding out her wrists as he tied the dangling ends of the cloth strip under Anna's armpits to create a makeshift harness.

Sorenson patted the rickety wooden railing. "Climb up."

Anna did as she was told. Only when she was balanced on the topmost rail, facing the mountain slope far beneath her, did Sorenson's plan truly sink in. "Wait a second," Anna said, twisting to face him. "You can't be serious."

"Hang on tight!" Sorenson pushed her – hard.

With a squeal, Anna slipped off the observation deck in a rush of wind and stars. She screamed. Careening down the mountain nearly felt like flying, but *definitely* felt like falling. The cable jounced and jiggled as she sped down the mountainside.

Wrapping her wrists in the tablecloth, she held on for dear life as her legs swung beneath her. From somewhere above, she could hear Elsa and Kristoff and Sorenson shouting as they zipped down behind her. Thank goodness they were safe!

Anna almost laughed – but the ground was rushing towards her, and coming up way too fast. Straining her eyes against the dark night, Anna followed the path of the rippling cable; it disappeared into the branches of a tree at the foot of the mountain, near the entrance to the mines. That much was good.

But what wasn't good was how fast she was approaching the very solid trunk. If she hit the tree at this pace, she would definitely break a few ribs, and that was *if* she was lucky. She needed to slow down.

"SNOW!" she yelled back at Elsa. "SNOW! SNOW SNOW SNOW!" She thought she heard Elsa shout back, but Anna couldn't tell. The wind stole whatever words left her sister's lips. She just had to hope and trust that her sister would know what to do, the way she always did.

Ten feet away from the tree. Now five. Now two. Anna released the tablecloth and set herself free. She tumbled through the dark air for what felt like a year but was likely only a moment, and then—

WOMP!

A cold tingle enveloped Anna, as refreshing and comforting as one of the bubbly drinks Oaken sold at his lodge. Soft, pillowy snowflakes had cushioned her fall. Elsa had done it again. But there was no time to catch her breath. Instead, Anna rolled out of the way as Elsa, Kristoff and Sorenson plopped into the snow pile like ripe apples falling from a tree.

Anna shot up. "Everyone okay? Where is it?"

Everyone nodded, then Kristoff pointed.

Anna turned. It was hard to see in the dark, but she could just make out a patch of shadow barrelling down the mountain like an avalanche of black snow: the Nattmara. Still on the hunt.

"The mines!" Anna said. "Hurry!"

"They're not safe!" Sorenson said. "Cave-ins and toxic air—"

"And Huldrefólk!" Anna said. "Elsa, remember the myth!"

Elsa gasped. "'Huldrefólk always find that which is lost.' Aren's sword!"

"It may be our only chance!" Anna said. "We have to find them and ask where the Revolute Blade is!"

"But—" Sorenson's protest was cut off by a long howl, a howl that rose in pitch until the very air of the kingdom became a scream and Anna staggered under its weight.

Clasping her hands over her ears, Anna ran past the warning posts, ripped back the wooden boards that had been nailed up over the entrance, and dived into the gaping mouth of the mines. Her friends followed her. The howl reached them even there, and Kristoff struggled with his traveller's pack to light his lantern, but at last they could see.

All around, there were passages: thin ones, wide ones, narrow ones, up and down and around. But which led to a dead end? And which led to chambers of poisonous gases or pits with sharp sticks or sleeping bears? Most importantly, which would take them to the Huldrefólk?

"Which one, Sorenson?" Anna asked.

But the old scientist looked perplexed. His long silver beard tufted in all directions, as if it, too, were confused.

Standing beside Anna, Kristoff swung his lantern, sending arcs of light rippling across the walls and floor.

Something glinted in the rock, and Anna looked down. She was standing on something long and metal: the tracks for mine carts!

"This way!" Anna said, taking off in a sprint as she followed the tracks.

A second later, they arrived in a large chamber where, at the far end, sitting comfortably as if it had been waiting for them all along, was a wooden mine cart.

Kristoff gestured to it theatrically. "Ta-da! Your chariot awaits, m'lady."

"Why, thank you, kind sir!" Anna clambered in, with Elsa and Sorenson climbing in behind her.

Kristoff pushed the cart, trying to get the rusty wheels to move forward. They rolled a bit then stopped, and Anna saw why. A rope had been tied around one end of the cart, anchoring it to a jutting boulder.

"May I?" she asked him, reaching for his lantern.

He handed it to her. "You may."

Anna held the lantern's flame to the rope.

The Nattmara's howl was even louder now, impossibly so, and the tunnel shook.

It had arrived.

Each step of its giant paws sent a tremor through the earth.

And Anna could see that her guess had been right – each time Elsa used her magic, the Nattmara seemed to have grown more fearsome and more horrible. It stood in the mouth of the cave, eclipsing the light of the moon, black sand sweeping around it as its eyes shone yellow.

In Anna's hands, the rope charred – blackening, thinning. Finally, it snapped. But the cart stayed put.

"Why aren't we moving?" Elsa cried out.

"We're too heavy for it," Anna said, desperation whirling through her. "Maybe if we rock a bit–"

"No need," Sorenson interrupted.

"What do you mean?" Anna demanded.

But the scientist only smiled – and then launched himself out of the cart. He sprinted towards the mouth of the mines... towards the Nattmara.

"Noooooo!" Anna yelled, though she couldn't hear herself in the ocean of the Nattmara's howl.

But Sorenson had done the trick. With his weight gone, the cart rose and the wheels rolled forward, slow at first, then faster and faster – and then the cart plunged, forcing Anna to drop Kristoff's lantern. It crashed to the floor of the cart, but the light didn't snuff out. Rough wood cut into her hands as she clung to the sides of the cart for dear life.

It barrelled down the tracks, screeching through jolting turns and sharp twists, threatening to buck them out at every turn.

"We're going too fast!" Elsa shouted. "Slow down!"

"The brakes aren't working!" Kristoff yelled back as he retrieved his lantern and held it out in front of them. "And the steering stick is stuck!"

Anna felt her mouth open in horror as she frantically tried to think of a solution.

"Lean right!" Kristoff bellowed.

Anna and Elsa flung their weight to the right, and the cart shifted on the track, following the curve of the rail. Kristoff continued to yell instructions. In this way – with Kristoff calling out and Anna and

Elsa leaning this way and that – they were able to direct the cart, zigzagging down into the mountain's core instead of dropping vertically. They would roll to a stop at some point. *Wouldn't they?*

And then, suddenly, there was light up ahead. An exit!

"What *is* that?" Elsa shouted. "We're nowhere near morning!" She was right, and as Anna's eyes drank in the light, she realised it held a strange aqua glow. Before she could wonder too much where it came from, Kristoff yelled, "LAKE!"

SPLASH!

In an explosion of lukewarm water, they careened into an underground lake. The cart rolled forward in the rippling water, then stopped, the surprisingly shallow body of water bringing their wild ride to an end. Kristoff's lantern went out, smoke snaking off into the air.

Anna allowed herself to be still. To feel the air in her lungs and hear the quiet of the subterranean world. But it wasn't utter silence. Far from it.

All around them was a soft splish-splash as stalactites dripped water into the reflective lake that was illuminated by the strange light. Anna looked down at the water and then up in wonder. She finally knew the source of the light. Dangling from the cave ceiling were a million tiny glow-worms, each one giving off a gentle light the colour of the bluest ice. They reflected onto the surface of the lake so that it looked like they were in a bathtub under a galaxy of stars. It was a secret world of sound and water and light, both comforting and glorious.

"Is everyone okay?" Anna asked.

Kristoff winced slightly, but said, more or less cheerfully, "Yep!"

"Yes," Elsa said. "I hope Sorenson is okay."

Anna hoped so, too, but she didn't want her sister to worry. "I'm sure he's fine," Anna said, mustering as much enthusiasm as she could. "That scientist has more tricks up his sleeves than appointments in your schedule." She stood up slowly. "And *everyone* will be okay once we have the sword to break the Nattmara's curse." Careful to keep her balance, she rose to her tiptoes and examined a glow-worm. "Wow," she breathed out. Each glow-worm looked like a beaded necklace and hung like an icicle, beautiful and perfect.

There was the sound of swirling water. Anna looked over to see that Elsa had clambered out of the mine cart and stepped into the lake. It was shallow, only coming up to her sister's waist. She didn't bother to lift her cloak out of the water, but instead let it float up around her, so that it almost looked like she'd grown a twinkling mermaid's fin. Now *mermaids* were something Anna wished were real. And maybe, just maybe, they were. Elsa waded to the rocky banks.

"Where are you going?" Anna asked.

Elsa stopped to look up at the steep track they had careened down only moments before. "I can't hear anything," Elsa whispered, as though they were little girls again playing hide-and-seek in the chapel and waiting for their parents to discover them.

"That's good, right?" Kristoff's voice was hushed. "The Nattmara couldn't have followed us. We were going impossibly fast, and there were too many tracks for it to know which ones we chose."

"Look up," Elsa said grimly.

Anna followed her sister's gaze. In the glow-worms' light, she could make out a dozen different passages above them, each one leading to somewhere. To *many* somewheres. Anna tensed. They had lost the Nattmara. They had lost Sorenson.

And now they were lost, too.

Chapter Sixteen

ANNA, ELSA AND KRISTOFF couldn't stay in the cave of crystal-clear water and glow-worm light forever.

Because now, even the quiet was dangerous.

It had been nearly twenty-four hours since Anna had last slept, and judging from the dark bags under Elsa's eyes, it had been even longer for her. But it was Kristoff who was suffering from exhaustion the most. Looking for his troll family, he'd already done a hard day's ride before arriving back at the castle, only to flee. He had been awake for too long. He needed sleep. They all did.

But if they slept, it might make it easier for the Nattmara to track them – and Anna knew it wouldn't give up. That was the nature of a nightmare

– one second, they were forgotten, and the next, they exploded into sharp memory. Anna, Elsa and Kristoff had to keep moving through the mines. They had to keep their feet shuffling forward, their eyes open. If one of them slept, it could be the end of them all. They had so many people to save.

And so, after gathering strands of glow-worms to hang around their necks and wrists, they decided on a tunnel – not because it was familiar, but because it seemed to go more *up* than the others. Using the skills he'd learned on the mountain, Kristoff had been able to help them all scale the wall with his rope to reach the highest passageway.

As they trudged forward, Anna tried to think about energising things: sunrises, sledging, playing with the children in town, Olaf. But instead of making her feel excited and awake, they only made her feel sad and even more tired. She wondered if she would ever feel awake again. Kristoff stumbled beside her. Instead of catching himself as he normally would, he dropped to his knees and sank back onto his heels.

Anna stooped beside him and rested a hand on his back. "Are you okay, Kristoff? You have to get up!" She nudged him.

Kristoff mumbled in reply and laid his head on the ground. "This rock is so soft."

Anna pulled on his arm, but instead of yanking him to his feet, she only succeeded in making herself more tired, and she, too, sank to the ground.

Kristoff was right. The rock was soft and still and it *wanted* her to lay her head down on it. It was warm, and from the depths of her sleep-addled mind, Anna remembered a lesson Gerda had taught her, about how the earth was a crust of dirt floating on top of hot magma, and that sometimes, little pockets of heat would spring warm water from the rocks underneath. Even though these carved tunnels within the mines had never seen the sun, they felt like a touch of summer – of lying on rocky beaches kissed by the sun. All Anna wanted to do was to stretch out her tired muscles and sleep there. *Anna!* From a long way away, she heard someone calling her name. *Anna, get up!*

"Just a few more minutes," Anna mumbled.

A slap of cold air hit her. Anna jolted upright. "Hey!" She wiped away what seemed to be the remnants of a snowball from her cheek.

"What was *that* for?" Kristoff protested, snow also flecking his face.

"I'm saving your lives," Elsa said. She conjured another snowball, which she juggled. "On your feet or it's more ice in your face. We have a deal?"

"Blargh!" Kristoff sputtered. "Just let us sleep!"

"Sorry, but I can't do that." Elsa shook head. "Anna! Oh, for goodness' sake."

Anna felt another slap of cold snow and jerked her head up. "Sorry, sorry," she mumbled, her tongue feeling too thick for her mouth. Snow glistened at Elsa's fingertips, and something niggled at Anna's mind. It was something important. It had something to do with Elsa and her magic. But what was it?

As Elsa wound her arm, ready to pitch another snowball at either one of them, Anna remembered. She shot up tall and nearly jumped.

"Elsa, stop!"

Her sister dropped her snowball to the ground, where it landed with a small *puff*. "You promise to stay awake now? Because there's more snow where that came from."

But Anna was no longer sleepy. Far from it. "You can't keep using your magic," she said. "On the observation deck, I noticed that every time you did, the Nattmara grew."

"Oh." Elsa folded her arms across her chest. "Great."

Anna rooted around in Kristoff's pack and pulled out the book, flipping open its pages to confirm her theory. But they were soaked through from the lake, the ink indecipherable. She sighed.

SNORFFF!

The sisters looked down to see Kristoff's eyes had closed again, a strangled snore escaping from him as his head drifted towards his chest.

"What are we going to do about him?" Elsa asked.

"Umm." Anna cast about for an idea – *any* idea. Usually, they came sharp and sure, but lack of sleep was making her feel fuzzy. All she could really focus on were their shadows thrown by the glow-worms onto the cave wall opposite them. Shadows. Shadows similar to the famous shadow puppets of Zaria. She'd read how the puppeteers were often as famous as singers, and could fill whole theatres with their performances. If they could ever defeat the Nattmara and make everything right again, maybe she would invite some of the puppeteers to come give a performance in Arendelle. Everyone had liked it so much last year when Kristoff had performed his musical...

"That's it!" Anna shouted. *That's it, it, it.* Her words

echoed down the rocky corridor. Crouching down to be at the same level as Kristoff's fluttering eyelashes, she began to sing: *"Goblin toes are ugly, and Hulder tails are sweet – but you would never catch me, sweep one off his'* ... paw!"

It was a silly song that Kristoff had made up for the last spring festival. The children in the village had loved it, and had performed it for the kingdom under Kristoff's encouraging eye. When Anna had first met the mountain man, he'd been snow-crusted and only grunted a few words to her. She never would have thought that underneath the rough exterior, and a dirt patch or two, his real language was song.

Kristoff had a gift for melody, and though he didn't mind the odd soup stain on his shirt and didn't care about the difference between a salad fork and a dessert fork, he was sensitive about song lyrics. Particularly to songs he had written.

"Huh?" Kristoff's eyes flew open. "It's supposed to be 'sweep one off his *feet!*'"

Eyes sparkling, Elsa sang the next verse. *"Goblins like to eat a lot, and Hulder like to sing – but you will never find one with a feathered'*... nose!"

"No!" Kristoff surged to his feet. "That doesn't

rhyme! And what does a *feathered nose* even mean?"

"Now we got him," Anna whispered to her sister, and she grabbed his hand. "Come on, Kristoff, sing it for us?"

And Kristoff – poor, tired, sorrowful Kristoff – sang.

Together, the three of them moved forward through the darkness, their voices echoing so that they sounded like an entire choir rather than just three fatigued friends hoping to survive, hoping to save the kingdom that Anna loved more than anything. She gave herself over to the sound, letting it sweep her along.

They sang about the Huldrefólk. They sang about Aren and his gallant sword. And then they sang a silly ballad about a goose who fell in love with a duck.

As they reached the end of the song, Anna thought about how beautiful Elsa's voice sounded. She hadn't known her sister could hit quite such high notes or even sing harmonies. Anna stopped singing, wanting to listen closer. And that's when she realised that Kristoff had stopped singing... and so had Elsa.

In fact, all three of them had fallen silent, and yet the song continued. It climbed around them, higher and higher.

It was as though the rocks themselves were singing. But that couldn't be – could it?

Elsa pointed down a passage to their left. "It's coming from there."

Anna turned towards it.

"Hold on!" Elsa grabbed her. "What makes you think we're going that way?"

"Why wouldn't we?" Anna said. "We're lost, and we need help. Besides, something so beautiful can't possibly be dangerous!"

Elsa stared at her. "Did you learn *nothing* from your engagement with Prince—"

"Shh," Kristoff interrupted. "The singing's stopped."

And so it had.

Anna turned on Elsa. "We missed out on someone who could have helped us!"

"Or maybe we missed out on whatever could have *eaten* us," Elsa said.

Kristoff gulped. "Or maybe they're right behind you."

"Very funny, Kristoff," Anna told him.

"No," he protested. "I'm... serious. Look."

While Anna had been talking with Elsa, they had walked into a new portion of the mines.

Unlike the other passageways, this one had never seen the tip of a pickaxe. Because all around were crystals – and not just any crystals. Each one was taller than Kristoff and as wide as a tree trunk. They jutted from the walls and the ceiling, angled every which way to form a forest of sparkling rock. Each crystal was a shifting white, as though when the crystals had formed, they'd been filled with smoke.

But it wasn't the crystals' unusual size or colour that made Anna gasp or caused Elsa to grip her so hard that Anna could feel Elsa's fingernails digging into her shoulder. Sitting astride a crystal as large as a pony was a little child.

At least, Anna *thought* it might be a child, as the figure was definitely child-sized, about as big as a three-year-old human. In the dim light of the glow-worm bracelet she'd put on, Anna could just make out the gleam of an eye, and soft-looking grey leggings that glimmered slightly as the child kicked out their legs.

The child began to sing again, though the melody had no words. Just clear, round notes.

With a gasp, Anna began to run towards the child, stubbing her toes and just missing occasional low-hanging rocks. But she didn't care. All that mattered was that there was a child under the mountain who had been left alone. And Anna never wanted *anyone* to feel alone or left out – not ever. Not if she could help it.

Worry pulsed through her, followed by guilt. She hadn't even *heard* of a child missing from the village. She knew she'd been distracted with Elsa's impending grand tour, but she couldn't have been so busy as to not have heard about a missing child. She wondered how long the child had been down there, where the guardians were, or – she realised with a lurch – maybe the question should be, what had happened to *them*? Did the Nattmara get them?

But before she could get more than a few feet from the child, she felt someone tug on the back of her cloak, yanking her.

"Anna," Elsa whispered, voice as low as could be, "do you see the ears?"

Anna squinted, trying to see what Elsa saw. At

CHAPTER SIXTEEN

first, she couldn't, as the child's curls bumped over where she expected the ears to be, except...

Anna squinted so hard now that she could see her own eyelashes.

And then, she saw them: the child's ears rose to slender points, like the tips of a dragonfly's wings.

Suddenly, Anna remembered a bedtime story from a long, long time ago, back when she and Elsa had shared a room. *They are tall and strong, with sharp ears. And they're sensitive. Which is why, little Elsa,* Mother had said with a tug on the hem of Elsa's pyjama bottoms, *if you ever see one, you must not mention their tail! It's rude.*

And if you do – a young Anna had popped up from behind her pillow fort, making a scary face and shaping her hands into claws – *they might eat you!*

Elsa had burst into giggles, which had only made Anna wrinkle her face more and add an extra growl.

All right, enough, Mother had said, scooping Anna up in one arm to plop her beside Elsa before she sat next to them on the bed. *Cuddle close. Scooch in.*

Anna had let her face fall back to normal, but she'd kept her fingers curled into claws as she cosied up next to her mother and sister and asked, *Mamma, what do their tails look like?*

No one knows, Mother had said, and fixed a ribbon in Anna's ponytail. *They keep them hidden under skirts or keep their backs to the wall at all times.*

But I wanna knoooow, Anna had whined, and her mother had kissed the top of her head and laughed.

Everyone is entitled to their secrets, she'd said. *Especially the hidden people.*

The hidden people.

Or, as the Arendellians called them...

"Huldrefólk," Anna breathed. And as she spoke the name aloud, Oaken's words came back to her, sharp as a stalactite.

Beware the Huldrefólk.

Chapter Seventeen

THE CHILD'S – *Hulder's* – melody flew off on invisible wings and faded again into silence.

Anna burst into applause; she couldn't help it. After all, the little Hulder didn't *seem* dangerous.

"That was *incredible!*" she exclaimed. "What's your name?"

For a moment, the Hulder seemed to stare at Anna in the glow-light, luminescent eyes boring into hers, and then the Hulder tumbled backwards off the crystal.

"No!" Anna said as she rushed behind the crystal to check on the child, hoping the tiny Hulder hadn't hurt themselves.

But as she rounded the tree-trunk-sized crystal, she saw that the Hulder was no longer behind it.

The child had disappeared, except for the sound of footsteps pattering down the dark passage up ahead. Without a second thought, Anna took off.

"Anna!" Elsa called from behind. "Wait! Slow down! You're going too fast!"

"Anna!" Kristoff shouted. Their warnings echoed off the rocks around them, but Anna disagreed with them both: she was going too *slow*.

The Hulder was quick – Anna wasn't sure if it was footsteps she was following now or just the quiet drip of stalactites in the distance. Still, they had come to look for the Huldrefólk, the only ones who might be able to help them find the Revolute Blade, the only ones of myth who might be able to save them all from Anna's terrible mistake. And so Anna ran on, only just missing the occasional low-hanging rocks. Suddenly, the Hulder screeched. It sounded frightened and Anna hoped the Hulder wasn't in trouble.

"Hang on!" Anna shouted. She ran faster and faster, and then her foot caught – on a rock, a divot or a root, it was too dark to tell – and she toppled to the ground, her hands out to cushion her fall.

Pain cracked through Anna's ribs as she slammed into the solid rock. She was going to have one giant bruise in an hour. Everything hurt. Everything but her right arm, which she'd flung out far in front of herself to try to break her fall. And as Anna looked at the glow-worm bracelet dangling from her wrist, she saw why: her right arm had not hit any rock at all. All that hand had hit was thin air. Anna was glad she was already lying on the ground, because she thought she might faint if she were still standing. She'd followed the Hulder – and had almost run off a cliff and into an abyss.

She could still hear the Hulder's cry. Tuva's warning from the trading post came back to her. *They're tricky. Sometimes, they help. Other times, they lure humans off the safest paths.* And maybe, Anna thought, lure them into an abyss. There was always a chance that the Hulder child had done this on purpose, had perhaps meant to distract Anna and Elsa and Kristoff away from the Huldrefólk's home.

But even as these dark thoughts gathered into a cloud, Anna scooted forward on her belly, towards the sound of the Hulder's cry. It didn't matter what the Hulder's intentions had been – but it did matter that the Hulder was stuck and scared. Once she wiggled to the edge, Anna leaned her chin out and peered down. The Hulder had tumbled over the edge, but by some luck or miracle, the child had caught themselves on a small ledge five feet down. It would be easy for Kristoff to lean over and reach the Hulder, but even as Anna watched, the rocky ledge was crumbling away under the child's weight.

"Elsa! Kristoff! Help!" Anna shouted as she inched forward even more, letting herself dangle over the edge, her hand outstretched. "Grab my hand!" she called down.

The Hulder raised a hand, but Anna was still too far away. She had to get *closer*. Wiggling forward, Anna lowered herself down inch by fraction of an inch. Just a little bit farther now... She strained her fingers forward, willing them to lengthen – and that's when she felt the crumbling of the earth beneath her own weight. What was once solid ground turned to gravel, and Anna skidded forward, head first into the dark abyss. She screamed.

But before she could shoot past the Hulder and plummet into the vast void, two pairs of hands grabbed her ankles from above. *Kristoff! Elsa!*

She lurched to a stop, face to face with the little cat-eyed Hulder, who was still mostly in shadow, and who, if Anna had to wager a guess, looked terrified of her.

"Hi," Anna said, trying hard to iron out the quiver in her voice. "My name is Anna, and I'm not going to hurt you." She offered out her hand. "Come with me!"

The Hulder hesitated a moment, then gripped Anna's palm. The child's skin was smooth and dry, like one of the little lizards Anna had read about that populated the Chatho deserts. But even with the Hulder so close to her, it was hard to see them properly. It was almost as though the child had been made of shadow or carved from a mirror. Trying to make out the details was a little like trying to hold tight to a bar of soap: the harder one squeezed, the quicker the soap slid away; the harder one looked, the quicker the Hulder seemed to vanish.

Gripping the child with all her strength, Anna called, "Pull us up!"

There was a grunt, and then Anna and the Hulder rose to safety, just as the little ledge deteriorated into nothingness. She and the child were dragged back onto solid rock. Before Anna had a chance to release the Hulder, Elsa and Kristoff wrapped Anna into a tight hug and she leaned into their warmth.

"Anna," Elsa said, voice tight. "I couldn't... I mean, you almost—"

"Key word: *almost*," Kristoff cut in with a wink.

Anna smiled at him. He always seemed to understand her, to know that if she thought too much about what had just *almost* happened, she would sit there forever and turn into a fossil.

"I'm here," Anna said. She could have stayed there forever in their arms, but for the wiggling Hulder she held.

The child pushed out of the group and plopped onto the floor – still far enough away that all Anna could really make out was a pointy elbow, but in more detail than before. Now Anna could see that the Hulder's skin was the exact colour of the bluish rock that filled the mines. Anna frowned. When she'd first spotted the Hulder, she'd thought the child's skin was a smoky white, similar to the crystal the Hulder had been sitting on. A funny, tickling idea crawled into Anna's mind: she'd been right both times. The Hulder had been smoky white *and then* a bluish grey. The Hulder's body had first looked smooth, then as rough as the stone wall. Maybe the Huldrefólk were like octopuses in the deeps of the Southern Sea, able to change not only their colour but also their texture.

"Wow," Anna said, trying to collect herself even as a stream of rapid thoughts dashed through her mind. First thought: *this is so cool!* She was thrilled to learn about this wonderful trait of the Huldrefólk. The second thought came fast on the heels of the first: if Anna could change colour and texture, she'd head to the portrait gallery, stand in front of all her favourite paintings, and feel what it was like to be Lieutenant Mattias, her father's old official Arendellian guard, for an afternoon. And finally, her third thought: the last time she'd been in the castle, she'd seen the wolf, and everything had changed. A shudder ran down her spine.

Elsa knelt before the child. "Hi there, little one. I'm Elsa. What's your name?"

The little Hulder burst into tears that sparkled like gems.

"Oh, no." Elsa jerked back. "Here!" She conjured a snowflake and presented it.

"Elsa," Anna hissed. "No magic, remember?"

The snowflake burst into water droplets. Elsa's cheeks turned pink and her hands clenched at her sides. "I'm sorry," she whispered. "I forgot." It was sad that Elsa had spent most of her life trying to suppress her magic. It truly seemed a part of her, as natural as breathing and blinking. Having to refrain from using it again was probably taking some getting used to.

Anna felt sorry about it. She took a deep breath. They had to get out of there. They had to find Revolute and defeat the Nattmara, not only for Arendelle, but for her sister. She couldn't let Elsa shut herself away again.

"Ow!" Elsa yelped.

Looking down, Anna saw her sister's thick braid held tight in a chubby fist.

"Ow-ow!" the little Hulder repeated, and gave another pull, as if Elsa's braid were a rope.

"Owowowow!" Elsa unwound her hair from the child's fists. "I'm not a horse."

"Horse!" the little Hulder said. "Horse! Horse! Horse!"

Elsa sighed while Anna covered her mouth to hide a giggle. She understood the Hulder's fascination with Elsa's braid. When she'd been little, she, too, had pretended Elsa was a racehorse and had ordered her sister to charge up and down the castle hallways. Once, she'd even got Elsa to neigh.

The little Hulder let go of Elsa's hair and toddled over to Kristoff. "Horse!" the child proclaimed.

"Hey," Kristoff protested as the Hulder ran around him. "You're one to talk."

"Hey! Hey! Hey!" the little Hulder said. "Talk, talk, talk!" Though the Hulder was running in circles around Kristoff, the child ran sideways, long gallops, keeping their back to the wall at all times.

To hide the tail! Anna realised with delight. Maybe she would finally be able to find out the answer to her childhood question about whether they all had tails.

"They're a bit... hyper?" Elsa tugged her cloak so that it would hang neatly again.

"No more than any other child," Anna said, thinking of the children she'd often run into in the village. "But most children wouldn't know how to get around a cave, while this little one might be able to lead us to the older Huldrefólk who can help us."

Tucking strands of hair back into her braid, Elsa looked doubtful. "Maybe?"

Taking note of what had happened to Elsa, Anna pushed her own hair back to make sure it wasn't easily accessible before getting on her hands and knees. "Hi," she said. "Do you remember my name?"

"Anna! Anna! Anna!" the Hulder screeched.

Anna blinked. She hadn't been expecting *quite* so much enthusiasm. "Yes, that's right. What's your name?"

"What's your name?" the Hulder repeated.

"Anna," Anna said.

"Anna," the Hulder repeated.

"Wait." Anna rubbed her forehead. "Your name is Anna, too?"

"Wait." The Hulder mimicked her again. "Your name is Anna, too!"

"Like I said," Elsa said, her lips twitching, *"hyper."*

"I might be wrong," Kristoff observed, "but I *think* they're just repeating everything you say."

"Hyper! Everything you say!" the Hulder echoed back.

Taking a deep breath, Anna spoke as quickly as she could, giving the Hulder no chance to repeat her words until she was done. "Hi, I'm Anna! My home is Arendelle, like you, but above the ground."

The Hulder looked at her in complete astonishment. "Home?"

Anna nodded. "Yes, *home*. Where do you live? We'd like to meet your family."

The Hulder looked at Anna, then nodded. "Home!" And then the Hulder was off – running backwards as easily as if they had eyes in the back of their head. And maybe they did. After all, as Anna knew from old bedtime stories, no one had ever seen a Hulder's back.

"Come on!" Anna shot to her feet. "We have to follow!"

The Hulder ran impossibly fast – and unlike Anna and the others, the Hulder was short enough to avoid low-hanging rocks, while Kristoff had to run at a crouch. Up, down and down again, they sprinted through seemingly endless corridors of crystals and sparkling rocks. Anna couldn't understand how the Hulder – Dash, as she mentally nicknamed them, taking a page from Olaf's book – was able to tell the difference between the tunnels. Maybe it was some special Huldrefólk trick. After all, Huldrefólk could always find lost things. Maybe it meant they could never become lost themselves.

A strange thought crossed her mind, and she wondered if that meant the Huldrefólk *always* knew what they should do next. How fantastic would *that* be? Maybe that's how Dash had found them so quickly. Or maybe Dash had found them because Anna, Elsa and Kristoff *were* the lost things.

Anna shook her head. She had so many questions, and there was so little time to attend to them all.

But there was one thing she could do. "Kristoff? Elsa?" Anna waited until they both looked at her, and then said, "I think I know what happened to the missing trolls. I read in Sorenson's tower that they always flee the land when a Nattmara appears."

Anna heard Kristoff let out a great sigh of relief. "Good," he said. "Then that means they're safe."

Soon enough, another sound began to play under the staccato of their footsteps. A strange, shuffling, creaking sound.

"Do you hear that?" Anna called back between breaths.

"Yeah," Kristoff said. "Do you think—?"

"Maybe," Anna replied, slowing to a walk. She didn't need him to finish his sentence to know what he was thinking: *Nattmara.*

"We should stop," Elsa said. "Take a moment to scout out what's happening. Huldrefólk can be mischievous... especially if they think we're here to take something that doesn't belong to us."

"But if we stop," Anna said, "we'll lose Dash!"

The corners of Elsa's eyes crinkled in confusion as she navigated around a large boulder that Anna had simply scrambled over. *"Dash?"* she asked.

"The Hulder," Anna explained. She turned back to see if Kristoff needed any help with the boulder, but he'd simply shoved it to the side, clearing the way.

"It's too late," he said. "We already lost them."

In the two seconds Anna had taken her eyes off Dash, the child had sped out of sight. "No," Anna breathed. "We have to keep up!" She broke into a run again, fresh fear giving her new-found speed. "Dash doesn't know about the Nattmara!"

But as Anna rounded the final bend, she saw where the sound had been coming from: an underground city carved out of the rock itself.

The secret home of the Huldrefólk.

Just as the world above, so was the world below. Cosy homes were carved into the blue-grey stone, and orange light spilled out from them, as welcoming as a smile. The pebble-lined streets were alight with glow-worms, so it was easy to see what various mine carts pulled: one held a pile of stalactites bundled like firewood, another was filled to the brim with glowing mushrooms the size of sun hats, and another was heaped with water-clear rocks that Anna thought might be large diamonds.

And the Huldrefólk. The adults appeared to be tall, built more like sapling trees than people, with long limbs and long necks. And similar to Dash, they were hard to see in the light of the underneath realm.

The glow-light wasn't the same as sunlight, bright and revealing, but the kind of soft glow that Anna associated with romantic candlelit dinners. It illuminated at the same time as it concealed, casting shadows that again helped to obscure the Huldrefólk. Still, even in the dimness, Anna could tell that they camouflaged into whatever it was that they were standing near, from onyx black to marble white and every shade in between. Some of the Huldrefólk looked as though they could be purple, others orange and green with sparkling, black-veined skin. The Huldrefólk – the hidden folk – could blend into any surrounding.

Which was great, Anna thought, but most important, they were *real.* Real creatures who would have real answers to where they could find the real lost sword of Aren. The thing of myth they needed to save the day.

"Wow," Elsa whispered. "How beautiful. And peaceful."

"If Sven were here," Kristoff said, "I bet he'd eat all those mushrooms, and then his teeth would probably glow for a week."

Sven. Anna wished the reindeer were with them. The way down to the village looked steep, and Sven was always good about finding the surest path down a craggy mountain. She scanned the side of the rock, looking for a pathway to the dwellings. Somewhere below, she was sure they would find the answers to how to set things right and heal Sven, and the rest of Arendelle, from the Nattmara's influence.

As she leaned forward to see better, Anna felt a sharp *something* prod her back.

"Kristoff," she said, swiping a hand behind her, "stop that. I'm just trying to see."

"I'm not doing anything," Kristoff said, standing to her left, a few feet away from easy poking distance.

The back of Anna's neck prickled.

Elsa stood to her right, her face pensive as she took in the city below them.

Suddenly, Anna became very aware of the feeling that someone was watching her.

Maybe even *a few* someones.

"Oh," she heard Elsa squeak.

Anna turned, only to come nose-to-nose with a spear. And not just one spear.

Many spears.

Chapter Eighteen

WHILE ANNA, ELSA AND KRISTOFF had been taking in the sights of the village below, it seemed as though a storm cloud had gathered around them.

Though, of course, storm clouds didn't exist in the belly of the mines, nor were they capable of holding a spear to one's throat. No. The roiling, shifting dark shapes gathering around them were none other than Huldrefólk warriors.

Like the littler Dash, these ones, too, stuck to the shadows. In the glow, Anna could only make out the glint of an eye here, and the back of a hand there. But she didn't need to be able to see their faces to sense how they felt about three human trespassers in their secret city: they were not very happy at all.

"H-h-hi," Anna stuttered to the spear tips, trying

to remember the etiquette of meeting a new group of people. It wasn't the exact same as meeting the prime minister of Torres, but she knew that dignitaries were sensitive, so polite manners seemed the safest bet.

Step one: introduce yourself and announce you are a friend.

She dipped into a curtsy. "My name is Anna of Arendelle, and this is my sis—"

A spear point jabbed closer to her and Anna went silent.

"Stop," a Hulder hissed. "Say no more, thief."

"I-I think there's been a mistake," Anna said, forcing a cheerful smile on her face. "We've come to ask for help. We're not here to take anything—"

"Take," the same Hulder spoke again, repeating Anna. "Take, take, take!"

"No," Kristoff said, his back against Anna's. "We're *not* here to take anything. We followed a little one—"

"Take little one," the Hulder repeated, and Anna could hear fury swell in the Hulder's voice. "Take little one!" The cry was repeated by another Hulder, and then another, until the entire shifting mass of spear-wielding warriors took up the chant.

Anna had a bad feeling. A *very* bad feeling.

"I think that they're accusing us of trying to steal Dash," she whispered.

"Ah," Kristoff said in a low voice, "well, *that's* not accurate."

"Wait!" Anna told the Huldrefólk, holding up her hand. "We weren't trying to kidnap anyone!"

The Huldrefólk's chant changed. "Liar, liar, every word!"

Anna shook her head, trying to make sense of them.

"We're not," Elsa spoke up, her voice smooth as ice, though Anna could hear the friction beneath the surface. "The little one found us. We were singing, and then my sister rescued the child from falling into a dark abyss—"

"The abyss!" another Hulder with a higher voice interrupted. "The abyss! Take to abyss! Take to abyss! Liar, liar, every word!"

Uh-oh.

"Um," Anna said with a gulp. "I think they want to—"

"Drop us off in the abyss?" Kristoff finished. "Yeah. I got that, too."

"Wait!" Anna tried again. "There's a giant wolf out there that'll be here before you know—" Anna's sentence was cut short as a warrior rushed forward and tied what felt like a handkerchief around Anna's mouth, making it impossible for her to shout.

But even if she could, would it help? They were so far underground, and the villagers who were still awake were far away, likely and hopefully already on-board Elsa's royal ship. Sorenson was gone, having been left to face the Nattmara. And next to her, Elsa and Kristoff were also being gagged. Hard roots pressed into the soft skin of Anna's wrists as her hands were pulled behind her back and bound.

After checking to make sure the knot was tight, the Hulder who had bound her nodded. "March."

Single file, they walked in front of the Huldrefólk. Anna kept her eye on Elsa's braid as it swung, and was grateful when Kristoff accidentally stepped on her heel. It made her feel better knowing they were both there. At least they were all in this mess together.

Anna thought the Huldrefólk would take them away from their hidden city, back to the abyss from which they'd saved Dash, but instead, the warriors marched them down a narrow path, away from the abyss and the swarm of glow-worms and fluorescent gardens. Anna's bad feeling only grew more insistent the longer they walked away from the city. Sweat beaded on her forehead, and her ribcage felt too tight as she breathed in the stale and stuffy air.

How far underground *were* they? Then the smell of rotten eggs punched her nose and her eyes watered. It was the smell of sulphur or else the Huldrefólk had some major issues with their plumbing. The air grew hotter still until it almost seemed to take on a rosy glow. A red light danced along the walls ahead of them, an unusual colour that typically could only be found in the most spectacular summer sunsets or in Tuva and Ada's forge, or... no. Anna's heart flipped.

Or in the centre of an active volcano. *Liar, liar, every word* plus *abyss* apparently equalled throwing the group of human trespassers from Arendelle into molten rock.

The red glow grew brighter, and while the Huldrefólk seemed as cool as ice cream in the middle of an eternal winter, sweat now drenched Anna. She imagined that if it got any hotter, her eyebrows would slide right off her face. Even if Elsa could use her magic here – even if it wouldn't draw the Nattmara straight to them – what chance did winter's cold have against the melting powers of red-hot magma?

Now it was in front of them, a round circle of red that pulsed like a beating heart. Anna stumbled to a stop, but the Huldrefólk shoved her forward, and though she could not believe it was possible, she grew even hotter.

"Stop," Anna garbled through her gag, her mind racing as she skipped over steps two to ten of diplomacy. "We'll give you chocolate!" The words came out muffled.

It wasn't actually a step of etiquette – truly, bribery didn't belong on the list at all – and nothing in all her reading had prepared Anna for the possibility of being thrown into a river of lava by a hosting nation.

But it didn't work. They pushed her forward. Even though it was hotter than Oaken's sauna, Anna went numb as she saw Elsa's boot hang over the edge, the toe turning red in the glow. Anna struggled harder. If they disappeared on their mission, no one would ever know how the Nattmara came to be or how it could be stopped. No one would survive it. Being thrown into lava wouldn't just mean the end of Kristoff, Elsa and Anna – it would mean the end of Arendelle. They would have failed. *She* would have failed. Emptiness yawned in Anna, threatening to swallow her whole.

All she had wanted – *ever* wanted – was to always do more and, out of true love for her sister, help her.

Although the whole kingdom had seen Anna save her sister three years ago, she had since wondered who *wouldn't* save their sister. And still, Anna couldn't get past that she was the one who had provoked Elsa into casting an eternal winter then, and now she was the one who had called a Nattmara to the land. She would never feed Sven a carrot again. She would never hear more about Olaf's warm philosophy on life. She would never get a chance to learn about the natural and celestial worlds from Sorenson. And it was all her fault.

From the corner of her eye, she saw Elsa whip her head so fast that her braid slapped her Hulder captor's nose, taking them by surprise, while Kristoff flung himself backwards, slamming his captor into the wall. The two managed to wrestle out of their binds in the process.

Come on! Anna told herself. *They're still fighting. You*

can, too! She wanted to cheer them on, but she needed to save her breath. And besides, there was still a gag in her mouth. Her guard dragged her forward, closer to the edge of the molten lake, while Anna freed her hands.

"HALT!" A deep voice reverberated around the rock, sending tremors through the earth.

But there was no way Anna was going to stop fighting. She lunged to the side, free of the Hulder's stony grip and tore off her gag. She took a few running steps away from them before realising she wasn't being chased. Instead, the Huldrefólk knelt to the ground as a fourth Hulder appeared in the red haze. This Hulder seemed to be the tallest of them all, their hair a wild black mane surrounding their face, and on their head they wore a circlet of something shiny. It took Anna a minute to realise it was gold.

The leader of the Huldrefólk.

And on the Hulder leader's shoulders sat a small, familiar figure.

"Horse!" Dash yanked on the Hulder leader's hair.

Anna sank into a curtsy, and after she coughed pointedly in Kristoff's direction, he bowed. Elsa, however, stayed as upright as an icicle, befitting her rank.

"Psst! Rule number one," Anna murmured loud enough so that Elsa could hear.

Elsa nodded and spoke. "Greetings. I am Queen Elsa of Arendelle, and this is my sister, Princess Anna, and her... er, our guard, Kristoff Bjorgman of Nowhere in Particular. We greet you in friendship."

Anna held her breath, wondering if the leader would accept.

"Friendship," the Hulder leader repeated. And then, to Anna's utter astonishment, the Hulder continued in full sentences. "I apologise for my family. They can be a bit overprotective." In the dim light, Anna saw the Hulder pat Dash's dangling knee. "Young Echo, however, has cleared up the misunderstanding, and she and I welcome you to our domain. I am the king of the Huldrefólk."

"You're not repeating everything," Elsa said, clearly too surprised to worry about manners.

The imposing Hulder king inclined his head. "We like to use other people's words so that we can wrap ourselves up and hide within them. It's very rare for Huldrefólk to actually have to compose something new. That's part of the reason why Echo found you – she wanted to collect your song. Songs are easy to remember. Easy to echo back."

"Echo!" Dash – now Echo, Anna realised – repeated the word from her perch.

Anna knew she should probably let Elsa do all the talking, but her curiosity was too much. "Why do *you* talk in your own words?" she asked.

"Because I am not only the king, but also the librarian," said the Hulder leader. "I've spent years visiting the world above, collecting items as well as stories, and I have enough words at my disposal. And so, I would like to apologise again for your initial greeting." The Librarian King reached for Echo and set the child on the ground.

"That's it?" Kristoff burst out. "We're almost thrown into a lake of lava, and all you can say is 'I'm sorry'?"

"I'm sorry!" Echo squealed, moving towards Kristoff.

"Does 'We're *very* sorry' make it any better?" the Librarian King asked. "Usually, the only humans who make it down this far want to take precious stones and gems from our mountain, or to capture a member of our domain to make them find iron ore deposits for their weapons and the like."

"We're not looking for stones, gems or iron," Elsa said. "We're looking for a sword of myth, the Revolute Blade. Can you please help us find it?"

The Librarian King's eyes flashed. "'Revolving moon and spinning sun, forged a crescent blade. From light and dark within the heart, the burnished sword was made.'" He looked down at them. "That's the one, yes?"

Anna nodded, feeling this was a good sign.

"And," he continued, "I suppose this has something to do with the Nattmara that has come to Arendelle?"

Anna gaped. "How did you know about the Nattmara?"

"Just because you can't see us doesn't mean we're not always there." The Librarian King studied them a second more. It was impossible to make out any expression on the leader's face. The Hulder's textured skin had taken on the appearance of the cracked rivulets of lava, and was hard to see against the molten backdrop. But then, he must have made a secret signal, because the guards bowed before each of them and then hurried away, keeping their backs to Anna and her friends. It only took the hidden people a couple of steps until they seemed to have disappeared entirely, though Anna knew they must still be there, great masters of camouflage that they were.

The Librarian King turned. "Now, all of you, come with me."

Anna's heart leapt. At last – she had *not* led them astray!

"We don't always know the answer – but we do know where to *find* it," the Librarian King continued.

Allowing the humans to walk in front of them, the Librarian King and Echo escorted Anna, Elsa and Kristoff away from the lake of molten rock and towards a tranquil tributary of water where rafts bumped and prodded against each other.

Anna looked at Elsa and Kristoff in the gloom and a smile spread across her face. "This could be it!" she whispered. "We may finally find the sword!"

"Let's wait and see," said Elsa, ever the one to freeze the excited mood.

Echo tugged at Kristoff's tunic and they began to toss stones into the water.

"My assistant will help. She will take you to the Library of Lost Things," the Librarian King told them.

"If my people ever came across the legendary sword, it will be there – that is, if the sword truly exists."

Elsa shot Anna a look, and Anna bit her lip. She hoped against hope that it did.

"We are sorry for bringing the Nattmara to your door," Elsa said. It wasn't lost on Anna that her sister had used the word *we*.

The Librarian King shook his head. "The Nattmara is one of the many natural enemies of the Huldrefólk – we both seek to reign the dark. But while the Huldrefólk love the night for its quiet privacy, the Nattmara prefers to use the dark as a weapon. Fear not: the Nattmara cannot pass into the borders of our domain. As long as you're within the Huldrefólk realm, the Nattmara cannot touch you. We are the hidden people. We keep ourselves hidden, and now that you're with us, we'll keep you hidden as well."

Relief filled Anna, and then a thought stirred. "Umm, I have a question for you," she said. "We lost a member of our group. Is it possible for the Huldrefólk to find him? He's kind of short and stocky, with a long silver beard that touches the floor, and he's grumpy." Anna paused, then added, "He's nice!"

The Librarian King inclined his head. "As you know, Huldrefólk are seekers of lost things. Collectors. If your friend is still free of the Nattmara, then I'm sure we can locate him."

"Land ahoy!"

Anna looked to the water, where a grey raft glided in front of them and bumped against the bank. A cheery-looking Hulder (as Anna thought she could make out a smile in the dim glow-worms' light) waved at them and leaned against the long pole she'd been using to steer the vessel.

"Ahoy! Ahoy! Ahoy!" Echo cried out, and left the game of skipping rocks with Kristoff to fling herself onto the raft and into the new Hulder's arms.

"This is my assistant, Obscuren," the Librarian King proclaimed. "She will help you find what you are looking for and will be your guide in my domain."

Anna scrambled onto the raft, settling herself next to Kristoff. It was only then that she noticed the unusual material it was made of. While rafts were almost always constructed of wood, this one seemed to be made of floating stone. As she peered closer, she saw tiny holes perforating the surface, making the texture of the raft seem more like bread than rock.

"I think this is a pumice raft," Anna said to Kristoff, who nodded.

"It is," he said. "Rock from the volcano."

Anna felt a tug on her hair as Echo crawled into her lap, quietly chanting, "Row, row, row your raft!"

"Say your goodbyes," the Librarian King instructed Echo. "It's time for dinner."

The little Hulder's eyes swam with tears. "Stay!"

"I wish you could," Anna said, and was surprised when she realised she meant it.

Miner's Mountain was beautiful, full of unexpected surprises and even more unexpected friendships. She liked the little Hulder and her penchant for flying ahead as fast as possible. Anna bet Echo could show her many things – glowing crystals, ice caves, maybe even a sleeping bat or two – but she needed to fix her mistake before she could explore the wonders of the mountain further.

"Besides, you'd be bored if you joined us," Anna said. "We won't be singing any more, and being on a raft makes it hard for you to dash anywhere."

Head tilted, the little Hulder considered this bleak

reality, then clambered out of the raft to join one of the Huldrefólk guards who'd seemingly materialised out of nowhere.

"Bye!" Echo proclaimed from the riverbank, waving. "Bye-bye-bye!"

Anna's heart squeezed. "See you later. Stay out of dark abysses, okay?"

Elsa was the last to step onto the raft. When she'd settled her cloak around her, she looked back at the Librarian King. "Thank you," she said. "For all your help. I promise we'll keep your secret, and we will keep the mines closed. Your city will remain hidden."

The Librarian King bowed in thanks, and then Obscuren pushed them across the glassy surface of the river.

The raft rocked as they navigated the underground waterway, the air refreshingly cooler now.

Obscuren took in their drooping eyelids. "You can sleep," she said. "I know my way around the river. And as the Librarian King said, you are hidden here with me, even from the Nattmara."

"Are you absolutely..." Whatever Kristoff had been going to say was lost in a yawn.

"The Nattmara cannot find our domain," Obscuren

reminded them. "We are cloaked from it. You can rest here, safely, without any fear of losing yourself over to its influence. Sleep. Rest. I'll wake you when we reach our destination."

Obscuren had barely finished before a snore ripped out of Kristoff, and in the next second, Elsa, too, was asleep. Anna, however, stayed awake. Though she had been daydreaming about sleeping, she found she couldn't close her eyes. Every time she did, her stomach hurt too much. Because each moment asleep was a moment she wasn't fixing her biggest mistake: the Nattmara she'd accidentally welcomed into Arendelle with a spell. Obscuren's voice interrupted her thoughts, and Anna pulled herself out of them.

"Sorry, what was that?" Anna asked.

"I said," the Hulder repeated, "that you should sleep, too." Obscuren pushed on the pole, and the water sighed as the raft sliced through it. The river flowed through winding tunnels with low ceilings, though here and there little beaches seemed to jut into the waterway, and Anna thought she could make out the distant shape of a Hulder or two watching them. This close to a Hulder who was *not* trying to kill her, she could finally make out a more definite shape.

Obscuren looked almost human but for an overall spindly appearance, pointed ears and changing skin. At the moment, the Hulder's eyes were a beautiful shade of orange, a colour that made Anna think of the end of autumn or the start of spring. They seemed to take in everything around them, and as Obscuren looked at Anna, Anna wondered if the seeker of things could find Anna's deepest secret in her eyes.

"Obscuren," Anna said, "do you know how the Nattmara came to Arendelle? I think I know, but I'm not entirely sure. The Blight started before the Nattmara arrived. I'm a bit murky on the details." She held her breath, waiting for Obscuren to somehow say the words that were blaring through her mind as loudly as a goatherd playing the tungehorn: the *spell.* It must have been the spell, as much as it didn't make sense that the animals and crops had grown sick before she'd read it. But after she read the spell, the wolf appeared. Of that much Anna was certain – just as she was certain it was her fault.

Obscuren was silent, but it wasn't the kind of sharp silence of being ignored. This quiet had a thoughtful quality to it, as though she were weighing each word before speaking.

"A Nattmara doesn't appear out of thin air," the Hulder said. "They are made, formed from an event in a person's life that grows so big they can't keep it inside any more, and the fear becomes so large that it takes on a life of its own."

Anna nodded. Yes, that was what Sorenson had said. *The fear is too big to keep inside.* "Sooo," Anna said, "you don't think that someone could have, I don't know" – she tucked a strand of ruddy hair behind her ear – "said a spell, or something, and brought the Nattmara to Arendelle?"

Obscuren gave a shake of her head. "I don't believe the poems that humans call spells are really anything other than just that: poems. They may be able to conjure a beautiful image or a moment of time, but that is a different kind of magic entirely."

Anna wasn't sure what to say, but she was comforted. Because Anna *had* read a spell... but it sounded like even if she had never said it out loud, the Nattmara still would have come to the kingdom.

Anna still would have accidentally called it, with or without a poem. Because the night that it had materialised from her dreams was the same night she'd heard Elsa holding a council meeting without her, and she had felt her heart break a little. It was the moment she had realised her greatest fear had come true: that Elsa really and truly had no need for her at all. And because of that, her nightmare – her *fear* – had manifested in the form of the Nattmara that was now stalking them all.

"And I guess," she said, trying to keep her voice light, "if there's no spell to call a Nattmara, then there's probably no spell to banish one, right?"

Obscuren shook her head. "I wouldn't think so. I've only ever heard of one warrior willing to face the Nattmara, and that was Aren, with his mythical Revolute Blade that contained a strange power."

Revolute.

With Kristoff and Elsa asleep and nestled against her back, and Obscuren in the front, keeping an eye on Anna and her friends, the mythical curved sword shone like a lighthouse in the dark river of Anna's worry, and, at last, she let her eyes drift shut to sleep.

Chapter Nineteen

WHEN OBSCUREN WOKE ANNA, she felt better rested than she had in a long, long time.

Next to her, Kristoff stretched, half his hair flattened against his cheek where he'd lain on it. "Up, up, and away," Kristoff said with a yawn.

Elsa, however, still managed to look regal, even though Anna could see the pattern of pumice pores on her face. Anna giggled, motioning to her sister's cheek.

"You should take a look at yourself," Elsa grumbled with half a smile.

Anna peered into the river. Sure enough, she looked the same as she always did when she woke up: a bit like a woodland creature with a slobber problem. Anna patted down her stray hairs with river water, and she found comfort in the way that some things stayed the same. Elsa smiled at her, and Anna guessed she was thinking the same thing, too.

"We're here," Obscuren said as they glided up to a post.

While they waited for Obscuren to secure the raft, Anna looked around, but even holding out her wrist with the glow-worm bracelet, she couldn't see any sign of a library... or where one could possibly be. The banks of the underground river were narrow, no wider than a foot or two, and as far as she could tell, nothing had been carved into the rock's surface except for a few crumbly-looking steps.

"Where is it?" Anna asked. It had been nice to sleep and all, but being awake again meant she was more aware than ever of the time that was slipping away. They had only one more day of sun and a single night left before the third sunrise made the Nattmara's reality permanent – assuming that the spell really had been what brought the Nattmara to Arendelle in the first place. Obscuren hadn't thought so, but Anna couldn't shake Sorenson's words. *All myths contain a kernel of hard truth.* The spell might not have been real magic, but that didn't mean the warning wasn't true. At any rate, Anna was not willing to risk it.

"Up, up, up and away," Obscuren said, seeming to settle into another's words comfortably, as if the conversation of the previous night had been a bit of a strain for her.

Elsa wobbled out of the raft first, followed by Kristoff. When he turned to offer his hand to help Anna step out, she ignored it and leapt over the side. Obscuren indicated with a nod that they should take off their glow-worm bracelets and leave the little creatures on the post. With a wistful sigh, Anna unwrapped the glow-worm and gave it a little pat in thanks.

"Will it be okay here?" she asked.

"Home is where the heart is," Obscuren said, and when Anna looked for clarification, the Librarian King's assistant explained, "I'll take them back with me. They're not needed where we're going."

And with that, Obscuren left the raft behind and stepped off into the darkness, silent as the moon sailing through the night sky.

Anna, Elsa and Kristoff followed her, not nearly as gracefully, but they managed to reach the beginning of the steps and started to feel their way up the side of the rock, following the carved path that wound its way to the cave ceiling.

"Stop a moment," Obscuren said, and there were a few quick taps, and then a *creak* as the Hulder pushed open a square hatch in the ceiling. Light streamed through.

Squinting her eyes against the unexpected brightness, Anna emerged from the dirt floor of a round room with stone walls carved with runes and windows blocked by grassy tussocks. She caught a glimpse of blue in the window. Her heart leapt. "Wait, is that *sky*?" she asked.

"We're in a turf house," Elsa said as she shrugged off her cloak and her mother's scarf before stepping aside from the trapdoor to make space for Kristoff to climb up beside them.

Of course! Turf houses dotted Arendelle's wilderness of scraggly birches and spruces. They were made by digging a dwelling-sized hole deep into the ground, which was then covered by a roof made of grass. Turf houses came in all shapes and sizes, but Anna's favourites were the ones that looked like Earth Giants sunk into the soil, the green grass of the roofs resembling troll hair. Anna looked around, hoping to see a neat row of books. "Um, Obscuren, are you *sure* this is your library?" she said.

It didn't look so much like a library as it did a too-crammed gift shop. Sure, there were a few books scattered here and there, with bleached covers that looked like they'd been forgotten long ago and left out to wither in the sun. But mostly there were *items*.

There were sideways chairs lying on top of rolled-up rugs next to a careful stack of mirrors. There was a pile of gardening tools, broken clay figurines and more than one pile of rusted old keys. And there were socks – lots and lots of mismatched socks.

"Welcome to the Library of Lost Things," Obscuren said. Above the ground and in the warm light of the turf house, the Hulder seemed to look less like rock and more like a tree, softly sprouting leaves where before there had been the rough texture of a pebble.

"Before you say anything, we did not steal any of these things. We simply find things that are lost and give them homes. That includes everything from missing spectacles, to hairbands, to legendary swords. Please," the Hulder continued, stepping aside, "feel free to roam."

"Thank you!" Anna cheered.

"Can the Nattmara find us up *here*? Or are we still hidden and all that?" Kristoff asked, peering out a window.

"With me, you are still hidden from the Nattmara," Obscuren said.

"Phew!" Kristoff said.

"That's a relief," said Elsa, peering through the mess of objects.

"We should split up," Anna said, then looked at Elsa. "Right?"

Elsa nodded, so the three of them began their search.

Some of the lost objects were beautiful – bronze vases from another age and even a necklace of heavy sapphires that Anna thought would complement Gerda's eyes – if Anna were able to turn them back from yellow, that is. She set the necklace down and hurried to the next pile. She picked up a round mirror. It was little, meant to slip into a pocket, and clasped cleverly to look like a clamshell. She opened it, then set it to the side. It was pretty, but not what she was looking for.

Scanning the room, Anna searched for a glint of metal, trying to find anything that could possibly be the sword of myth. She moved aside a rickety chair and a mountain of missing socks and tried to push down her disappointment, but it kept rising, like a hot-air balloon, not wanting to be weighed down. There had to be *something* in this library. Anna's thoughts skidded to a halt. Her eye had caught on a statue in the centre of the room. It was a figure of a human girl in a sky-blue dress with a glittering train, and a platinum blonde braid. It looked to be about as tall as Elsa's knee, and it also happened to look *a lot* like Elsa.

Anna gasped as she stepped closer. It *was* a statue of Elsa. Specifically, the one the sisters had installed in the town cuckoo clock a few years before. Last spring, the Elsa figure had disappeared in a sudden storm, blown away by unusually strong winds. Anna peered at the statue.

A little green wreath with candles had been perched on top of statue Elsa's head, and Anna had the briefest thought that the statue looked more comfortable here, surrounded by other wondrous things, than it had looming above the masses, day in and day out. She was glad the Huldrefólk had found a new home for it, and so she kept searching.

But no matter how hard or long they looked, they did not find the coveted sword in the turf house.

The closest things to a mythical sword they'd managed to unearth were a few shields and helmets from the time of King Runeard, but nothing older than that. Anna's shoulders slumped. If the Huldrefólk didn't have Revolute, and if Sorenson was lost, and if the trolls had fled the Nattmara... what were they going to do? They were running out of places to find answers.

"There's not a single sword in this library!" Elsa said to Obscuren an hour later as the gang flopped in front of a large fireplace to eat from Kristoff's traveller's pack.

Obscuren sighed. "So it appears." The Hulder's skin had taken on the runes of the turf house walls, and speaking to Obscuren now almost felt like talking to alphabet soup. She seemed to droop slightly, and it was clear to Anna that Obscuren wasn't used to having to converse so much.

"Why not?" Kristoff asked. "Arendelle's history seems to be full of swords, as far as I can tell. Why didn't the Huldrefólk ever find one? Maybe it's at another location?"

"Sometimes," Obscuren said, settling down onto the dirt floor to rest, "great swords are buried with their heroes."

"*ARRGH!*"

Anna's heart began to pound furiously as a cry that sounded a bit like a seagull reverberated through the turf house. Wide-eyed, Anna turned to see what had made such a terrifying sound – expecting to see the Nattmara or a mob of yellow-eyed villagers coming for them – but all she saw was Elsa, who'd leapt to her feet.

"Well, that's just great!" Elsa's blue eyes flashed and her cheeks reddened. For the first time in a long time, Anna thought that her sister looked visibly upset.

"What's wrong?" Anna scrambled to her feet, too. "We just need to find out where Aren was buried—"

Elsa snorted, and it was such an un-Elsa-like sound that Anna grew quiet.

"We *can't* find where he was buried." Elsa paced the floor. "Don't you remember the story? Aren was swallowed by a dragon!"

Anna blinked. "He *was?*" She'd forgotten that. She glanced over at Kristoff, who was looking at Elsa with something like awe, as though he couldn't quite believe that calm and collected Elsa was panicking.

"Yes," Elsa said, exasperated. "A dragon came to the fjord and it threatened to eat everyone! And so Aren, our greatest leader besides King Runeard, who loved his home and people more than anything, decided to go face the dragon... who" – Elsa paused, then changed to her most dramatic voice – "'lives where the sea is a sky', and never came back." Elsa took a deep breath. "Because the dragon swallowed him. And dragons don't exist, and neither does this sword, and Anna, oh, I've tried listening, but there's nothing we can do!"

"Curious," Obscuren called out. During Elsa's tirade, the Hulder had gone to a stone wall. "That's not what *all* stories say." She waved a delicate arm at the walls around them. "In that long-ago time when Huldrefólk and humans were more comfortable with each other, we would meet here, in a place of compromise between earth and sky. Each community carved their stories into these walls. This is one of the oldest turf houses. And here, the myth of Aren changes, slightly.

"This" – the Hulder pointed at a carved rune that looked like a sideways S-shape – "according to *our* legend, says that a great danger came from the waters, and in order to save his home and people that he loved, Aren set out in a boat and was never seen again."

"How is *that* any better?" Elsa asked, and Anna was shocked to see her sister's foot twitch, as though she had just resisted the urge to stomp her feet. "That just means Revolute is probably somewhere at the bottom of the ocean, and even if it *were* possible to scour all the waters, we just don't have time." Elsa turned sharply, sending her braid whipping out behind her and almost smacking a shocked Kristoff across the nose. "So you see," she addressed Anna, "we're never going to find Revolute!"

But actually... Anna *did* see.

Anna opened her mouth. "Elsa—"

"The Nattmara is still out there, the Blight chokes the land, and all of our friends are probably stuck in a nightmare by now!"

Kristoff flinched at her words.

"You wanted to visit the Huldrefólk because they were supposed to be able to tell us something," Elsa continued, "to show us the way to a made-up sword. Is there anything else, any other clue—"

"Elsa—"

Her sister threw her hands in the air. "The people are all counting on me!"

"ELSA!"

Elsa's furore stumbled to a halt, and, panting, she looked over at Anna, who pushed away a smile.

"How can you be so *calm* at a time like this?" Elsa demanded, and Anna had to stop from giggling.

"I'm calm because I learned from the best," Anna said, and she could feel a fiery hope burning bright in her chest. "And because I know where Revolute is."

Chapter Twenty

"WAIT, WHAT?" ELSA SAID.

Anna couldn't help smiling now at hearing her signature line coming from Elsa's mouth.

"What do you mean, *you know where Revolute is?*"

Somewhere along the way, it had clicked as Anna stared at the carvings on the walls and listened to Obscuren's tale. The Arendellians' story and the Huldrefólk's story were different, but the same. Like Anna and Elsa. And just like the royal sisters, the stories made the most sense when they were together.

"Why can't *both* things be true?" Anna suggested. "Why can't he have been eaten by a dragon, as our story says, *and* be sent out on a boat? It's all in the stories – Aren was swallowed by a dragon who lived in a place where the sea is a sky."

"But for the sea to be a sky, you have to be under the..." Elsa's voice trailed off and her eyes lit up. "The Earth Giant's Passage! It goes under the fjord, which means the sea is the sky. And that's where the *dragon* boat is!" Elsa's hand flew to her mouth in wonder. "The tumulus," she said softly. "It's Aren's tumulus, which means..."

"That's where Revolute is buried," Anna finished with a nod. "Exactly."

"Way to go, Anna!" Kristoff said. "You solved it!"

"Thanks!" She flashed him a smile. "This means we have to go back to the castle," Anna said, looking up at the Hulder, who stood there tall and impassive as they spoke. "And we need to get there as soon as possible! Elsa, can you..." Anna twirled her finger.

"*Magic?* But it'll draw the Nattmara right to us," Elsa said.

Obscuren chimed in. "If you wanted to use your magic without the Nattmara sensing it, I think it would need to be now."

Elsa nodded. In the safety of the turf house, she crafted a sleigh of ice – ice so clear that Anna could see right through it. It was practically invisible. And then Anna felt a whoosh of cold air blow by her, and she shivered as snowflakes danced in the air, shaping themselves into a massive snow bear, who loomed much too large in the tiny turf house.

"Elsa," Anna said, taking in the snow bear with wonder, "he's beautiful."

The bear growled.

"He says his name is Bjorn," Obscuren translated.

"I can hear my reindeer, Sven, talk, too," Kristoff said to the Hulder. His voice sounded glum, and Anna knew he was still worried about his best friend. She hoped Sven was all right, and, at the very least, safe on the royal ship.

Obscuren rested a hand on Kristoff's arm and flashed a sad smile. "The Huldrefólk are known for finding things that are lost, because we know how to listen," she said. "But we're not the only beings who listen. Animals can, too. They can tell a kind heart from one filled with cruelty. And I suspect, Kristoff, that you're someone who knows exactly what Sven is saying to you."

Kristoff shook his head. "I just hope he's okay."

"If we leave right now, he will be," Anna said, trying

to say it with so much confidence that it would just *have* to be true.

As quickly as they could, they buckled the snow bear up to the sleigh, and then said their farewells to Obscuren.

"In my family," the Hulder said, "we don't say goodbye."

"What do you say, then?" Anna asked.

"We say, 'Till we see you again.'"

Anna smiled. "Till we see you again."

"Maybe," Obscuren said, already disappearing behind a stack of lost and broken plates. "But I'll probably see you first. Unless you look very, very closely."

Obscuren reached out an arm and cracked open the door. There was a second while the Hulder took in the land, and then she flung the door open wide for the bear and the sledge. "Remember," the Hulder called as they slipped from the safety of the turf house and slid out under the sky. "Home is where the heart is. Good luck, friends of Arendelle."

"Goodbye, friend," Anna said.

But Obscuren was gone.

As Bjorn loped away from the turf house, home

did not look like home any more. Anna saw a haze had settled over Arendelle as colour drained from the world. It was as though the earth itself were afraid, turning pale with fear. Anna held out her hand, studying it in the sunlight. It still looked pink in the cold. Glancing at Elsa, Anna was comforted by the fact that her mother's scarf, wrapped around Elsa's shoulders, was still burgundy, while Kristoff's hair was still the colour of wheat. The colour that wheat was *supposed* to be, Anna corrected herself. But there was still time before sunset. There was still time to remedy this all.

"It looks like the forest after a fire," Kristoff said, glancing at the terrain as he guided the snow bear around a bend with a careful tug of the reins.

"What do you mean?" Elsa asked.

"The way the ash drifts," Kristoff explained. "It floats on the air instead of falling."

"Maybe," Anna said, trying to force cheer into her words, "that's a *good* thing. I read in the library that forest fires are necessary to clear the bramble and make way for new life."

Kristoff shook his head. "Tell that to the people who've lost their homes." He jounced the reins, and the sleigh went faster.

Anna held a spyglass of ice from Elsa up to her eye, scanning the horizon for any sign of the Nattmara. So far, so good. There was no sign of the wolf. Well, no signs other than this pale shadow of their home and the fearful thump of Anna's own heart.

Except, what was that? A dark smudge seemed to move from the washed-out green of the spruces.

"Elsa," Anna whispered, and slipped the spyglass back to her sister. "Something's moving. Over there."

Elsa peered over her shoulder, then looked ahead again. "You're right," she said. "I think it's following us."

Kristoff snapped the reins harder and Bjorn veered right, sending a swirl of pale white leaves into the air. Anna looked back. The smudge also veered right. Yes. Whatever it was, it was definitely following them. Bjorn's ears swivelled, and then Anna heard it.

A cry: *Ahhhhhhhh!* It seemed to come from the direction of the smudge. And it wasn't the bone-cold howl of the Nattmara. This noise sounded almost human, as though someone were trying to call out a name. In fact... *Ahhhhhh! Naaaaaaaa!*

"Stop!" Anna lurched upright. "It's Sorenson!"

Elsa gasped. "What?"

Kristoff pulled the reins, flinging Anna into Elsa as they sped back to the scientist. As they got closer, the cry became clearer. "Annaaaa! Elsaaaaa!"

"Sorenson!" Anna shouted, relieved he was okay.

Or was he? The scientist looked the worse for wear. His coat was torn, shredded by the Nattmara's claws, and he limped, his ankle swollen. But he was alive, and not only that, his eyes didn't appear to be either pitch black or yellow.

"Stop the sleigh!" Anna said, and Kristoff pulled Bjorn to a walk.

The snow bear snorted, protesting the change in pace.

"Sorenson!" Anna called as she swung out of the sleigh and hurried towards him. "We're so glad to see you! How did you escape?"

"Hello to you, Anna, and to you, Your Majesty," Sorenson said. He spoke in a strange cadence, as if he had somehow managed to twist his tongue as well as his ankle. "I'll tell you all about it in a minute. Just let me catch my breath."

"We don't really have time," Elsa said, looking to the sky. The sun was definitely low now, approaching dinner time. "How about you tell us in the sleigh?"

He nodded. "That's a good idea, but we can't take a sleigh where we need to go."

"And where do we need to go?" Anna asked. She stepped over to Kristoff's traveller's pack and sifted around for a spare splint. Aha! There it was. She knew Kristoff rarely left home without it. The splint was for ice mountain emergencies, but Kristoff liked to tease her that he needed to make sure he had one on hand at the castle for the amount of times she'd managed to trip or stumble over something.

Anna sat down and offered the scientist the splint. "How did you escape the Nattmara?"

Sorenson said, "I found a thing of myth."

Anna's eyebrows shot upwards. "You found Revolute?"

Sorenson tilted his head, and with his long silver beard, he looked a little bit like a confused dog. "Did you figure out where it was hidden?"

Anna grinned. "Yes! Well, we know where to look. It's in—"

"What did *you* find, Sorenson?" Elsa asked, stepping in between them. She'd arranged their mother's scarf around her shoulders like a cape.

"Ah, I found a cure," Sorenson said, and he tapped his fingertips excitedly together. "But it's hard to explain. I'd rather show it to you first. It won't defeat the Nattmara, but I believe it will clear up the Blight from the animals and the crops."

"What?" Kristoff, who'd been waiting in the sleigh, jumped out. "There's a cure? We can help Sven?"

"Allegedly, yes," Sorenson said. "And the Huldrefólk have it."

"I don't know about that," Elsa said, tugging on the fringe of her scarf. "They're our friends, I think, and they didn't say anything about having a cure."

"Yes." Anna nodded. "And they are *definitely* our friends."

Sorenson's face crinkled and he shook his head while he sighed. "Whatever they told you is wrong," he said. "The Huldrefólk are thieves. You should not have trusted them."

"No," Anna said, standing up for Echo, the Librarian King, and Obscuren. "They find lost, unwanted things and give them homes. They find 'that which is lost', like your book says, sir."

But Sorenson kept shaking his head, his long beard waving like one of the windswept pennants on the castle wall. In the lengthening light, his beard looked more white than silver. "Then my book must be wrong, because the Huldrefólk have a thing of myth hidden in their hot springs, not more than a mile away. I discovered that if a Nattmara-touched animal drinks the water, they will be cured, even if you *don't* defeat the Nattmara by sunrise of the third day."

"Let's go!" Kristoff said, the hope so bright on his face that it hurt Anna to see. "If it's only a mile, we could get a cup of the water from the hot springs, just in case, and still make it back without losing that much time!"

Bjorn's snuffle was louder now. The bear wanted to move. He wanted to *go*. Yet Anna was torn... until she saw the expression on Kristoff's face.

Kristoff's best friend was sick. And he had no way to know what had happened to Sven in the time they'd been gone, but he'd risked his life over and over again just for the chance that he could help make Sven feel better. How could Anna say no to that?

"Elsa," she said, turning from Sorenson, who still nursed his ankle on the splint, and from Kristoff, who looked like he was about to go sprinting in any direction as soon as he heard where these curing springs were. "I think we should get the water, as a precaution."

Again, Elsa looked at the sky and bit her lip. As Anna saw her sister take a deep breath, she knew she wasn't going to like whatever she was about to hear.

"We can't risk it," Elsa said, still keeping her gaze on the sky, and on the floating bits of ash that looked like snow but weren't. "I'm so sorry, Kristoff, but we can't. Even if the spring water *does* work, there's no way we can bring back enough for everyone in all the kingdom... and what about the sword?"

The look on Kristoff's face was unbearable. "So *now* you think the sword is real?"

"Elsa!" Anna said, looking between her sister and the man she loved.

"I understand your responsibility to the kingdom," Kristoff told Elsa, "but Sven is family to me."

"Kristoff," Elsa cut in, and her eyes were wide with hurt, though Anna didn't know why her sister would be upset. "I'm saying *no* because it endangers too many people!"

Anna took a deep breath, ready to argue more, when Bjorn let out a great bellow.

Whirling round, she turned to see that Sorenson

had taken Kristoff's pickaxe from the sleigh and was trying to yank the bear out of his harness.

"Sorenson?" Anna said, forgetting her frustration with Elsa as she took in the man's peculiar actions. "What are you doing?"

"Nothing, nothing," Sorenson said, reaching down to fiddle with a buckle. But as he bent down, Anna noticed something falling from his pocket.

If the world had been its normal colour – dark emerald hues mixed with the rich blue of the mountains and the oncoming colours of fall – she would never have noticed it. But the world had turned ashy white, so what tumbled from Sorenson's pocket stood out like a stain. It was sand.

Black sand.

Chapter Twenty-One

"NATT–NATT," ANNA SPUTTERED, trying to get the warning out.

But it was too late.

Already, as she watched, sand swirled from out of Sorenson's eyes to reveal not dark brown irises as Anna had thought, but eyes the colour of a hornet's jacket. And then the sand swirled into Sorenson's heart. A place for the Nattmara to roost until the sunset. *Trolls tremble at the Nattmara's howl while the Nattmara flees from the sun like a shadow.* But nightmares could still hurt, even in the day.

"Nattmara!" Anna finally bellowed, and it was as if her shout had broken some strange enchantment. A moment ago, she'd felt utterly suspended outside of herself, and now she was moving faster than she could think. "Run!"

But Kristoff and Elsa had already seen what Anna had not been able to say. Kristoff took a running leap for the driver's seat of the sleigh while Elsa grabbed Anna's hand and pulled her safely inside.

"Mush!" Kristoff shouted, and Bjorn, already deeply unhappy about the break from the run and nervous around the man who did not smell quite right to him, shot off.

"Go! Go! Go!" Anna yelled when she was able to make her mouth move again. She twisted around just in time to see Sorenson bare his teeth, and then he reached into his coat pocket and pulled out a glittering vial of violet powder – the Highly Flammable and Very Dangerous Combustion Powder. The scientist, now the Nattmara's puppet, raised the vial high into the air.

"FASTER!" Anna cried, just as an explosion fell short of them, barely missing the sleigh.

They careened out of control, the ride far from smooth as it was still early autumn, and the ground was only just hard enough for the sleigh's runners to work. Any other sleigh would not have been able to make it across the rough terrain of scrub, brush and rock, but an Elsa-made sleigh was as slippery as could be, and twice as fast.

Another vial of powder whistled by Anna's ear, and she turned her head just before violet fire could engulf her. From the corner of her eye, she saw Elsa raise her hands.

"No!" Anna yelled. "You can't! The Nattmara will only get bigger and more powerful!"

Elsa lowered her hands, and Anna faced forward.

"What's that?" Anna asked, pointing at a dark line in the earth that loomed ahead.

"That," Kristoff said with a gulp, "is a canyon. A very, very, very *wide* canyon."

Another whistle hit the air. Another blast.

"We have to lose it!" Anna yelled. "Faster! Faster! We'll be able to clear the canyon!"

"No, we won't!" Elsa shouted. "We're too heavy!"

The dark line was thicker now, the chasm closer and wider. Just a few more seconds until they would be able to try to clear it, to try to soar over the deep trench.

"Elsa, here!" Kristoff thrust the reins into Elsa's hands before turning to Anna. "I think I can hold

Sorenson off until sunset," he said, looking straight into her eyes. "Tell Sven I said he should listen to you." His words came too fast, and the meaning came too slow.

Anna shook her head. "Wait, what?"

But then Kristoff was kissing her. His lips pressed to hers, warm and light and as strong as a promise... but a promise for what? Before Anna could gather up her thoughts and piece together what he was telling her, her lips were suddenly cold again. The kiss, over.

And Kristoff was turning away from her, balancing on the edge of the sleigh...

"No!" Anna gasped as his words became clear.

But she was too late. Kristoff leapt from the sleigh, and Anna screamed.

"What's happening?" Elsa yelled, tearing her eyes from the chasm and looking back just as Kristoff landed hard on the ground, both knees bending to absorb the impact, somehow managing to stay on his feet. And then he was off, running towards Sorenson.

"KRISTOFF!" Anna shouted. But without his added weight, the sleigh slipped faster.

The bear's heavy paws sent mud flying as he barrelled his way towards the chasm, taking Anna farther and farther from Kristoff.

"KRISTOFF!" Anna shouted again. "KRISTOFF, COME BACK!"

But Sorenson had seen him now. The old man raised Kristoff's pickaxe, its two hooked ends gleaming like wolf fangs as he moved towards Kristoff, who was now armed with only a fallen tree branch.

In any other circumstance, the victor of the fight would have been unquestionable. Kristoff was young, strong as an ox, and fresh from a summer of hauling blocks of ice up and down the mountain and from doing handiwork around the castle. Sorenson, on the other hand, was wizened with age, his face a crinkled map, his short limbs thin from years of sedentary study.

But the Nattmara had lent Sorenson its predatory grace and ruthless instinct. Sorenson moved like hot oil, fast and crackling, guaranteed to cause pain, sliding so fast it was hard to tell if Sorenson was now man or wolf or both. His swollen ankle did nothing to slow him.

Sorenson chopped down with the stolen pickaxe, Kristoff only just whirling away from being sliced in two. He barely had time to look up before Sorenson was on him once more. The pickaxe swung down again and again with the deftness of a sewing needle. Still, Anna could see Kristoff's shaggy yellow hair dipping and dodging, tucking and rolling, just as the trolls had trained him to do. Anna wanted to leap off the sleigh and run to his side more than anything.

"Do we go back?" Elsa called, the older sister asking the little sister what to do. And of all times, Anna thought.

Elsa's cloak snapped in the wind, and though she looked shaken, she still gripped the sparkling reins with the same steadiness as when she'd held her coronation sceptre. They were almost upon the chasm. "You need to tell me, now!"

Yes. With the whole of her heart, Anna wanted to grab the reins from Elsa's hands and tug the bear back towards Kristoff and the Nattmara-possessed Sorenson. But she couldn't. She wouldn't.

The shadows were already long. Night would soon be here – and then there would be dawn. The *third* dawn, the last dawn if Anna couldn't get Revolute first. Kristoff had given her a gift – a chance to undo what she had done. And she couldn't let it go to waste.

"Keep going," Anna croaked, even as her heart

cracked. Hot tears flew down her cheeks, mingling with the ash from the sky as Elsa tightened the reins and Bjorn jumped.

Anna's heart dropped into her stomach as they soared over the chasm.

For a long moment, they seemed to dangle in the air, suspended by nothing thicker than spider's silk over the gaping mouth of the earth. If they didn't make it across, the sharp rocks hundreds of feet below were ready to rip and chew them apart.

Anna tried to cling to the sleigh's sides, but Elsa's creation was flawless. There was no rough patch of ice she could grab hold of. No uneven knot she could clutch. And so Anna clung to the only thing she could: her sister.

Seconds seemed to pass, and still the other side felt as far away as forever. And then, with a bone-rattling thump, the bear's paws touched back down on the ground, and the sleigh and the sisters slammed down behind him – hard. They had made it.

"Anna, I can't breathe!" Elsa squeaked out.

Anna let go of her sister, whirling round to see what had happened to Kristoff. She could just make out two figures beyond the chasm, but she could no longer tell which blur was the pickaxe and which was the branch. They grew smaller and smaller as the bear lengthened his strides and the ground flew by, but Anna kept her eyes on the battling figures.

Anna knew this dance could only last so long. In just a few hours, the sun would drop behind the horizon, and then the Nattmara would stop hiding in Sorenson's body and resume its full power as the fearsome wolf.

Or would it possess Kristoff before then? Would Kristoff be smothered by a nightmare reality? He'd live in his own horror-scape, where there were no trolls or reindeer, or quiet mountain solaces, or Anna. A nightmare world that might last forever, unless she and Elsa could stop it first.

"Can we go any faster?" Anna's throat was so tight that her question was barely more than a whisper. In fact, she wasn't actually sure she'd said anything at all. She felt about as substantial as a shadow and just as useful. She wasn't sure Elsa had heard her until she felt her sister's hand squeezing hers.

"We'll go as fast as the wind," Elsa promised, both hands back on the reins.

They slid through the rocky terrain of the mountains,

hurtling at a breakneck pace until Bjorn's wild run ended at a cliff-side. A river rushed nearby, gaining speed and sound as it hurried to the mountain's edge. They had reached the waterfalls – and the entrance to the Earth Giant's Passage, to Aren's tumulus.

"We're here." Elsa stumbled out of the sleigh. "Hurry!"

Looking down, Anna could make out the distinct shape of Arendelle Castle. The ice bubble Elsa had so carefully and beautifully made had fractured, leaving sharp shards of ice around it, a terrain as dangerous as broken glass. Next to it, Anna could see the village, the colour of its homes still cheery despite the terror that Anna knew it now housed. But at least, she saw with relief, the ice dome Elsa had made for the village still held.

She looked towards the port. The royal ship, too, was gone, and Anna hoped that Sven, Olaf and the villagers were far away by now, and safe. She couldn't handle it if one single soul more was hurt because of her. Because Kristoff... No. She couldn't think about Kristoff. Not now.

Slipping out of the sleigh, she helped Elsa free the snow bear from his harness. Without it, Bjorn looked ten times fiercer and ten times wilder, and Anna was aware that with just a single paw, he could crush her as easily as she could crush a crocus. But then, the bear shook himself, his fur rippling like seaweed, and pushed his cold nose into Anna's hand. He snuffled, and Anna flung her arms around his snowy ruff.

"Thank you," she said, squeezing Bjorn and allowing herself a moment of wonder. She was hugging a bear. *She was hugging a bear!*

Elsa nodded. "Yes, thank you, Bjorn."

Bjorn waited for Anna's one last squeeze and looked at Elsa. He seemed to nod his head in her direction. But then he pulled away – and ran in the direction of the Nattmara and Anna understood.

He'd helped them as best he could, and now he would try to lure the Nattmara away from them while they searched for Revolute.

"Come on," Anna said, excitement rising in her chest as she headed towards the waterfall. "If we're right, we're about to fix everything!"

Elsa wrapped her scarf tighter around her shoulders. "But if we're wrong, then..."

Anna was glad Elsa didn't finish her thought, because she couldn't bear to hear it.

Chapter Twenty-Two

THEY WERE WRONG.

Anna was wrong.

In the light of a torch that Elsa had found and ignited, Anna looked again at the dragon boat's empty hull, a lump filling her throat.

Once, there might have been mounds of gold, pottery, lush cloaks and jars of rare spices to help send Aren the warrior on his valiant voyage.

Once, this might have been a splendid place of sleek polished wood, a fitting resting place for Aren and his mighty sword.

But now the rotten boards were barely strong enough to hold a dusty footprint, let alone a thing of myth. Elsa stood in the hull with Anna, turning over a small clump of dirt with the toe of her boot.

A cloud of dust trailed into the air, and Anna sneezed.

"We're too late," Elsa said as she stepped over the remains of what might have once been an oar, "by a thousand years, give or take. Maybe Revolute was here once – maybe this had even been Aren's final resting place, but..." She trailed off, her eyes lingering on the holes in the porous old wood. "I think this boat has been empty for a long, *long* time."

No. They had come too far, risked too much.

"Revolute is around here," Anna said, kicking another clot of dirt with her boot only to reveal... more dirt. She knew many boats had secret watertight compartments in the floor, but she had searched and found none. "It just has to be here!"

But even as she said it, Anna knew that wasn't necessarily true. In fact, nothing *just had to be* anywhere. If *just had to be* counted for anything, then a great storm would have never met Mother and Father's ship. It would mean that King Runeard's life wouldn't have been taken by dangerous northerners, and that young Elsa and Anna would have known their grandfather. It would mean that Sven would have never got the Blight and that Anna would have never called a Nattmara to the kingdom by manifesting it from her fears and nightmares.

Suddenly, it was *just all too much.* Anna felt the weight of all the earth and sea and castle fall onto her shoulders and crush her, snuffing out her last bit of hope. She had not found the Revolute Blade and she never would. She would never be able to defeat the Nattmara. She would never see Kristoff or Olaf or Sven ever again. She stepped out of the boat and lowered her head into her hands and tears began to fall.

"Oh, Anna," Elsa said, following her.

Anna felt pressure on her shoulder as her sister crouched down next to her in the flickering torchlight.

"Please, please, please don't cry," Elsa said. "It's not your fault. If I had been doing a better job, I would have recognised the signs, and we could have stopped the Nattmara before you called it into the kingdom."

Anna knew Elsa was trying to be comforting, but her words only made Anna feel a hundred times worse. They were just more proof that Elsa didn't need Anna any more – that, in fact, Elsa might even be better off without Anna.

Anna dragged her face away from her hands, and leaning against the rough-hewn wall, she put her head back and looked up at the dragon figurehead, its mouth opened in an eternal snarl, unable to ever really stop thieves from stealing its treasures. Anna closed her eyes, shutting out its accusing wooden eyes.

Maybe it would be best for Elsa and all of Arendelle if the wooden dragon could just come to life and swallow Anna and her great disappointments whole, like how the wolf had swallowed her in her nightmare. She wasn't exactly sure *what* that would do, but... Anna's runaway thoughts lurched to a halt as an idea grabbed on to them. She looked back up at the wooden dragon, its mouth gaping open.

"Elsa!" Anna rose to her feet.

Elsa lifted the torch as she stood, too. "What is it, Anna?"

"I think I know where the sword is!" And without waiting for her sister to interrupt, Anna continued to barrel ahead. "We were just looking in the hull of the boat, because that's where one would end up if you were eaten – in the belly of a dragon or in the boat. But the myth doesn't say that the dragon *ate* Aren, it says—"

"He was swallowed," Elsa said, eyes growing wide. "Revolute could be hidden in the dragon's mouth!"

Anna nodded. "Exactly!"

The dragon's snarling mouth reared several feet above their heads. Usually, Elsa would be able to wave her hands and make a staircase out of ice. But they weren't under the Huldrefólk's protection any more. If Elsa used as much as a lick of her magic, the Nattmara would be upon them in seconds.

Crawling out onto the dragon's neck also wasn't an option. The boat was a thousand, maybe even *thousands* of years old, and the peeling, splintering wood had as many holes as a sponge. The whole thing looked like it might collapse if Anna so much as breathed on it.

Elsa planted the torch in the ground and crouched down. "All right, get on."

"What?" Anna looked at her sister, confused.

"We need to get someone up there. I think you can reach it if you get on my back."

"A piggyback ride? Really?" said Anna, a grin breaking across her face. "You haven't offered me one of those since before the gates closed."

"Well," Elsa said with a smile, "I guess I owe you at least one more."

Kicking off her boots, Anna scrambled up onto her sister's back. Then, balancing herself against the wooden hull, she placed her feet on Elsa's shoulders and pulled herself into a standing position so she was eye to eye with the dragon.

Even though centuries had scrubbed it clear of most of its details, up close, Anna could still see the hatch marks that hinted at scales, and the expression of the dragon. From below, the expression had seemed to be of a snarling angry beast, but now, Anna thought maybe it wasn't angry, just protective. Nerves bubbled throughout Anna's body.

This was it. Their one shot. Their last chance.

The Revolute Blade, the very thing that had carved out Arenfjord and made a home for a wandering people. A sword forged from a curved sunbeam with an unusual power, a gift from the sun herself. They would defeat the Nattmara. They would cure the crops and animals and people of the Blight, and free everyone she loved from their own terrifying nightmares.

"Do you have it?" Elsa asked from underfoot.

CHAPTER TWENTY-TWO

Whoops. Anna's mind was running away again.

"No, not yet!" Anna said, reining in her galloping thoughts.

"Well, hurry up! You don't exactly weigh the same as you did when you were five."

No, Anna wasn't five years old. She was capable of making serious mistakes, but she was also just as capable of fixing them. And so, she reached her hand into the dragon's mouth.

At first, there was nothing there. Frowning, Anna leaned farther into the dragon's gaping maw, her elbow disappearing, followed by the rest of her arm, until the wood hit her armpit. Worry crept through her. If the dragon's head was hollow, would she need to crawl all the way in? She wasn't sure if she would fit. If only Olaf were there, he'd be able to send his hand down inside. Or even Sven would have been helpful, with his sensitive nose. But they weren't, so Anna would have to do it herself.

"Anna," Elsa said, "your foot is starting to dig into my shoulder."

"Sorry," Anna said. "Just one more second." Taking a breath to balance herself, she rose to her tiptoes, stretching, reaching until her fingers brushed something cold and metal-smooth. Something that fit comfortably in her palm as she wrapped her hand around it. Something that sent a note of anticipation through her. Anna pulled.

At first, there was resistance, and then a whisper of metal, a noise that almost sounded like a dragon's sigh as its secret came loose. And then Anna's hand was back in the rippling orange light of the torch.

Could it truly be?

The hilt was wrought from gold, and in the centre of the pommel, like a miniature sun, sat a yellow diamond. The gold of the handguard had been worked to look like little rays of the sun, leading down to the blade.

And the blade... it was made of a blue-black metal – the same colour as the meteorite in Sorenson's observation tower. It curved, the slight S-shape mirroring the inlet of Arenfjord, where myth said Aren had made the legendary cut.

But Anna hardly dared to believe that what she held was what she needed it to be. Not until she'd carefully slipped down from Elsa's back. Not until Elsa tore a scrap of cloth from her split dress and began to polish the top of the blade, right below where it met the hilt. Not until she could read the letters that had been etched into the sword itself did Anna believe:

R-E-V-O-L-U-T-E

They'd found it. The carver of the first fjord.
The myth and the solution.
The Revolute Blade.

Chapter Twenty-Three

"WE DID IT!" Anna shouted, forgetting the need to be quiet and embracing Elsa.

"Careful!" Elsa twisted the sword away. "You don't want to accidentally stab us."

Though Elsa's warning wasn't really all that funny, for some reason, it planted a seed of humour in Anna. A giggle slipped out, and then, a bloom of laughter. And instead of trying to trap it down, Anna let it rush through her, throwing back her head and laughing long and loud. Elsa looked confused, which only made Anna laugh harder.

Then, ever so slowly, Elsa's lips began to turn upward, and she giggled; then she, too, laughed, loud and free. Their laughter echoed around the Earth Giant's Passage, bounding and rebounding, patching the tiny rip in Anna's heart caused by constant worrying.

Because Anna had done it. She'd proven to Elsa that she still needed her little sister who made mistakes. She'd proven that she could actually accomplish exactly what she had planned to do.

Suddenly, Elsa stopped laughing, and it was only Anna's laughter that bounced around the walls, sounding alone and by itself.

"Hey," Anna said, somewhat breathless. "What's wrong?"

Elsa held her finger to her lips and Anna listened. Without the protective barrier of laughter, she could now hear another sound coming from beyond the waterfall and the passage. A long, low angry howl.

The Nattmara was nearing.

"We need to get out of here," Anna said, slipping her boots back on. "Or else it'll trap us in the tunnel."

"Agreed." Elsa nodded. Already, she was tightening the band around her braid. "But Anna, I think—"

"That we need a plan," Anna said, finishing her sister's sentence, as they so often did. "Yes, you're right! The plan – the-plan-the-plan-the-plan... You use your magic to distract the Nattmara – only for a second or two! – and then I'll surprise it with Revolute. That's a *brilliant* idea, Elsa!"

"But I—" Elsa began, and that was all Anna could really make out, because she'd already tugged Revolute from Elsa's hand and begun to sprint down the passageway for the exit and the Nattmara. Fear thrummed through her veins, and yet, she had Revolute.

She had hope.

Anna squeezed the hilt tight, the yellow diamond pressing into her hand. It almost hurt, but still she kept running, trusting in the power of the myth and trusting her sister to follow behind her with an icy blast or whirl of hard wind.

The still-frozen waterfall sparkled up ahead, and Anna squeezed herself out onto the narrow ledge and exited the passageway only to stop in her tracks. Because the land sprawled before her was not the home she knew.

Her home had a cheery village with painted houses, a fjord full of rich blue waters and a vibrant display of autumnal colours that would have made her paint set jealous. But the land before her was bleached white, as though this reality were being erased to make way for the nightmare that was settling in for eternity. Like storm clouds rolling in, the Nattmara prowled the village edge.

When Anna had first spotted the wolf in the Great Hall, it'd been bigger than any wolf she'd ever seen, but not abnormally so. Then it'd become twice the size of a normal wolf, then the size of a bull, then the size of a knoll. But now, its eyes were level with the second-floor windows of the village townhouses.

It was exactly as Sorenson had foretold. Each hour that the Nattmara had not been banished, it'd grown in strength and size as it gorged on the fear that had swept over the land. Each stride of its paw seemed to cover a mile, and wherever it passed, the trees twisted away from it, as if they, too, could sleep and dream and wanted none of the Nattmara's offerings. As if poplars and aspens and spruces, too, wanted to run away.

Anna had thought that the Nattmara would come directly for her, its accidental summoner, but instead of tearing up the path that would take it to the waterfall and to Revolute, the Nattmara turned... and loped back towards the village.

In the time that it took Anna to blink, the giant

wolf had arrived at the edge of the protective ice dome over the village. Rearing back on its hind legs, it struck the dome with a heavy paw.

THUMP!

The ice stayed whole and smooth. The dome was working – but for how long? The Nattmara swung again.

THUMP!

Anna frowned. Had that thump been followed by a cracking sound? The Nattmara only needed to make a fissure as thin as a hair for it to be able to trickle though Elsa's barrier in its black sand form.

"Anna!" Elsa said, flying out from behind the waterfall to join Anna on the ledge overlooking the village. "I need you to—"

"We have to go help them!" Anna yelled, desperation making her voice shrill. The villagers – they had no idea of the danger they were in. They were all asleep! She took a step forward to run – but her foot stayed put, rooted to the ground as though it had been locked in place.

What? Anna looked down to see a lacy frost pattern rising up from the ground, snapping together like links on a chain and wrapping around her foot.

While Anna gaped, something tugged on Revolute, and without thinking, Anna let go. Too late, she realised what she'd done. Looking back up, she saw Elsa standing in front of her, holding Aren's sword with both hands. She no longer looked like Anna's older sister, or even a queen. She looked like a soldier.

"Elsa." Her words sounded small even to her own ears. "What are you doing?"

"I'm sorry," Elsa said, and Anna could hear the truth in her sister's words, but still, Elsa made no move to stop the advancing frost. It circled around Anna, shuttling back and forth on itself like yarn on a loom to form a white tapestry, rising higher and higher. "I failed to protect the kingdom," Elsa said, "but I'm not going to fail you, too!"

Failed? Anna didn't know what Elsa was talking about. Elsa never failed at *anything*.

"Elsa," Anna said as the frost crystals scattered up over her head, dancing into a domed roof. "I don't *need* to be protected!"

It felt like Anna's whole being had contracted and collapsed in on itself, like a black hole or a dark abyss. She felt as though she'd become no bigger than the head of a pin. The last frost link clicked into place, finishing not a tapestry, but a bubble-like tent. Anna found she could move her feet again, the frost chain that had held her to the ground slithering away to weave itself into the structure. It didn't matter, though, if Anna could move her feet or not, because Elsa hadn't bothered to make a door.

"I love you," Elsa said, sounding for a moment like she was younger than Anna or even Echo. And then she was running, sprinting down the dirt path to the village below, Revolute a curved gleam in her hand.

"Come back!" Anna yelled. *"Elsa!"* She pounded her fists against the frost, but the walls were so strong, so solid and so cold, that each pummel felt like a bite. The frost links held fast, keeping Anna locked away.

Anna was useless as she watched Elsa reach the end of the path and run towards the Nattmara. Useless as the Nattmara caught Elsa's scent and turned towards her sister, its fearsome claws extended. And useless as Elsa strode forward, ready to become the great ruler that Arendelle needed... just as Aren had done. But it would be okay. *It would be okay it would be okay it would be okay.*

Elsa wielded the myth that could defeat the myth. She held in her hand the crescent blade that had carved their home on Arenfjord. If Revolute could do that, *surely* it could defeat a Nattmara summoned by a scared little sister. Still, Anna held her breath as she watched, too far away to help, yet at the same time too close, because she could see it all.

A howl of wind clashed with the howl of the wolf as Elsa intercepted the Nattmara at the base of the Bridge of Arches. Elsa looked like a doll in front of the monstrous wolf, which had grown so tall that its ears were at the height of the castle's waving flags. Even from a distance, Anna could see the slip of saliva that hung from the Nattmara's fangs as it began to circle her sister, its great yellow eyes locked on Elsa.

This was a thousand times worse than any of Anna's nightmares. In all her nightmares but the last, she'd been in some sort of control. She'd always been able to puzzle her way out somehow, or distract the creature long enough that she could wake up. But even if Anna *could* break free from the frost bubble, she would not be able to wake up.

The wolf and her sister circled each other.

Elsa's cloak and scarf flapped in great gusts of wind as she twirled one hand and clutched Revolute with the other. But something was wrong. Even though Elsa was controlling the gusts of ice, no matter which direction she commanded the snow and ice to go, the wolf would force her to turn her back into the magic so that her hair and billows of icy magicked air constantly whipped into her eyes. There was no way for Elsa to clearly see.

And then, the Nattmara attacked.

Elsa and Revolute whirled away, the Nattmara's teeth snapping on thin air. It retreated for a moment, then struck again. This time, a terrible screech filled the air as a fang scraped across the blade. Or maybe the screech was Anna's own scream. Because Elsa now lay between the Nattmara's giant paws, sprawled like a spider, her limbs askew and her hand empty.

Revolute flew through the air, a blue-black streak, and landed several feet behind Elsa. Anna saw Elsa's hand sweep out, trying to feel for the sword without taking her eyes away from the Nattmara.

"REVOLUTE!" Anna shouted, though she knew Elsa wouldn't be able to hear her. "TO YOUR LEFT!"

The Nattmara licked its maw, its fangs poised above Elsa.

For a moment, Anna saw in startling detail the gleam of the Nattmara's claws and rise in her sister's chest as Elsa took a deep breath.

Then, the Nattmara lunged down.

But in the space that it took for Anna to blink, Elsa had lunged, too. She grabbed for Revolute's hilt. In one fluid movement, she held it up in front of her – the ancient blade flashing in the light of the setting sun – and thrust it into the roof of the Nattmara's mouth.

Anna waited for the Nattmara to fall and disintegrate into dust, defeated at last by a thing of myth, just as Sorenson had said that it could be.

Instead, the world slowed and stilled as the Nattmara bit down. And Revolute – the great, mythic sword of Aren's oldest hero, the sword that had carved the Arenfjord from the mountains, slain beasts, and conquered nightmares – shattered like glass. Bits of the meteorite blade sparkled as they sprayed uselessly to the ground, raining down on Elsa, who now lay completely defenceless in front of the Nattmara.

"ELSA!" Anna roared, pounding at her prison of frost. "ELSA! Use your magic!"

Maybe it was a trick of the wind, but Elsa appeared

to turn her head in the waterfall's direction. For one second, it almost seemed that Elsa looked at her. Glancing down, Anna saw that the frost bubble had started to dissolve into thin air – not good! If Elsa's magic was dissolving, that must mean that Elsa was weakening, too.

But Anna was now free!

She began to run down the path even though she knew that she would not make it in time, but still, she had to try. Elsa would have – no, Elsa *had* – done the same for her.

The Nattmara threw back its leviathan head and howled its victory. And as it rose once more above her sister, its white fur shifted into a glittering black as the Nattmara morphed into a cloud of sand that stood out starkly against the faded landscape. The bits and pieces swirled together, forming a spinning column.

And then the sand slammed down into Elsa's chest... and disappeared.

"Elsa!" Anna sobbed, stumbling into range. "Elsa!"

Her sister sprawled on the ground, her eyes closed and her blonde hair coming loose from its braid and spilling onto fallen leaves. Scattered around her like a broken halo were the blue-black shards of what had once been the great sword Revolute.

And though Anna knew what would happen next, she still wasn't prepared for when Elsa's eyelids fluttered open to reveal glowing yellow eyes.

Anna's stomach heaved at the sight of the wolf's eyes in her sister's familiar face. Her stride slowed. "Elsa?" she called out hesitantly.

Elsa opened her mouth... and screamed.

And then she raised her hands, blasting Arendelle with her powers, her usually white snow and white ice now replaced by *black* snow and *black* ice.

No, not black snow *or* black ice. Black *sand*.

As Elsa continued to scream, the sound swept through Anna, hollowing her out like the wolf's howl had, until there was nothing left except for Elsa's scream within her, reverberating against her ribcage, echoing again and again in her complete emptiness. In her utter aloneness.

Revolute had shattered and Elsa's eyes were yellow.

"Elsa," Anna sobbed, not knowing what do. "Elsa... Elsa... Elsa!"

But the figure who had been her sister did not even turn to face her.

With great heaving gasps, Anna gathered the shards of the sword into her cloak pocket – a futile hope. Because Revolute, the famed sword of myth, had not been enough to defeat a beast of myth. The myth was no longer a myth. It had not saved her sister. And the sound of Elsa's scream – or was it the wolf's howl? – pulled her into the black dots gathering at the edge of her vision. Anna didn't know which was which, but the nightmares stormed in and dragged her down.

"Elsa," she managed to croak out one last time. No longer knowing what was real and what was a nightmare, or if they were now truly one and the same, Anna saw Elsa at last turn to her.

Elsa raised her hands and black sand erupted from her palms towards Anna.

Darkness swirled around Anna, and then, at last, there was nothing at all.

Chapter Twenty-Four

ANNA WOKE TO HER MOTHER singing a lullaby.
She knew it was just a dream, and so she kept
her eyes shut, letting herself drift in the familiar and
comforting melody. Though she couldn't make out
the lyrics, she had a sense of the story behind it. A
story from long ago, in that time before time, when
the world was sprightly green and the rivers bubbled
with enchantment. That time when the sun would
step down from the sky and walk along the earth,
just to feel the grass tickle her feet and to discuss
philosophy with the wind. It was an olden song, a
song of strength and meekness, revenge and love. The
sound was sweet, but it was not real. Anna knew that.

Mother was gone. Father, too. And now Elsa...

Yellow eyes and a haunted kingdom. Tears dripped from

beneath her eyelashes, but Anna still didn't open them. She wanted to stay suspended in the dark, cocooned away until someone had cleaned up her mess.

Something cold patted her cheek. "Anna, quit joking around. Wake up."

This voice was familiar, too.

Anna opened her eyes to find herself nose to carrot with Olaf.

"You're leaking," he informed her, referring to the tears she was shedding.

"Olaf, what are you doing here?" Anna swiped at her eyes and looked away from Olaf's nose to see branchless trees swaying above her. No, not trees – masts. Three tall ones, each strung with the ropes and nets of a working ship and boasting wide billowing sails.

Above the slap of the waves, Anna could hear singing – but it wasn't her mother, it was Tuva the blacksmith, who stared out at the dark night over the royal ship's rail, her lilting voice filling the salt-sprayed air.

"Anna's awake!" Olaf shouted.

"How did you get here?" Anna asked Olaf. "How did I get here?" She looked around and saw Sven wrapped in a large blanket, still fast asleep, though his legs twitched and sweat sheened his almost now completely white coat. Only a little patch of brown fur remained on his flaring nose.

"Hoo-hoo!" Oaken said, stomping into view, his cheeks a bit redder than usual from the cold sea air. "We watched everything from the harbour! When Scary Elsa vanished inside the castle, we crept ashore and carried you back. We thought both you and Sven would rest better next to one another."

"I thought you had already sailed away!" Anna said, perplexed. She also wondered why she hadn't fallen under the nightmare sleep. She studied her hands, not sure what she expected to see.

"We were going to," Tuva called from the ship's stern, her hands on the helm. In the yellow lantern light, the blacksmith looked ragged and her curly hair had been tugged into a cloud of frizz by the wind. Her brown eyes, however, remained warm as she looked at Anna. "But then we had a change of heart. And a good thing, too – or else we wouldn't have been able to pick up SoYun."

"Since I live on the outskirts of the village," SoYun said softly as she appeared from behind the post, a coil of thick rope in her arms, "the wolf ran straight by – and at that very moment, the rest of my herd fell asleep. I realised I had to go seek a solution myself. So I rowed out onto the sea, hoping to find someone awake on the water, and that's how they" – she gestured to Tuva and Oaken – "found me."

"I'm so glad," Anna said, and she was pleased to note that while SoYun's long black braid wasn't yet in its usual tidiness, she looked less terrified than when she'd come upon Anna and Elsa in the woods. In fact, SoYun looked determined.

"But," Anna said, looking back at Tuva, "what kind of change convinced you to return?"

"You," Tuva said simply.

Anna blinked. "What do you mean?"

Tuva turned the wheel and the sails above rippled in the night breeze. "I mean," she said, "that if a young woman like you could stick around, even though all was falling apart, and you don't have powers of snow and ice, and I doubt you can lift a blacksmith's hammer above your head for even a minute – then why couldn't we? After all, Arendelle is just as much our home as it is yours.

"We'd only sailed out a little way when we realised

that we *needed* to return. And so, we agreed to turn around in case you were still out there. And you were. So we scooped you up just in time and carried you to the ship, and now we've set sail again."

"We're keeping an eye on the castle," SoYun added. "Elsa... she's..."

"Still in there," Tuva finished darkly.

"Thank you. H-how long have I been asleep?" Anna said. Her thoughts reeled with the vision of Elsa falling victim to the Nattmara.

"Only a few hours!" Olaf called from the prow. "Which is actually a short amount of time when you take in the eons of our galaxy."

Anna's heart sped up. It was still the same night. "And when's sunrise?"

"In just an hour," Oaken said.

An hour. Arendelle had a single hour before this terror became permanent. Uneasy, Anna rose to her feet and headed to the railing. She stared down at the black waters of the Arenfjord. They slapped relentlessly against the ship's hull, giving rhythm to the terrible thoughts that swarmed through Anna's mind: Elsa, failure, Elsa. A tear coursed down her cheek. Anna's greatest fear wasn't a wolf. It never had been.

It had been losing her sister.

Olaf took Anna's hand in his. "You're melting," he said. "I wish I could share my permafrost with you."

Anna smiled as she wiped her face with the back of her hand. "I'm okay, Olaf." She paused. "Actually," she admitted, "I'm not okay. All along I wanted to go on the grand tour with Elsa on this very ship, but now... It was supposed to be a journey that Elsa and I did together."

And though Anna didn't say it, she thought: *Just like taking care of the castle is something we're supposed to do together, too.* But even after the trip to the Huldrefólk, Elsa still hadn't trusted her to get rid of the Nattmara, and now, their one and only chance of defeating the nightmare – Revolute – lay in tiny jagged pieces in her cloak pocket.

Sven suddenly bellowed and Anna looked just in time to see him thrash wildly, his legs moving as though he were running for his life, even as he slumbered.

Anna ran over and sank down beside him, her skirt billowing around her. Careful to avoid his hooves, she reached out and tenderly began to pat his nose. Slowly, Sven stopped kicking, but his ears continued to twitch.

"I ruined it all," she said, continuing to pet Sven gently on the head. "I thought I finally had the answer. But" – she drew a long, shuddering breath – "I thought wrong. And Elsa – she was right not to trust me to come along on her grand tour or to defeat the Nattmara or to do anything at all."

"Ah-hem," came a familiar throat-clearing. She turned to see Wael climbing up out of the ship's hull.

Quickly, she looked away and kept her head bent towards the water, using her hair as a curtain. She didn't think she could stomach the nosy journalist's judgement. She barely felt like she could handle anything at all.

"Ah-*hem*." The throat clearing became more insistent. "I couldn't help overhearing, but, well... have you been belowdecks yet? To Elsa's study?"

Anna shook her head. She'd been to the royal ship to help unload rations, but she had made it a point to avoid Elsa's cabin, unwilling to see it piled high with the luggage that would accompany Elsa far from home.

"Then I suggest you check it out."

"I don't know," Anna said, thinking of the wild hair that now fanned around Elsa's face and the yellow eyes of the Nattmara set into her sockets. That image would haunt her forever, she was certain of it. "It—it would hurt too much to see right now," Anna said.

Olaf slid his hand into hers. "Sometimes, you walk into a cave thinking you'll find wolves inside, but they turn out to be puppies."

With a heavy sigh, Anna shuffled after Olaf, following him and Wael downstairs to Elsa's study. As she walked, she kept sneaking glances at Wael. She was surprised that he'd been willing to come back and help her.

Wael caught one of her glances and exhaled. "I know what you're thinking," he said as he stepped onto a groaning stair.

"You do?" Anna said, her cheeks warming slightly.

Wael nodded. "You think that because I ask you and your sister hard questions about the kingdom, that I must not like you or Arendelle very much." He opened the door to Elsa's floating quarters and paused a moment to look at Anna. "But the truth is, I ask hard questions because I *love* Arendelle so much, and because I believe in you and Elsa. You know, asking questions is often the first step to accomplishing something."

And Anna was surprised to realise that yes, she *exactly* knew. She smiled at Wael and said, "Thank you so much for your questions, and for coming back to help us." And she meant it with the whole of her being.

Wael returned the smile and stepped back so that she could enter.

Anna gasped. Everywhere, there were sunflowers. Painted sunflowers danced across wooden beams and were carved into the handles of the cupboards. A plush sunflower rug, cheery yellow and spring green, lay at the base of the stairs.

Sunflowers weren't Elsa's favourite flowers. They were *Anna's*. Elsa must have asked that the entire study be decorated to remind her of her sister. To remind her of home. And in the centre of the room hung a newly commissioned portrait of two little girls, one with white-blonde hair and the other chestnut brown, skating across a frozen pond. The entire room felt like a hug.

Wael went to the desk and pulled out a page

from the stacks that had already accumulated in anticipation of Elsa's grand tour. "This is the one that I thought you might like to see," Wael said, handing it to her before slipping out, leaving Anna alone with Olaf.

Anna peered down at the paper, then did a double take. It was a proclamation written in Elsa's elegant handwriting:

I, Elsa, Queen of Arendelle, do hereby proclaim my sister, Anna of Arendelle, Keeper of the Kingdom while I sail on the grand tour. She is kind, thoughtful and loves Arendelle with the whole of her heart. There is none better than her to watch over the kingdom while I am away.

At last, Anna had an answer. The reason Elsa had not invited her on the grand tour – it wasn't because Elsa thought Anna was incompetent. It was because she *knew* Anna was helpful, and she needed Anna at home to keep an eye on things. Of course Elsa didn't want Anna leaving Arendelle. Arendelle needed Anna just as much as Anna needed it.

"Now that's true love!" said Olaf, who had angled his head to read it.

"It is," said Anna with a sad smile. All this time, Anna had thought that Elsa believed she was useless, but maybe that wasn't the case at all. Maybe the only person who hadn't believed that Anna was helpful... was Anna *herself*.

She remembered the ice bubble that Elsa had enclosed her in. She'd thought it had been Elsa doing one more protective big sister act, but what if it was meant to be more than that? What if she wasn't trying to be protective of Anna, but she was instead *arming* Anna, forcing her to wait and watch, because she trusted her to figure out the solution if the worst should happen?

"Olaf," Anna said, "would you mind getting Tuva down here, please? We don't have much time."

Half an hour later, though, Anna's fragile hope had once again unravelled. She'd laid out the collected pieces of Revolute across Elsa's desk to see if Tuva could piece them together, but the blacksmith shook her head. "The pieces are too small, and the metal – I've never seen anything like it before. Maybe I could do it if Ada" – her breath caught on her wife's name – "were around and I had access to our forge, but there's no way it can be fixed in time, and definitely not on this ship without the proper tools."

"Why would you fix it?" Wael called from the doorway. "The sword didn't work the first time – what makes you think it would work *this* time?"

"Because," Anna said, keeping her eye on the porthole. *Was the night sky beginning to brighten?* "You can only defeat a myth with a thing of myth, and Revolute is definitely a thing of myth. Besides" – she turned her head to look at the map of Arendelle pinned to the wall. It reminded her of the map she had uncovered in the secret room, the one where her mother had written one of their father's many sayings – "my father used to say the past has a way of returning."

"And what goes around comes around again, like a sneeze in the wind," Olaf added. He sat at the desk, examining the pieces of the shattered sword. "Maybe you should look at Revolute and Aren's past."

Anna sighed. "I would, but I don't exactly have a copy of the *Saga of Aren* on me at the moment and Elsa's not here to declaim."

"Ah-hem," Wael coughed. "Elsa is not the only one who studied the classics."

"Apologies, Wael," Anna said. "Please perform, but quickly." Unease filled her, but she tamped it down. "We're running out of time."

"'Revolving moon and spinning sun, forged a crescent blade...'" Wael began, and Anna half listened as she tried to skim the other documents that might be helpful.

"Hey, Anna," Olaf said, "don't you think it's funny how you can find love in the most curious places?"

Anna tried not to sigh. She loved when Olaf discussed philosophy – *usually* – but now, mere minutes before sunrise, was not the time. "Yeah, sure I do. Why are you asking?"

"Because," Olaf said, "it's sitting here on the desk."

Anna looked over, trying to see what he was talking about. She had not realised that Olaf had been rearranging the broken pieces of Revolute, specifically the top part of the blade that had held the inscription of the sword's name, which now spelled out:

L-O-V-E R-E-T-U

"'The sea rushed in as hidden power flowed from the gleaming sword'," Wael continued to proclaim – and Anna's heart skipped a beat.

A hidden power.

Anna's heart began beating again, but twice as fast, as thoughts tumbled through her mind and she took in the other letters. A grin spread across her face.

"Oaken!" she yelled up to the deck. "Turn this ship around again! We have a kingdom to save."

Chapter Twenty-Five

ANNA KNEW WHERE TO FIND HER SISTER.

The nearer the night drew to sunrise, the more foreign Anna's home had seemed to become. Knobby branches twisted every which way, as if a forest of shadows had taken root in the land. And overhead, a great sandstorm spun, its centre positioned directly over Arendelle Castle. Its great winds raised up high waves, and Anna and the rest of the crew covered their noses and mouths with the silk scarves that were originally meant to be gifts to the court of Corona, but now acted as shields so that they could breathe without inhaling sand as the royal ship glided closer.

Oaken steered the ship while Tuva barked commands at Wael, and SoYun and Anna helped with a complicated system of ropes and pulleys. Wael looked a little green around the gills, and Anna was grateful that she herself had a strong stomach.

But it was Olaf, a snowman who was used to falling apart and rolling in several directions at once, who was the biggest help. He made sure that the items on deck didn't slam into anybody and that the still-sleeping Sven stayed safely out of harm's way.

"Sharp turn!" Oaken warned, and the next second, he'd turned the royal ship to be parallel to the castle gates. But there was still a sizable distance between the ship's deck and land.

"This is as close as we can get without smashing the ship!" Oaken called.

Anna stared down at the choppy grey water. Black sand sullied its usually white foam. She'd have to jump! But then she saw SoYun's rope. Remembering how she'd escaped the Nattmara from Sorenson's tower, she called to SoYun to throw the rope and latch it securely to a street lamp.

When it was done, Anna clambered up onto the top rail. "Wish me luck!" She took the free end of the rope from SoYun – and jumped! Three long seconds passed as she soared into the air and over the water, and then, let go. With a thump, she landed on the castle grounds.

Anna winced, not because of the pain, but because she should have made a quieter entrance. Two pairs of glowing yellow eyes suddenly appeared at the front entrance to Arendelle Castle: Kai and Gerda. And their hair, too, had turned snow-white.

They still opened their mouths in a scream, but only a rasp came out. Anna shook her head in sorrow. Kai and Gerda had been trapped in a screaming nightmare reality for almost three whole days. It was a wonder they had any voice left at all. Unfortunately, they still seemed able – and eager – to wield their household weapons. The glint of Kai's fire poker and Gerda's sharp scissors still cut through the black sand.

What to do what to do what to do!

"Hoo-hoo, yellow-eyed wolf helpers!" Oaken called as he swung over the water and landed with surprising ease next to Anna. "It's not polite to attack guests!"

"Oaken! Get back on the ship!" Anna instructed. "It's not safe!"

"Don't worry, Anna," Oaken said with a nod to the ship where Wael, SoYun, Tuva and Olaf were calling out to Kai and Gerda from the deck, distracting them from Anna. "We've got this, *ja*? We'll lure them away and make sure they don't come to any harm – or cause any. Now, go help Elsa!" He turned to Kai and Gerda, and waved his arms. "Over here!"

Anna nodded her thanks and rushed inside to find her sister... if there was anything left of her. She didn't have a solid plan, but she was brave and she had hope. And that would have to be enough.

The sand seemed thickest near the entry of the Great Hall, so Anna ran there as fast as she could on the strange combination of sand and hardwood. It slowed her progress, but still Anna pushed forward towards the double doors. Sure enough, as she drew closer, she could hear sobs. Shoving the doors open, Anna raced in.

Her sister sat on her throne, her yellow eyes staring unblinking into a dream that Anna could not see. As Elsa wept, strange flurries of black ice circled above her head. Anna's heart squeezed.

"Elsa?" she whispered. "Elsa?"

But her sister's expression didn't change. Not wanting to startle Elsa, Anna slowly moved towards her. Suddenly, from the corner of the room, she heard a long, low growl. It was happening again! Her

nightmare! It prowled out from behind the pillar
– and attacked.

But Anna was prepared. She'd left her cloak
unclasped for this very reason. And as the wolf
leapt at her again, Anna flung her cloak off her
shoulders and for the first time, instead of running
away from the wolf, she ran *towards* it. She held her
cloak above her head like a banner as she sprinted
between its two front paws, each one as large as a
boulder. The wolf realised a moment too late its
prey's route. Its teeth snapped down around the
cloak, catching only fabric as Anna let go of it and
raced under the protection of the wolf's belly.

Holding her breath, she paused just long enough
to hear the shred of cloth as the Nattmara's teeth
ripped the cloak, not quite yet realising it was only
a decoy. The charade would not last long, but it had
bought her precious seconds.

Scurrying out from under the wolf's tail, Anna
hurled herself towards the throne.

Twelve feet left. Six. Three. She was almost
there!

Aroooooooooooooo!

The Nattmara had realised she had tricked it!

Anna's blood turned cold as she glanced back. She shouldn't have.

Because the wolf was upon her.

Claws the length of butcher's knives raked across her back. She squeezed her eyes shut, waiting for the pain... but it never came.

In fact, Anna didn't feel a *thing*.

Her eyes flew open just in time to see the Nattmara attack her again, but instead of colliding with her, it sailed right through Anna as though *she* were the one made of sand instead of the wolf. Her heart slammed into her chest. She hadn't felt any pain. Had she become a ghost?

The Nattmara snarled, clearly as confused as she was. It lunged again, this time teeth first, but Anna felt nothing more than a light breeze as its fangs grazed her throat, leaving not a scratch. Like wind grasping at her. And for the first time, Anna didn't feel the suffocating pull of the Nattmara on her thoughts, making her think terrifying and helpless things. Again and again, the Nattmara attacked her, but nothing it did could hurt her.

Anna's mind whirled at a frantic pace. Whenever she had been around the Nattmara before, thoughts of not being good enough had filled her and held her down. But now – now Anna knew, recalling the proclamation in Elsa's travelling study, that she *was* good enough and that she had always been.

The truth in those inked words seemed to have mended the cracks in her heart.

She was no longer afraid. The Nattmara could no longer harm her... so why was Anna's nightmare still there?

Anna couldn't concentrate! Elsa's scream dug at her, and though the Nattmara's fearsome claws could not hurt her any more, each time Elsa wailed, Anna felt as though she'd been physically punched.

"Elsa!" Anna cried, staggering towards the throne. "Whatever you're seeing, it isn't real! It's just a nightmare!" Her thoughts dashed frantically and she grabbed onto one before it slid by. "Remember Mother and Father!" she said. "Hot chocolate! Cosy stories—" Anna broke off.

Wait a second.

Pretending to give her nightmares to Frigg the Fisherman had never helped Anna. But now she recalled Elsa's words from two days earlier. *Mother's trick worked for me. I haven't had a nightmare since.*

Another thought darted by, this time, a memory of Sorenson's voice, and his confusing words suddenly had meaning: *The act of burying fear is what manifests the Nattmara*, he'd said.

And now Anna understood. Fear only grew the longer it was ignored. Avoiding a nightmare only made it more powerful, more terrifying when it finally erupted again. And if Elsa had ignored her fears for years – if she had banished her nightmares away, then maybe they had taken on their own life, taken on their own shape....

Ulf the Wolf was always my favourite, Elsa had said in Sorenson's tower. What if, instead of handing her nightmares over to a friendly fisherman as Anna had tried, Elsa had imagined feeding her fears to a hungry wolf?

Anna's ideas came to her even quicker. Elsa's rejected nightmares and fears, unable to latch onto Elsa but more powerful than most people's fears, had weaselled their way into another scared, lonely child's dreams – a child whose loneliness had gaped wide within her, leaving room for black sand and dark dreams to creep into her heart. A heart that had cracked when the child had been separated from her sister. *Anna's* heart.

Realisation thundered through her: Anna had not

created the Nattmara – not with a spell or her own great worries. The wolf that had first appeared to her on that night sixteen years ago was not a manifestation of Anna's fear. There had been another scared and lonely child in the castle beside her then, one who had also feared being separated from her sister: *Elsa.*

The Nattmara was Elsa's nightmare! It was *Elsa's* fear that they needed to conquer!

But... Anna had no idea what her sister was afraid of. Elsa was the strongest person she knew, a great queen, brave in the face of danger, determined and regal.

What to do what to do what to do!

The Nattmara, frustrated by its futile attempts to inflict harm to Anna, let out an ear-splitting howl. The sandstorm whipped up faster. While Anna might be safe from the beast's attacks, Arendelle was not.

Anna ran towards Elsa, and though her stomach hurt as she looked at Elsa's yellow eyes, she didn't look away. The Nattmara had only come when they'd been separated – either by their parents when they were young or by Elsa's queenly responsibilities.

So it would only be defeated, Anna guessed wildly, when they were together.

All Anna needed to figure out was what scared Elsa – but she truly had no idea what that could be.

"Elsa!" she cried as she approached the throne. "Elsa, I'm here! What's wrong? What are you so scared of that you can't tell me?"

Elsa just screamed harder and the rush of black sand still spilling from her palms came quicker. It began to pile into a barrier between them, filling up the Great Hall. Eventually, it would reach the rafters and then the ceiling, burying Elsa on her throne. Wait a minute – the throne!

They were in the Great Hall; the Nattmara had chosen it, so it must be Elsa's least favourite room in the castle. And as Anna looked at the flurry of sand circling Elsa's throne, spiralling up above her head to form a glittering crown of darkness, the answer came to her: Elsa was scared of being a bad queen.

"The people are all counting on me!" Elsa sobbed in her nightmare-scape. "Please! I'll be better!"

Anna, no longer afraid of the Nattmara – but much more afraid of losing her sister forever

– sprinted up the dais and grabbed Elsa's hand. Elsa yanked it away from her, but Anna held tight.

Suddenly, Anna could see into Elsa's nightmare: the endless meetings that Elsa felt awkward leading, not knowing what to say to people after having had very little social interaction for most of her life. Anna had always just thought Elsa was a good listener. Everyone seemed to think she was so wonderfully collected, but in truth, her quietness wasn't composed thinking, but a deer-in-the-path-of-an-arrow kind of fright.

And the Nattmara had made her a bad queen – with the Blight. It all made sense to Anna now. Before the Nattmara had the strength to take on the physical shape of a wolf, it had seeped into the kingdom as a sickness, stalking the kingdom the same way it had stalked Elsa's mind. And with the Blight came the people's constant worry and questions, and Elsa had become more overwhelmed and even more fearful that she could not protect them. She had begun to crack at the seams while trying to keep it all inside. She had not been able to sleep... and so, Elsa's suppressed nightmares had found another sleeping, worried sister to haunt until, at last, the fear in Arendelle – Elsa's fear – had grown so great and powerful that the Nattmara could at last be seen by everyone. Because above all, Elsa feared hurting the kingdom – again. Of hurting Anna, again.

"Oh, Elsa," Anna whispered, her heart aching. "Why didn't you just tell me?" Anna held on to her sister's hands, even as black sand pelted them from all around. "You're perfect just the way you are! You're a *great* leader! You pay attention to details, and your quietness gives you space to listen. I'm so proud of you, Elsa. You're a wonderful sister, and you're a role model for me. You're someone I look up to!"

Was it just Anna's imagination or was her sister now squeezing her hand back? Ignoring the thrum of the Nattmara's anger around them in the form of black sand spraying Anna's face from all sides, Anna continued to talk, focusing all of herself on her sister – letting her know how she felt about her, just in the same way Elsa's proclamation had shown Anna the truth.

"You know that I am better than who I think I am!" she yelled over the wind and battering sand. "I was so scared that you didn't need me any more since I wasn't invited on the grand tour. But then I saw that the tour had nothing to do with me, and I realised that you are right – I am helpful and I am always here for you and for our people, no matter what! Just as I know you are here for me!" Anna wasn't sure if she was getting through to Elsa, but still she hung on, despite the growing swarm of assaulting black sand.

Elsa's eyes shut tight. And then... "Anna?"

"Elsa!" Anna cried. "I'm here! I'm always here!"

Elsa turned her head and Anna saw that her eyes were no longer yellow, but back to their usual beautiful shade of light blue. "Anna," Elsa said, voice raspy from all the nightmare-induced screaming. "Of *course* I need you."

The Nattmara threw back its head and howled in rage, the sound echoing endlessly around the hall.

Elsa clutched tight to Anna's hand. "Why is it still here?" Elsa whirled her other hand up, ready to blast it with ice.

"No!" Anna shouted. "You can't fight your fear – it only makes it stronger! Just as you can't ignore your fear, because out of sight, it grows in strange ways and mutates."

"Then what should I do?" Elsa asked, her voice cracking. "Dawn is almost here!"

"Accept it," Anna breathed, praying she was right. "It's okay to be afraid, Elsa. You just can't let the fear take control of you! Fear is the shadow of love. You only fear because you care so much about Arendelle and about me, and that's what makes you a great queen and a great leader. And a great sister. That's why we *love* you, Elsa."

It was the riddle that Olaf had helped her solve when he had rearranged the letters of the sword. Not *R-E-V-O-L-U-T-E* or *L-O-V-E R-E-T-U*, but *T-R-U-E L-O-V-E* was the way to defeat the Nattmara. And *that* was a thing of myth.

Elsa didn't say anything, but then she held out her hand again. The giant wolf paused, the winds calmed down and with each step the wolf took towards the sisters, it grew smaller. By the time it reached Elsa's outstretched hand, the wolf was the size of a little wolf-puppy. It still had sharp teeth and claws, but it was manageable and could be contained.

"My fear," Elsa said in awe. "I was so afraid of being a bad queen, but I don't need to worry about that any more. Because I've got you, Anna."

Anna smiled and stayed put as the white wolf pup approached. She wasn't scared of Elsa's fear – it was a part of her sister, and she could never be afraid of her. The Nattmara's power was truly done at last.

The puppy touched its nose to Elsa's hand and turned into a cloud of sand, shimmering in the air and then... just a single grain of black sand lay before the sisters. With a flick of her wrist, Elsa captured it in an ice crystal and caught it in her hand. Then she held it up to the dawn's first ray of light.

"How?" she breathed. "How did we defeat the Nattmara without a thing of myth?"

"Because," Anna said, peering at the crystal, "we *do* have a thing of myth – we've had it all along. Aren didn't become a myth because he just so happened to own a fancy sword. Swords and crowns don't change who we are."

Elsa slipped the single grain of sand into her pocket. "Then what does?"

"True love," Anna said, referencing the hidden power that the *Saga of Aren* spoke of. "The power that carved out Arenfjord. The same power that gave Aren the strength to go out in his boat to face an unknown danger or up a mountain to face a dragon. It doesn't matter which really happened – what matters is the choice he made."

Suddenly, it hit her how sleepy she was, and her thoughts came to her like a lap of quiet ocean waves.

"It's like how Sorenson said all myths contain a kernel of hard truth. It wasn't a magical sword that carved out a home on the fjord. The myth wasn't about the creation of the *actual* fjord – it was a myth about how, through love, Aren and the others in his generation believed in each other and trusted each other and loved each other enough to settle here and carve out a home for themselves, and for their future children, families and friends. For us. A place where Arendelle's flags could always fly strong."

"True love," Elsa mused. "The thing that can move mountains and defeat nightmares."

"Exactly," Anna said. She led Elsa over to the window, to the curtain she'd first spotted the wolf hiding behind. "Our love is worthy of the great myths. Us. The royal sisters of Arendelle." Anna pulled back the curtain.

Sunlight rushed in. Dawn had fully broken and the sun streaked across the horizon, brilliant gold in a grey-satin sky, shining down on a land full of vibrant colour. No trace of the angry black sand or deathly pale rot remained.

And as she squinted in the direction of the rising sun, Anna noticed a figure walking towards the castle. There was something about the clothes and the shaggy hair that looked familiar...

"Kristoff!" Anna shouted.

Elsa rested a hand on Anna's shoulder. "Go get him," she said.

Anna grinned at her sister, then took off, flying into the second great hall and outside the castle, and then Kristoff was in her arms, kissing her again and again. She kissed him until the memories of the past few days faded away, and for the first time in a long time, she felt like everything was going to be good again.

With tears of joy streaming down her face, she took Kristoff's face in her hands. "I'm so glad you're okay," she said.

"You know I will always come back to you," Kristoff said, giving her a playful wink.

"Me too!" a new voice commented.

Anna looked up to see Olaf sitting on Sven's antlers. Sven's fur was still mottled white, but his eyes were bright and shiny once again. The smell of the sea lingered on his coat.

"*Sven!*" Kristoff cried with delight. Planting one last kiss on Anna's cheek, he hurried over to the reindeer and hugged him tight, while Sven nuzzled him back. "You're finally awake!"

He wiggled the reindeer's lower lip and added in Sven Talk, "And you look like you're half asleep."

"Group hug," Elsa said as she approached, and she enveloped everyone in her arms.

And with a happy yawn, Anna leaned her head against Elsa's shoulder as the village bells began to toll across the fjord, calling all to rise and wake.